CHASING
Riddick

CHASING

Riddick

ALEXANDRA ST PIERRE

CONTENT WARNINGS

- Explicit scene with implied/dubious consent
- Somno
- Death of a loved one
- Fist fights/Hand to Hand Violence

AUTHOR'S NOTE
(Please read)

Hello psychos!

I just wanted to be transparent and let readers know about the nature of the content you are about to read. If you have no triggers and prefer to go in blind, you can skip this.

HOWEVER! Considering this book is much lighter than most of my other works, I anticipate this may reach a wider audience than I am accustomed to. So for that reason, I would like to make it abundantly clear that if you are a reader who requires full and enthusiastic consent in all on-page spice scenes to enjoy a book, this may not be the book for you.

There is one scene where consent is only implied. It happens while one of the characters is asleep, so he cannot give *true* consent in this scene.

If this is a trigger, please proceed with caution.

I do not condone this type of behaviour in real life. This is a work of fiction telling a story that involves flawed characters.

The only acceptable form of consent in real life is loud, vocal, enthusiastic consent.

Everything else in this book should be relatively safe. We do deal with the death of a loved one and a fist fight that is instigated in the defence of a woman who is physically struck by a male villain.

I will also warn readers that this book is extremely emotional, and is designed in such a way that you will finish this story with some very big feelings.

I consider the ending to be a happy one, however I do acknowledge that some readers may disagree – and that's okay! Reading is subjective!

With all that out of the way, I hope you all love Finn and Riddick's story, and find yourself getting lost in the quaint coastal town of Stars Cove.

*To anyone who feels like they're drowning – This one's for you.
Just keep swimming.*

SURF SLANG AND TERMS

- **Amped** – Super excited, usually before a big wave or surfing session.
- **Bail** – To jump off the board to avoid a bad situation, like an impending wipeout.
- **Barrel** – When the wave is hollow, allowing the surfer to ride inside.
- **Barrel Riding (Tube Ride)** - Surfing inside the hollow part of the wave (the "barrel")
- **Big Air (Aerials)** - Launching off the lip of the wave and landing back on the face.
- **Carve** – Making a sharp turn on the wave, a stylish, skilled move.
- **Cutback** - Turning sharply back toward the breaking part of the wave to stay in the critical section.
- **Drop in** – Catching a wave that another surfer is already riding, which is poor etiquette.
- **Double up wave** - a type of wave in surfing where two waves merge and combine their energy, creating a larger, steeper, and often more powerful wave than usual.
- **Double wave hold down**: Being caught under water for multiple wave sets. This can result in loss of life.
- **Epic** – When conditions are perfect.
- **Foamies** – Soft-top boards, often used by beginners.
- **Floater** - Riding over the breaking section of a wave
- **Gnarly** – Can mean challenging, dangerous, or impressive.
- **Green room** – Being inside the barrel of the wave.

- **Hang ten** – When a surfer places all ten toes over the edge of the nose of the longboard.
- **Kook** – An inexperienced or clueless surfer, often unaware of surfing etiquette.
- **Late Drop** - Taking off steeply on a wave at the last possible moment, just as it's about to break.
- **Layback** – A move where the surfer leans back dramatically into the wave.
- **Lineup** – The area where surfers wait for waves to break.
- **Off the lip** – A maneuver where the surfer rides up and then back down the wave's crest.
- **Ripping** – Surfing really well; also referred to as "shredding."
- **Swell** – The waves rolling in from the ocean, often the result of distant storms.
- **The Washing Machine:** Being trapped under a wave in the undercurrent. The water is so strong in these instances that a person can be pulled around violently under water like 'a t-shirt in a washing machine.'
- **Wipeout** – Falling off the board, usually in a dramatic way.

TYPES OF SURFBOARDS MENTIONED

Shortboard: Usually 5-7 feet in length, with a pointed nose and more rocker (curve) to handle steep waves. Best for high-performance maneuvers like carving, airs, and cutbacks on powerful, steep waves. This is the most common choice for professional competitions because they're designed for speed, agility, and responsiveness.

Fish: Short and wide, typically 5-6 feet with a swallowtail design and less rocker. They're thick, providing float and speed in smaller waves. Best for Small to medium waves, particularly in summer conditions when waves are slower and less powerful. Professionals may use fish boards for fun, smaller waves when they're not in competition. Great for generating speed on small days.

Longboard: Typically 8-10 feet or more with a rounded nose, lots of volume, and a flatter rocker. Used on Small to medium, mellow waves and classic, smooth surfing styles like noseriding and cross-stepping. Often used by pros in longboard competitions and by surfers specializing in traditional surfing styles.

Gun board: Long, narrow boards (usually 7-11 feet) designed for big waves with a lot of volume to improve paddling speed and stability on steep waves. Used in Big-wave surfing, especially waves over 15 feet, such as at Jaws in Hawaii or Mavericks in California. Professionals use guns when riding massive waves because the length and narrow shape allow them to paddle into and handle steep, fast-moving waves.

Soft Top / Foam Board (Also called foamies): Made with a foam deck for safety and buoyancy, usually longer and wider for stability. Best for beginners or for playful days in the surf when falling is likely. Foamies are rarely used by professionals except for casual, fun sessions or when teaching others.

PLAYLIST

Playlist available on Spotify! Search: Chasing Riddick

CHAPTER

One

Finn

Alexa Play: Coastline by Hollow Coves

Maybe if I were capable of feeling fear, I would have heard the name *Leviathans* and had the good sense to stay away.

But, as it was, I don't process fear the same way most people do. I don't get all jittery and frightened when faced with things that could kill me.

Nope.

Instead, I get *excited,* and my body gets this warm, *rushing* sensation.

So, if you tell me there's a wave so badass they named it after a demon that came straight from Hell, I'm gonna surf it.

No question.

That's pretty much how I ended up in the quaint little coastal town of Stars Cove: Home to a beach that produces waves so gnarly that the dudes who named it got all biblical on us.

It's said that the swells in Leviathans, California, can hit twenty-five feet in as many seconds.

Twenty-five *feet.*

In twenty-five *seconds.*

Let me put that in perspective for you.

Here's my list of things that are roughly twenty-five feet (in no particular order):

- A Two Story House
- Half the Hollywood sign
- Four refrigerators
- An orca
- A telephone pole
- My dick (HA! Just kidding, that would be terrifying.)

No, but seriously.

Riding twenty-five feet of pure *power* is not for the faint of heart. It's not something many people can say they've done. Not even most surfers can say they've successfully ripped a twenty-foot swell.

Waves like that are for professional big-wave surfers. It takes training, dedication, and perseverance to tame a wave like the ones that break at Leviathans every winter.

It's something I'd always planned on working toward in my lifetime; I just didn't expect to be chasing this dream so soon.

But here I was, signing the final sale documents for the small beach shack I had found listed for a *steal* in Stars Cove.

Apparently, local Stars Cove surfers had been sitting on this secret beach for years, knowing that the waves that swelled in the winter months would attract surfers from all over the world once word got out that there was a California beach that could produce such monsters.

As I signed my name on the dotted line, ignoring the quizzical look of the realtor as she watched me fritter away my entire inheritance in less than thirty seconds, I had to smile at that.

I supposed they had been right.

I was not from California, but here I was. Ready to show these local Leviathan tamers what I could do.

I was born near Virginia Beach, and that's where I actually got my start surfing. The waves were small, but so was I at the time.

Despite being a beach known to be best for beginners, the surf culture was strong, and that's where I learned the basics of the sport. I rode my first wave on a foamie at eight years old, and I still remember my best friend, Turtle, grinning and whooping like an idiot as I skated across the water on my own two feet for the very first time.

My mom and I didn't have a lot of money, but it never seemed to matter. She always managed to put food on the table for us. She had to work two jobs to keep a roof over our heads, and because of this, she had always been really supportive of my love for surfing.

It kept me busy and out of trouble.

My dad bounced before I was born, and it used to bother me when I was younger. I asked my mom about him a lot in the beginning.

'Why doesn't he want us, Mommy? Why'd he leave us all alone?'

'You're not alone, sweet boy. I'm right here!' she used to tell me with a wink.

As I grew and saw just how much my mom tried to be the best of both parents for me, I stopped hoping he would someday come back for me.

Of course, it sucked that he didn't want me... want *us.*

But my mom was right; we had each other, and that was enough.

Until one day, Mom didn't come home from her shift.

I had just turned eighteen and was wiped from spending the day at the beach with Turtle.

She wasn't in the single-story bungalow we had been renting since before I could remember, which wasn't out of the norm. She often worked late and just ate when she got back.

I made dinner for us and passed out on the couch, waiting for her to come home and tell me about her day. She worked at our local

Comfort Inn, and she often had *hilarious* stories about the guests who stayed there.

I woke up around midnight, and she still wasn't home. I'll never forget the sinking feeling in my gut the moment it occurred to me something was wrong.

Every time I tried to call her, her phone went to voicemail. I tried to convince myself I was overreacting, but I just couldn't shake the feeling that my life was about to change forever.

I called Turtle in a panic. My mom and I shared a car, and she had taken it to work that day, so I had no wheels. Turtle picked me up, and together, we drove around for hours looking for her.

It was around three am when I received a call from the police, informing me that my mother had been involved in an accident with a drunk driver, and they needed me to come to the morgue to identify her body.

Turtle held me while I sobbed, and my entire life fell to pieces around me.

She was gone, and now, I really *was* alone.

My mom left me everything she had, which was more than I expected her to have squirreled away. I don't know if she had been planning to use this nest egg to send me to school or what, but she had managed to save roughly sixty grand.

I didn't touch any of it for years. Turtle and I both dropped out of school and went on a road trip across the US together, chasing waves.

Or that's what I told myself. It was easier to believe I was chasing something instead of running away from the pain of losing the only family I had.

When we first heard about Leviathans, Turtle and I were living out of the van he bought for us in Cape Hatteras, checking out the East Coast scene.

Our plan had always been to eventually end up in Hawaii and level up into the big wave scene the islands were famous for... So, to learn that we could find twenty-foot swells without shelling out surf tokens on a plane ticket?

Say less!

We packed up the next day and drove for almost two full days from North Carolina to Stars Cove, California.

The *second* we entered the tiny town, I was overcome with this unnerving sensation that I would never leave this place again.

Turtle drove us through the single main road that cut through Stars Cove in the direction of the beach, and I drank in our new home with so much gusto you would think I'd never seen a surf town before.

It was identical to almost every other town we had passed through in the last four years.

The main strip was flanked by pastel-colored surf and souvenir shops. There was a bigger outdoor beach restaurant by the boardwalk called *'Sharkies'* with a **NOW HIRING** sign out front.

This place had everything a couple of surf bums could want or need, including a beach-side trailer park for Turtle to park his van, Shelly.

Get it? *Shelly?* 'Cause turtles have shells? HA!

We'd unpacked and slept in Shelly that night, but I was already itching to explore by morning.

Turtle didn't seem as enamored with the place as I was.

Don't get me wrong, he was *pumped.* He pointed out that the waves were nice (perfect pipelines), but they were a far cry from the twenty-footers we had driven across the entire country to surf.

After poking around, we learned that the waves we were chasing were seasonal and could only be found in the winter months on a much more secluded beach called Leviathans, just outside of town.

That was how I found this shack that I just spent all sixty thousand dollars of my inheritance on.

Now, you might be thinking: *Finn!* That's crazy! Sixty thousand dollars for a SHACK?

To which I say: Bruh. *Look at it!*

I can't believe it was only 60k, if I'm being honest. Sure, the structure itself is small, but it's all about *location*.

It's right by the water, nestled a couple hundred feet back from a crescent moon-shaped *private beach* with consistent *perfect* swells.

It was only a mile away from Leviathans and sat just outside of Stars Cove, making it the perfect halfway point from town and the beach where I planned to make a name for myself.

The place also came fully furnished, and you could just tell the dude who lived here before me was rad as fuck.

The beige, shiplap walls were covered in framed posters of some of the greats. Black and white action shots of Grant "Twiggy" Baker, Mark Foo, and Keala Kennelly filled me with an aching sense of belonging as I handed the completed documents to the realtor.

"Congratulations, Mr. Summers. You're officially a homeowner."

I winced. "Mr. Summers is my father... or he would have been if he stuck around. Oh shit—that was too much information... sorry..." Fuck what was her name? "Brenda! I'm sorry, Brenda. Thanks. For all the, um, help with the paperwork and stuff."

God.

Can you tell I haven't communicated with someone who doesn't eat, sleep, and breathe the ocean for a minute?

This poor gal in her pencil skirt was looking at me like I was some gnarly sea creature squirting ink all over the place.

"Not at all, Mr. uhm, Finn. Welcome to Stars Cove," she said by way of parting, then she let herself out and left me alone in my new digs.

I glanced around at the small but comfortable space, taking in my new bright red couch and cream shag rug. The shack consisted of a split living room/kitchenette, one tiny bathroom with a standing shower, and a small bedroom. It had everything I could possibly need, and a huge grin spread across my face.

I fist-bumped the picture of Mark Foo and sighed happily.

"Home sweet home."

CHAPTER

Two

Finn

"**Y**ou *bought a house!?*"

Turtle's mouth was hanging open in shock. His wavy, chestnut hair was tied in a low bun at the nape of his neck, and he had a Billabong hat on backwards.

Both of us were toned and tanned from spending so much time in the ocean, but Turtle was naturally darker than me overall.

He was wearing a loose tank with the sides cut out, showing off his stick and poke tattoos. There was a goofy cartoon shark on the chest of his shirt, and his navy blue boardshorts had white pineapples on them, making him look like the beachy himbo he was.

I, in contrast, had a mop of sandy hair with some pretty shocking white streaks from all the sun and the salt water. I was also wearing a white tank, but mine just had the Volcom logo on it. Though I was just as fit as the Turtle Man, I was leaner and about a head shorter.

We passed a few local girls on our way to Sharkies, where Turtle said he'd already secured us both jobs as busboys. Which was awesome, considering I was officially house-poor.

I watched the girls check us out as we walked by, and I shot them a big, flirty smile, enjoying the way their cheeks flushed and the gentle sound of their tittering giggles.

"Yeah, man. It's dope as fuck. You should come live with me."

"*And abandon Shelly!?* BRO, who even *are you?*" He gasped, holding his hand over his chest like I had mortally wounded him.

"Yeah, I guess you're right. You and Shelly need each other." I laughed.

"Shelly and I need you too, bro. What about our plans to travel to every beach in the world together!? The adventures of Turtle, Shelly, and the Finn Man—over before they could even begin!" I didn't bother pointing out that it would be impossible to drive Shelly to every beach in the *world.* We wouldn't even be able to take her to every *state.* We obviously couldn't drive to Hawaii.

Instead, I shoved him playfully in the arm as I walked onto the boarded deck that made up Sharkies' dining room. The place didn't open until nine am, so it was deserted. We'd been asked to come in early for orientation, and it was nice to get a sense of the place before it got busy.

I looked around the open-air structure and grinned.

It was *awesome.*

The entire place was open to the elements and so close to the water you could hear the waves as they lapped greedily at the shore.

The border of the dining room was basically just a line of big, thick nautical rope strung through waist-length wooden posts.

The roof was thatched, and there was a big square bar in the center of the wooden floor, surrounded by fifty or so tables.

Turtle assured me Sharkies was almost entirely staffed by kids our age who were just as obsessed with surfing as we were. I was looking forward to getting to know more people in what I was now considering my home.

"I don't know, man. I have a good feeling about this place. I want to stick around."

In typical Turtle fashion, he quickly got over his initial distress and smoothed right into the flow of things.

Shrugging, he grinned. "No worries, Finn Man." He roughed up my hair, and I laughed, shoving him away from me again. "You wanna grow some roots? We'll grow 'em together. Imma probably still chill with Shells, though. I can't leave her, man. Not after everything she's done for us."

I nodded solemnly. "I understand. I would never get between a man and his van."

"You have a van?" A pretty feminine voice chirped from behind us.

We both turned to find a petite blonde girl with a surfer's tan smiling at us. She had straight, white teeth and was wearing what looked like a lifeguard's T-shirt and little red shorts. Upon closer inspection of her shirt, it was actually a Sharkies' shirt, made to look like a lifeguard uniform, which I guess made sense for the beach theme of the restaurant. She was holding two men's versions of the same shirt, and she handed one to each of us as she approached.

I took mine on reflex and grinned at the girl, and Turtle gave her a flirty wink.

"Yeah, babe, wanna come meet her? Shelly loves making new friends." Turtle smiled, and the girl rolled her eyes, though she was still smiling good-naturedly.

"Does that line work on all the girls?" She laughed, and Turtle chuckled, shrugging.

"Some of them."

She snorted and shook her head in amusement.

"I'm Blake." She smiled, reaching out a hand to shake. Her wrist was covered in those colorful friendship bracelets made of thread and knots, and I smiled. Blake seemed cool.

"Hey, I'm Finn, this is Turtle."

"Oh, I know who *you* are," she informed me, her bright blue eyes shining with curiosity. "You're the kook that bought Jake Whittling's old place."

Huh?

"Who's Jake Whittling?" I asked dumbly, and Blake's eyebrows rose.

"You're telling me you bought that place without learning anything about it first?" she asked, sounding shocked.

Turtle and I exchanged a confused look, and I shrugged.

"I dunno, it was right on the beach and a sick price. I just snatched it up."

"Oh my god, dude. You didn't *snatch* anything up. No one's bought that place for a reason."

My good mood was quickly evaporating and being replaced with a small twinge of doubt. I had been so excited about buying that place. The last thing I wanted was to learn that I had wasted all my mom's money on some shack that was condemned and full of black mold or something weird like that.

"What? What do you mean?" I yelped, hating the high-pitched squeak my voice seemed to have taken on.

Blake gave me a sympathetic look before reaching out and giving my arm a comforting squeeze.

"Jake Whittling was, like, a local surfing *legend.* He died last year surfing Leviathans."

Turtle squawked next to me in shock. "What!? Dude *died*?"

Blake nodded, her eyes shining with what I could have sworn were tears. She swallowed so hard I heard it.

"Yeah. It was awful. Everyone *loved* Jake so much. He was such a rad person. No one's bought his spot because I think it hurts too much, you know? Like, that's *his* place. It has been for as long as I've lived here. He was one of the original guys who discovered Leviathans. It's messed up that the beach that made him famous is what ended up killing him."

Guilt welled up in my chest at the real pain in Blake's eyes as she told me about the tragic death of someone she'd clearly really cared about.

"Shit, I'm sorry," I croaked, gripping the T-shirt she had given me tighter in my fists.

She shook her head gently as if trying to brush the painful memories away. Her bleach-blonde ponytail swished behind her in the early sun.

"It's not your fault, Finn. Just... don't be surprised if you get a little pushback over buying his place. People around here have this weird thing about it. Like only someone worthy of it should live there or something."

"What, like, only another Leviathans' rider?" Turtle asked the question I had already been thinking.

"Something like that."

I brightened slightly and gave Blake a reassuring grin.

"Well. Good thing it's my plan to shred Leviathans this winter. That's why I'm here."

Blake barked out a laugh, then seemed to realize I was being serious. The second she took in the earnest look on my face, the blood drained from hers.

"What? No! You can't! Leviathans will eat you alive, Finn."

I frowned, suddenly feeling annoyed and defensive. "You don't know that. You don't even know me! I've been surfing my whole life. I can handle it."

Blake looked me up and down. She clearly didn't mean it in a judgemental way, but it came off that way anyway. I bristled further.

"I may not know you, Finn Summers, but I know Leviathans, and I know you can't surf those waves without someone to coach you."

I was about to argue further when what I assumed was the manager walked into the bar and called Blake's name.

She abandoned our conversation to head over to where the manager was starting to stock the bar, but she paused after a few steps and glanced back over her shoulder at us.

"Let's meet up after work. I'll take you to Leviathans and show you what I mean."

"Deal," I barked back, a little more abruptly than she deserved.

Turtle tossed his lifeguard/uniform shirt over his shoulder, his usually carefree brown eyes dark with concern.

"Well. She's got the tea; I'll give her that," he said, shamelessly staring at her pert ass as it swayed back and forth in her little red Sharkies shorts.

"Apparently," I mused, though I was much less interested in Blake's ass than I was in her complete and utter lack of belief in me.

She didn't even *know* me.

I wasn't one to boost myself, but I wasn't exactly a beginner. I knew what I was doing, and I planned on training all year to ride this wave.

However, when she came back and got to work teaching us the ins and outs of the restaurant and what would be expected of us in our new roles, I couldn't shake the cold pit that had formed in my gut.

Had buying that shack been a mistake?

Had coming here at all been a mistake?

I watched Turtle flirt with Blake and did my best to keep up with what she was telling us, but I was too distracted.

Dead surf prodigies and the monster waves that devoured them filled my mind.

Clenching my fists at my sides, I felt a stubborn swell of determination roll through me.

No.

I was doing this. I was Finn Summers, and I knew I was born to surf since the first day I stood on a board by myself.

If this town wanted to see someone *worthy* of living up to this Jake Whittling guy's legacy, then that was what I was going to give them.

CHAPTER
Three

Finn

Alexa Play: Grow Up by Late Night Thoughts

Our first shift went quickly. It was on the shorter end since it was our first day, and honestly, it wasn't complicated.

See a table with dirty dishes? Clear dirty dishes.

Rinse.

Repeat.

Until you die.

Just kidding, that's a little dramatic, hahaha. But after my seventeenth lap to the dishpit, I was starting to see why Blake had warned us against 'getting lazy.'

I was an adrenaline junkie, constantly on the hunt for my next hit of dopamine. Repetitive shit like bussing tables was the definition of my worst nightmare.

Happily, Turtle was used to keeping my ADHD ass from getting fired, and he immediately turned it into a competition.

He assigned points to all the different types of dishes and started a tally. First one to get to a thousand points got first dibs on the next day's swells.

Nothing lit a fire under my ass like a friendly competition, and by the end of our shift, both the manager and Blake were shaking their heads in awe.

"You two are the best bussers we've ever had," Blake said as Turtle and I met up with her at the host stand. We'd changed out of our uniforms and were ready to check out Leviathans with our new local guide.

I snorted. "Pretty sure *I'm* the best busser you've ever had. I hit a thousand points way before this joker." I laughed.

Turtle smirked at me and shrugged before winking at Blake. "This guy's a little competitive."

She giggled, her blue eyes twinkling with amusement. "I can see that." The light in her eyes dimmed slightly as she realized what that meant. Competitive dudes tended to do dumb shit like riding monster waves despite the warnings of cute local girls.

Turtle was right. I *was* competitive. I was also prone to severe hyperfixation.

The *second* we'd learned about Leviathans while surfing in the East, my mind latched onto the notion of riding these monsters like a super magnet.

It was a familiar feeling, and I knew the signs of my next great obsession brewing. Once I got it in my head that I was going to do something, there was quite literally nothing on the planet that could stop me, not even myself.

I ran at two speeds. Either completely enthralled with something to the point that I ate, slept, and breathed it or completely uninterested to the point that I couldn't even focus if someone mentioned the topic.

'It's always feathers or steel with Finn,' my mother used to tell people, almost as if it were a good thing to be completely incapable of finding the middle ground on anything.

Seeing the concerned look in Blake's eyes, I knew she was already starting to see this dangerous quality in me.

"You gonna take us to Leviathans or what?" I asked, and she nodded slowly. Her brows pinched together as if suddenly wondering if showing us the beach at all was a good idea.

I'd bought that shack because I knew it was close to Leviathans, but I hadn't been able to find the beach itself yet. It wasn't like it was marked. According to Blake, even local surfers were wary of the treacherous waves.

Blake drove an old Volkswagen Golf. I noted her fish board strapped to the roof and grinned. *Nice.* Knew she was cool.

I let Turtle ride shotgun since he was clearly trying to get with her. She surprised me by driving us only four minutes down the road from my beach shack. She parked on the side of the road and turned off the car, motioning for us to get out.

"Down this way," she said, leading us into a nearly completely hidden dirt trail that led into the brush.

As soon as we passed off the road and into the wild terrain that surrounded the rocky coast, I felt a thrill rush through my body.

My pupils blew, and all the blood in my body seemed to rush to the surface of my skin, making me feel both hot and cold at the same time. I trembled as we walked, and each step closer to the distant crash of waves sent my heart rate into a tailspin.

I hadn't physically reacted to something like this since the very first time I felt the sand between my toes, and I swallowed, somewhat unnerved at how powerful of a reaction I was having to my environment.

At the end of the trail, we stood on a rocky outcropping off the edge of a cliff, overlooking a small, hidden beach.

The cliff had what looked like a manageable stairway of natural stone that would be easy enough to climb down if you were careful.

However, I couldn't move.

The second my eyes processed the view before me, my bones locked up, and my breath caught in my throat.

My entire body was tingling, and I shivered as one of the most powerful surges of dopamine I had ever experienced ripped through my veins.

Here, the water wasn't the bright blue I was used to, but a deep navy so cold it felt like a warning. The white caps on the waves were violent peaks of salt, marking the beginning and end of each swell. I nearly panted with excitement as the water crashed against the rocks and sand in savage bursts. My fingers tingled as I watched the sharp edges of the waves cut through the terrain like a hot knife through butter.

We were high enough up that the waves below us appeared diminutive, and it was only experience that told me they were much larger than they appeared.

Every swell that rolled into that small, dark sheet of sand at the foot of the cliff must have cleared at least fifteen feet.

A little over half the size of the twenty-five-foot Leviathans I hoped to see this winter, but still.

The sheer *power...* the *energy* of the ocean below me called to every single one of my pleasure centers.

I could almost hear the ocean calling my name, challenging me to conquer it.

The hyperfixation that had been brewing within me solidified in that instant.

There was a *'snapping'* sensation in my chest, and I knew I would conquer this beach or fucking die trying.

"See what I mean, Finn? This isn't even the high season. This beach is *dangerous*. More experienced surfers than you have literally *died* here. You need to take this really seriously," Blake said. She glanced at me, clearly hoping that this little field trip would have convinced me to stick to safer swells.

However, Turtle took one look at my face and chuckled. He knew what Blake had just done was having the complete opposite effect on me.

It was fucking *on.*

"I'm going to *shred* this beach to pieces," I vowed, my voice coming out low and breathy. I was so excited at the thought that I was borderline turned on. I felt a throb between my legs that had nothing to do with the hot blonde that had shown me the beach that had just fundamentally altered my brain chemistry.

"You're a psycho," Blake whispered, her blue eyes wide and her face so pale she looked like she might pass out.

I gave her a grin that I was sure confirmed I was, in fact, a psycho.

"I need to learn everything there is to know about how these waves break, and I need to learn fast," I told her, and she shook her head, looking at Turtle like he would take her side in this matter.

He just shot her a *Lazy Turtle Smile*™ and slipped his hands into the pockets of his board shorts.

His shoulder-length, wavy brown hair whipped around his handsome face as his dark eyes shone with a look likely very similar to mine.

"Baby Girl, when the Finn Man decides he's gonna ride, not even the devil could stop him. No talking him out of it now."

"Be serious. You could *die.* "

I watched another fifteen-foot wave crash against the beach with the power of a small bomb. White sea foam shot into the salty air like shrapnel, and my grin widened.

"Then I guess I'll die happy."

CHAPTER
Four

Finn

Turtle and I spent the rest of the afternoon shredding up the much more manageable pipelines on the main beach of Stars Cove.

Blake joined us, and it was cool to see her ride. She was pretty fucking good, which really hammered home her warning about Leviathans even further.

Not that I was going to listen to it... but still. There was definitely some hammering going on.

If someone as skilled as Blake was *that* terrified of that beach, I would definitely need to train and study. Best case scenario would really be for me to get an actual coach. Someone who had experience with that specific beach and could run me through all the ins and outs.

See, the trouble with a hidden, local secret like Leviathans is that there wasn't any information online about the wave patterns. More popular beaches like the Banzai Pipeline in Hawaii, for example, have a plethora of information you could study before diving in.

Learning why waves formed the way they did was important to keep yourself safe, as they usually formed due to underwater hazards such as coral reefs or rock formations.

Knowing what you were getting into was half the battle.

As Leviathans was a closely guarded local secret, I couldn't find anything online about the beach, so I would need to dig up an expert to guide me if I was going to be successful.

The trouble was that Blake hadn't been kidding about the townspeople of Stars Cove not being thrilled about me buying Jake Whittling's old place.

As we bobbed on our boards, waiting for our turns to drop in, Blake introduced us to some of the local veterans. None of them seemed interested in *speaking* to me, let alone coaching me.

"Tough crowd," Turtle mused as we turned in for the night. We strapped our boards onto Shelly's roof, and I shrugged, not dissuaded in the slightest.

"They'll warm up to me." I winked at him. "No one can resist the dimples."

"You swore you would only use your dimples for good!" Turtle cried dramatically as he tore a joint out of his wet bag before climbing into the driver's side of the van. "You were the chosen one! Your dimples were meant to bring balance to the force! Not destroy it!"

I cackled as he perched the joint between his lips but didn't light it. He knew better than to drive under the influence, especially with me in the car. After what happened to my mom, I refused to smoke or drink.

Turtle still did, but he never did it before he had to drive. He just had a bit of a hand-to-mouth fixation and liked to play with his joints before he smoked them.

Hopping into the passenger seat, I waved goodbye to Blake as we pulled out of the boardwalk parking lot.

Turtle alternated from glancing at Blake and his rearview as he reversed, and I grinned at him.

"She's cute, huh?" I offered, and he grinned at me.

"She's more than cute, bro. I wanna split that girl in half."

"Jesus," I snorted. "Slow down, we just got here, maybe you shouldn't shit where we eat."

"Who said anything about shitting? She could be wifey material. Mrs. Turtle has a nice ring to it." He grinned as he pulled onto the main road and headed toward my new shack.

"I'm going to start calling you Rabbit instead of Turtle. You're moving at the speed of light, bro; I have whiplash."

His smile just widened. "I figured it was just 'cause rabbits like to fuck a lot," he joked, and I shook my head, laughing.

"Just get me home, you d-bag," I muttered, suddenly glad we weren't sharing the van anymore. The last thing I wanted to do was be up all night listening to Turtle jerk off to visions of Blake in her little red Sharkies shorts.

"Aye, aye, captain." He winked and turned on the stereo, cranking Noah Kahan's soft acoustic notes.

CHAPTER
Five

Finn

'd intentionally left the curtains in my new bedroom open, so when the coral and tangerine glow of the morning sun filtered in, I was up and ready to get started.

Before crashing, I spent about an hour cruising online trying to find anything I could on Leviathans, but I came up empty.

Resolving to worry about finding a coach, once I had managed to get the townsfolk to warm up to me more, I decided to spend the day working on the physical part of my training.

There was a lean-to on the side of the shack that had a bench press with a bar and two 45-lb plates. There was also a free weight rack with dumbbells, which was more than enough for the strength training part of the regiment I had sketched out over a cup of coffee and a bowl of plain oatmeal.

Also, to be clear, *yes,* I agree oatmeal is disgusting. But it's cheap, and it has the carbs I need for energy. So, mushy and bland as it is, I forced that shit down.

I was stretching out my quads, getting ready for some barefoot sprints in the sand (running in sand is *insanely* hard; you should try it!), when a man I'd never seen before strode right past me.

He was shirtless and in black swim trunks with a teal shortboard tucked under his arm. He was older than me. I couldn't tell *how* much older, but if I had to guess, I would say he was in his late thirties. His shoulders were broad, and he was at least two heads taller than I was, with biceps the size of cantaloupes.

He had a chiseled jaw covered in coarse but well-groomed stubble, and his hair was shoulder length like Turtle's, though this man's hair was a swirl of golds and browns.

Like me, he had some pieces that had clearly been bleached by the sun and the salt water.

The man looked exactly like every other old-timer I had seen during my beach bum career while also giving me the sense that he was completely different from anyone I had ever met.

Something about him tickled my brain, like a strange sense of familiarity. I felt like I *knew* him, or was *supposed* to know him, in some weird way.

The sensation was similar to the feeling of deja vu, and I found myself wondering if I had seen his face in my dreams because I couldn't for the life of me think of a place where I could have met this man before.

I mean, I'd surfed a lot of beaches, and the way this guy was heading for my private shoreline like the ocean owed him something told me he wasn't a kook. So maybe I've seen him around..?

Wait.

That's right... This was MY *private shoreline!*

What the shiz? This dude just walked right by me without even *looking* in my direction!

This was *my* property!

Not that I had a problem having people come surf my beach, but maybe at least ask? That was reasonable? *Right?*

I'd never owned property before, but I was almost *positive* it wasn't cool to just roll up onto someone else's land and use their shit without permission.

Remembering what Blake had said about the people of Stars Cove likely having a problem with me buying this shack, I wondered if this was some sort of weird power play.

Like this dude was rolling up here to show me that it didn't matter if I bought this place, it still belonged to the town, and they could come and go as they pleased.

I wouldn't necessarily classify myself as a *hot head*, but between the T man and me, I was definitely the more... uhhh, *spunky* of the two. That's the word my mom used, at least.

So when the initial shock of seeing the man passed and my temper flared, I didn't really think of the consequences as I stormed after him.

"Hey!" I shouted, kicking sand up as I bulldozed toward him. His back was now toward me, and he didn't respond or even look at me.

Dick.

"HEY! Douchebag! I'm talking to you!" I barked. This made the man pause. He glanced back at me, his stern brows drawing together in a sharp frown. I was struck suddenly by just how blue the man's eyes were.

They were *so* strikingly blue, like the color of the ocean in those over-edited travel magazines. They were even more blue than Blake's eyes, and that was saying something. Those two swirling shards of pure aquamarine locked onto my face, and I watched as his frown line smoothed out into a look of surprise.

His mouth parted slightly, and I watched him trace the tip of his tongue over his bottom lip as I approached, my temper still flaring hot beneath my skin.

"Yeah, *you!* This is private property, buddy. You can't just use my beach without asking me if it's ok!"

I was right in front of him now, standing less than a foot away, and I needed to tilt my head back to look him in the face.

A chill rolled through me as I realized how much bigger than me the man was. Maybe confronting him head-on hadn't been the smartest move I'd ever made, but *still*.

The man looked me up and down, then glanced back at my beach shack before cocking his head to the side in curiosity.

"*You* bought the shack?" he asked. I don't know what I expected his voice to sound like, but I wasn't prepared for the deep rumble that felt like a physical thing as it rolled over me. All the hairs on my arms stood on end, and I suddenly felt very young and small standing next to him.

His entire body was corded in thick, lean muscle. He looked like a brick fucking wall, all hard lines and sharp edges. His skin was a deep, golden brown, and his chest was covered in groomed but coarse hair, framing his dark nipples, which stood out in stark contrast against his honey-gold skin.

I blinked, feeling weird that I was looking at this dude's nipples when I should be kicking him off my property.

"Yeah. You got a problem with that?" I snapped. He didn't react to the obvious venom in my tone. Instead, he just stared at me like I was some big, complicated puzzle he couldn't seem to figure out.

He glanced over his shoulder as if checking to see if we were alone, and then he dragged his gaze back to meet mine.

It literally felt like he removed a weight from my chest when he looked away, then slammed the weight back into me when our eyes met again.

My breath caught in my throat.

What was up with this guy? Why was I having such a strong reaction to him?

I shook off the strange sensation, chalking it up to the fact that I was just on edge because he was so boldly trespassing without any signs of remorse.

"Why would I have a problem with that?" he asked, his tone even and dry. It didn't sound like he actually cared about my answer.

"I don't know. A lot of people seem to have an issue with the fact that I bought Jake Whittling's old place."

The second I said the name, I regretted it. The man's face crumbled like I had physically struck him.

There was a heavy, pregnant moment of silence, then finally, he seemed to recover and spoke again, his voice an octave lower than it had been before.

"Jake Whittling is dead. What does it matter who buys his place?"

My anger was quickly disappearing. The heat in my veins was being replaced with a sense of remorse. This man had clearly known Jake Whittling. The pain in his eyes when I mentioned his name was so raw I felt myself swallow.

"Uhm. Some people in town yesterday already made a big deal about it. I thought you were here to, I dunno, make some sort of a statement against me," I admitted, rubbing the back of my neck awkwardly while the strange dude continued to stare at me like I was the one trespassing on *his* property and not the other way around.

"I don't give a fuck if you bought the shack, kid. I'm just here to surf."

"Well, this is *my* beach. If you want to surf here, you need to ask permission."

Suddenly, the sadness in the man's eyes disappeared and was replaced with a steely sort of dominance.

On reflex, I took a step back and cursed myself internally.

Way to stand your ground, Finn.

"You want me to ask permission?" he challenged. That low, rumbly voice sent a shot of something that felt very similar to an adrenaline high through me. Something low in my gut tightened, and there was a confusing moment when my mouth flooded with saliva.

What the fuck?

He stepped toward me, and I forced myself not to back away as he hovered inches from my face.

"I've been surfing this beach since you were in diapers, kid. I'm not asking you for shit."

He turned to walk away, and suddenly, my temper was back.

I reached out without thinking and grabbed his arm, my fingers flexing over his warm, solid flesh. His skin was soft and hot from the steady beat of the early morning sun. Despite the heat, I shivered as he turned those icy blue eyes on me again.

He glanced down at where my fingers were wrapped around his forearm, clearly shocked that I had the balls to touch him.

Hell.

I was shocked that I had the balls to touch him.

We stood there, frozen for a moment, before I realized what I was doing and ripped my hand away. He continued staring at the place I had touched him for a long moment, and I cleared my throat awkwardly.

"Uhm, sorry. It's just—"

He slowly locked his gaze on mine again, and I shook my head, beating back the strange submissiveness his presence seemed to be drawing out of me.

Forcing myself to straighten, I met his insanely intimidating gaze head-on. I had an idea. If he really had been surfing here for over twenty years, then he definitely knew about Leviathans. Even if he hadn't ridden the waves himself, he had to know some local lore he could share with me. I shot him one of my most charming grins. It was the smile I used to get girls out of their panties and free shit from surf shops.

I hadn't met anyone yet who was immune to this particular grin, and I was willing to bet this dude was no exception.

"How about we work out a deal?"

He narrowed his eyes.

"What sort of deal?"

"I'm looking for someone to coach me."

"Coach you?"

"Yeah, coach me."

"Coach you on what?"

"I need someone to coach me on the best way to tackle Leviathans. I'm shredding that beach this winter, and I need help getting ready. If you agree to help me out, I'll let you surf my beach as much as you want, no questions asked."

If I thought I'd made this dude angry before, it was nothing compared to the pure rage that ripped through his features at my offer.

Suddenly, he was in my face again, his lip curling up in a snarl, flashing perfect, straight teeth.

"I'm not in the habit of leading *little boys* to their deaths, kiddo. Now get the fuck out of my hair and go back to whatever pussy ass workout you were about to attempt before you decided to so *rudely* interrupt me."

Then, before I could respond, he was gone.

I watched him sprint full tilt for the beach and leap onto his teal shortboard, paddling like a bonafide expert out into the surf.

CHAPTER

Six

Riddick

The kid followed me into the water, and I gritted my teeth in frustration. No one had surfed this beach in nearly a year... not since *the incident*.

I had no idea that someone had bought the shack, and honestly, while I knew I should have been happy that Jake's... *legacy,* for lack of a better word, was finally starting to be erased, I really just felt annoyed that this little prick was here disturbing my peace.

Because it was a *good thing* that the town was finally moving on. The boys had done everything in their power to keep the accident from becoming this big, sensationalized thing. And most of the fail-safes they had installed to keep Leviathans a secret seemed to have been held up. Or so I had thought.

The last thing I wanted was people like this dumbass kid swarming to Leviathans and killing themselves riding waves they had no business riding.

I'd always been against keeping the shack as some sort of weird shrine, no matter what Jake's death meant to the town... what it meant to *me*.

Selling the place meant that the tragedy would fade into the past where it belonged, and I could finally rest in peace knowing that my foolishness wouldn't put an entire new generation of surfers at risk.

I wished the guys and I had never discovered Leviathans in the first place. Now, with this punk-ass kid paddling out after me on his highlighter pink board, I regretted it more than ever.

"Fuck off, kid. I surf alone," I snapped over my shoulder, tossing my wet hair out of my face as I prepared to drop in.

"Yeah, except you're surfing on *my beach,* dickhead. The least you could do is hear me out!" the little shit called after me as I caught my wave.

His protests melted away, however, as the water tumbled and rolled beneath my board. I leapt to my feet, completely forgetting about the annoying kid the second I caught traction. I fell into the familiar feeling of carving through the green room, running my fingers across the warm wall of water as I passed through the barrel of the wave. Already lost in the magic of the sea, I caught myself smiling at the cacophony of sparkling whites, blues, and aquamarines that made up this temporary world of liquid glass.

A moment of true peace possessed me as I edged my toes over the nose of my board, hanging ten, and I thought: *This* must be what heaven is like...

The thought was fleeting, however, as that punk-ass kid suddenly ripped past me, carving out in front of my board in a clear attempt to force me to bail.

Rage flared through me.

Dropping in on someone else's wave wasn't only bad etiquette, it was fucking *dangerous.*

And this asshole wanted to ride Leviathans?

Fucker!

I wiped out just as the wave broke, and my board shot out from under me. My tether snapped taut, both keeping my board from getting lost in the ocean and causing a small spark of panic to shoot through me.

As I rolled through the aftermath of the wave, instinctively righting myself and following my tether to the surface, I hauled myself out of the water and straddled my board.

I could hear the kid cackling in the distance, and anger like I hadn't felt in *years* ripped through my veins.

I locked eyes on him, and suddenly, he wasn't laughing anymore.

Laying down on my board, I started paddling toward him. This little shithead *clearly* had a death wish.

He wanted to kill himself on Leviathans? I would make it easy for him and drown his skinny ass right here, right now.

He gulped when he realized I was out for blood, and he plastered himself to his own board, catching a baby wave into shore.

I cursed under my breath and followed suit.

By the time I was in the shallows, he was already sprinting through the sand back to the shack, and I almost laughed.

He was sorely mistaken if he thought he would be safe from me there.

I'd basically grown up in that shack. I knew things about it that no other living person knew, like the fact you could disable the lock mechanism in the door handle by pushing it in slightly and giving it a clockwise, quarter turn.

Sprinting after him, I ripped the quick release off my ankle tether, abandoning my board and following the kid into the shack.

Predictably, he tried to lock me out, and he yelped in terror as I exploded through the door like I owned the place.

"Dude! It was a joke, relax!" He was babbling, holding up his hands and backing away from me.

He was so small. Just a little pipsqueak, and I forced down my amusement at the fact that he felt brave enough to fuck with me. I wasn't done being pissed with him. No time to admire the giant balls he must have hiding under those Hawaiian swim trunks.

Ignoring his protests, I crowded forward until he was backed up against the wall, smack dab between the black and white portraits of Mark Foo and Keala Kennelly.

I slammed him against the wall by his throat and marveled at how easily my hand swallowed him whole.

"Jesus, dude! I'm sorry, ok!?" He was kicking his feet and clawing at my hand as I watched him struggle beneath my grip. I stared, fascinated, as he scraped his blunt fingernails over my skin, carving deep red marks into my wrist.

I'd avoided people since the accident, so even though his marks hurt, they were oddly comforting.

They were better than feeling nothing.

Now that I had him pinned, I took a second to really look at him.

He had a mop of golden hair that had a few sun-bleached strands poking out.

His cheeks, which were currently flushed pink from the physical exertion, were dusted with a light smattering of freckles. His hazel eyes had looked blue outside but were now leaning toward a soft green. Each eye was lined in thick dark lashes. I was so close I could nearly count them.

There was a drop of saltwater on his pouty, pink lips, and I watched his tongue dart out to lick it off as he continued to buck and arch against my ironclad grip.

"You think it's cool to drop in on someone else's wave?" I asked, my voice low and calm. The more he struggled, the tighter I squeezed, relishing in the way his pink cheeks began to turn an alarming shade of red.

He coughed and shook his head.

"No, I just... I didn't know how else to get your attention!" he croaked. I could feel his heartbeat in my fingertips, and I forced myself to let up a bit so he could breathe.

"You have my attention now," I growled, and his cheeks turned an even deeper shade of crimson. His skin was flushed and hot beneath my palm, and he squirmed again, though he seemed less desperate now.

He was looking at me in a way that suddenly made me feel off balance. I couldn't put my finger on what it was, but my heart skipped a beat.

"Listen..." He coughed again, and I reflexively backed off a little more, letting him take in a big gulp of air he clearly needed. "I need your help. You want to surf on my property; it's a win-win."

"I don't need your permission to surf here. You can't stop me," I pointed out, tilting my head toward his prone, sea-slick form. He was hairless and lean.

So... young and...*vibrant.*

My throat caught, and I let out a slow breath through my nose, pushing back the ever-present trauma of the accident that haunted my every waking moment.

"I'll call the cops!"

I barked out a laugh and leaned in closer to him, enjoying the way the color in his cheeks continued to deepen at my proximity. He smelled... *amazing.* Like the ocean and sunscreen... but also something more masculine and raw. Something that I was pretty sure was just his natural scent. I resisted the sudden urge to lean in closer to inhale.

Instead, I growled, "Go for it, kid. They're not gonna do shit."

His expression flickered from angry to frustrated to devastated and then, finally, defeat.

He sort of deflated against the wall and hung his head.

I should have felt happy that I won.

But something about watching all the fire melt out of him just pissed me off even more. It reminded me too much of myself and everything I lost the day that wave killed Jake Whittling.

"That's it? You're giving up?" I found myself saying, my tone much more accusatory than it should have been.

His head whipped up, and he narrowed his eyes on me.

"I won't ever *give up*, dude. If you're not willing to help me, I'll still find a way to do it on my own. I'm surfing Leviathans. It's happening. Help me or don't," he spat, and I snarled, my fingers tightening around his throat again.

I stroked my thumb over his heartbeat, gritting my teeth in frustration.

Thump, thump, thump.

Strong. Vibrant. *Alive.*

"You have a fucking death wish, kid?" I snapped, and he chuckled, giving me this sly, mischievous little smile that I was sure got him out of all kinds of trouble. He had dimples on both cheeks, and I would bet money he could convince the devil to give him a hall pass with that smile.

"I won't die if you help me." He smirked and shrugged despite the fact that I still had him pinned to the wall by his throat. "If you don't help me... well. I guess I *will* probably die." He sighed, checking his nails like I wasn't about to crush his damn windpipe.

Little fucker.

He met my gaze dead on, and that impish smile of his spread wider. He knew he had me.

With a snarl, I released him and spun away, running my fingers into my hair and tugging at the roots in frustration.

This wasn't heaven. This was fucking hell.

Fuck this kid.

"What is *wrong* with you?" I hissed at him. "Do you not value your life at all? Did you not hear about what happened last year? About why this shack was even available for you to buy?"

He rubbed his throat gingerly, watching me with one eye squeezed shut as if it hurt to touch the bruise blossoming on his neck.

Guilt crashed through me, and I immediately regretted losing my temper like that. He couldn't be older than what? Twenty? Twenty-one?

It wasn't his fault he was a little prick. He would grow out of it.

I had...

I think.

"Yeah, I heard. It sucks, but I'm not that Jake guy. I'm gonna do it, and I'm gonna live to talk about it."

I glowered at him.

So *arrogant*.

I ignored the voice in the back of my head that reminded me *I* had been arrogant once, too. We all had. We hadn't had anyone to coach us or teach us.

Maybe if we had, things would have been different.

Looking at this stubborn little asshole in front of me, I knew nothing I said to him would talk him out of doing it.

I knew it because nothing would have talked *me* out of doing it.

"Fine," I barked, and the *smile* that broke out on the kid's face... Both his dimples popped, and I scowled.

"Really!?" he asked, leaping up in the air like a Mexican jumping bean.

I pinched the bridge of my nose and sighed.

"Yeah. Really."

"What, like, now?"

I glared at him as I headed for the door.

"No, kid. Not, like, *now,*" I mocked. "We'll start tomorrow. *Now,* I'm going to finish my morning sesh. Try not to fucking drop in on me again, yeah?"

He nodded his head eagerly, his megawatt smile so big I swear the corners of his mouth were going to touch his ears.

"Yeah, yeah! No problem... Mr..."

"Riddick. You can call me Riddick."

"You got it, Riddick!" he chirped happily, and I paused at the door just as I was about to leave.

"One last thing..." I trailed off, clearly wanting him to tell me his name.

"Finn."

I nodded.

"One last thing, Finn. If you tell anyone about our little arrangement, the deal's off, got it?"

His giant smile slipped a notch, and he frowned.

"How come?"

I sighed. "My buddies and I have been trying to keep Leviathans from getting swarmed for years. No one's going to be thrilled to hear that you're training to ride the wave that killed Stars Cove's poster boy."

This didn't seem to sit right with him, and I scoffed.

"So you're in it for the glory, then? You need the crowds and the titles and the accolades or what, it's not worth it?"

His frown deepened, and he set his jaw, locking his fierce, impish gaze on me.

"It's not about that. It's about proving to myself that I can do it," he insisted, and my lip twitched.

"Well then, you shouldn't have a problem keeping your damn mouth shut. Welcome to the club, kid."

"There's a club!?" he asked excitedly, following me out of the shack, much to my dismay.

"Yeah, there's a club," I grumbled.

And the only way out is in a fucking body bag.

But I didn't tell the little imp that last part. That was something he was going to have to learn on his own.

CHAPTER
Seven

Finn

I spent the day surfing with Riddick.

Well, WITH Riddick was a stretch. He barely acknowledged I was there. But I was with him, whether he wanted me to be or not.

He was better than me.

He was better than anyone I had ever met, if I was being honest. I could understand why he was so pissed at me for dropping in on his wave after watching him for only an hour.

Riddick didn't wipe out.

Like, *ever.*

And it's not like he was just carving up the pipe; he was casually doing super sick, advanced shit with his eyes basically closed.

Riddick doing a layback was one of my new favorite things. I wanted to be able to do the things he could do.

I wanted to *look* how he looked while he was doing it.

He was *amazing*.

Watching Riddick surf felt like I was witnessing something sacred. The complete look of serenity that took over his expression each time he caught a wave was mesmerizing to me.

Then he would lock eyes with me, and that look would disappear and immediately be replaced with a hard, grouchy scowl.

I didn't think he liked me very much, which was unusual for me. Most people loved me, so it bothered me that Riddick didn't.

He ignored me every time I tried to chat him up and rolled his eyes whenever I tried to ask him a question about himself.

And I had *a lot* of questions.

How long have you been surfing?

Have you surfed in Hawaii?

Who taught you to hang ten?

Can you teach me to hang ten?

Have you been in any surfing competitions?

You're good enough to be in surfing competitions. Do you think I'm good enough to be in surfing competitions? There's one I've always wanted to go to in Australia.

Ever been to Australia?

I've heard surfing is sick there. Do you think that's true? They have a lot of sharks, though.

Ever seen a shark?

What would you do if you saw a shark?

Are you scared of sharks? I don't really know what it feels like to be scared of stuff, but sometimes I wonder what would happen if a shark tried to chomp on me, but then I forget about them once I'm riding... Does that happen to you, too? Do you ever think about sharks chomping on you?

"ENOUGH!" he finally snarled at me as he rode his last wave onto the beach.

We got out of the water, and I trotted after him, slinging my board under my arm. He was quite a bit taller than me, so I had to take two steps for every step he took to keep up.

"Where are you going? Do you have a ride home? How did you get here? Where do you live? I can call my friend Turtle, and he can give you a lift if you need one…" I babbled happily as he ripped off his ankle strap and shook his head roughly as if trying to get water out of his ears.

"Do you ever *shut up?*" he snapped, whirling on me, and I grinned.

"Nuh-uh," I replied honestly.

He stared at me for a long moment, and I just stood there, grinning at him.

C'mon big guy. Admit I'm adorable. No one can resist these dimples.

That's what my mom used to always say.

She said my dimples would be my key to taking over the world one day, and so far, they haven't let me down.

Riddick was stubborn, sure, but he couldn't resist me forever. I was loveable as fuck, and I knew it.

"No, I don't need a ride," he finally said, his blue eyes flashing with something I didn't understand.

"I'll be back here in the morning. Five AM. Be ready."

"Five AM?! Dude, I have a shift tonight at Sharkies. It's a close; I won't be done till two."

Riddick shrugged. "Not my problem."

Fuck.

I was going to have to ask to switch off closing if he was going to insist on starting so early every day.

He was staring at me, his face an impassive wall, and I knew he was challenging me to argue with him.

I nodded and saluted him, not wanting to give him an excuse to accuse me of not being committed.

"Yessir. Five AM. I'll be ready."

He narrowed his eyes.

"A few other things."

I grinned, perking up. "Yeah? I'm all ears!" I wished I had a notebook to write down whatever sage wisdom I was sure he was about to impart upon me.

His frown deepened, but he continued as if I hadn't said anything.

"If we're going to do this, there will be rules."

"Yeah, you already said." I nodded, pretending to zip my mouth shut.

His expression remained blank and serious. I had the distinct feeling he was watching me closely, and my reaction to his next words was important.

"From now on, you're not to drink, smoke, or party."

Was that all? I shrugged.

"No problem. I don't drink anyway."

Riddick's eyes widened in surprise.

"You don't?"

I shook my head. "Nuh-uh. My mom was killed by a drunk driver. I haven't been interested in alcohol at all since then. I don't smoke either. The sober life is the life for me."

For a split second, I thought his ice-blue eyes softened, but I must have been imagining it because I blinked, and the next second, his expression was hard as stone again.

It made my stomach feel all twisty.

I wanted him to be impressed that I didn't drink. I had the feeling he was, but I needed him to validate my suspicion.

I wasn't sure if it was from watching him surf all day or the fact that he was probably the first person I had ever met who didn't immediately warm up to me, but I needed his approval like I needed my next breath.

"Fine. One more thing."

"Yeah?"

"No fucking."

I felt like he'd physically struck me.

"W-what?"

"I don't repeat myself," he said, turning on his heel and taking his board toward my lean-to.

"Wait! No fucking? Why not?"

"Fucking leads to relationships. Relationships are distractions. You don't have time for distractions if you want to survive Leviathans. I need you to be focused one hundred percent on your training. You're not focusing on your goals if you're out chasing tail or worrying about some chick breaking your heart."

That made sense, actually.

I nodded as I followed him into the lean-to, where he slapped his board into the rack next to my boards.

Oookayyy. Guess he was keeping his boards here now.

"Alright. I can do that."

I think…

Fuck. That was the one rule that was going to be the hardest.

I thought of Blake and how likely it was that Turtle was going to be on a mission to get in her pants. Usually, we acted as each other's wingmen. It was going to be hard to explain to Turtle why I couldn't join him in the great chase for pussy… especially without being able to tell him about Riddick.

Riddick shot me a skeptical look and raised an eyebrow as if he doubted I could do it.

I scowled.

"Don't look at me like that. I can do it! I can still jerk off, right?"

He cocked his head to the side.

"I'll let you make that decision on your own."

"What does *that* mean?" I asked, my mouth hanging open.

"It means exactly what you think it means," he said, turning away from me and walking back out onto the beach.

"I don't know what I think it means! Why'd you say it like that? Are you trying to tell me I can't fuck *or* jack off?" I was scrambling to chase after him as he headed for my property line. He was already disappearing into the brush in nothing but his swim trunks by the time I caught up to him.

"*Riddick!* I'm twenty-one! If I can't fuck *or* beat off, I'm pretty sure my balls will explode!" I was calling after him as I chased him into the brush.

"Ow, fuck!" I cried out as I stepped on a sharp rock. Grabbing my foot, I hopped up and down on one leg, scanning the overgrown ferns and palms for Riddick.

I couldn't see him anymore. The only indication that he'd been there at all was the now distant rustle of branches as he wandered farther into the untamed land that surrounded my property.

Damn, he was fast.

He wasn't even wearing shoes!

I glanced down at my foot, relieved to see that the rock hadn't broken skin, though I might get a bruise.

That hurt like a bitch!

Did he seriously not want me to jack off?

My mind was spinning, and I didn't know what to think.

Surely having the bluest balls on the planet would be just as bad of a distraction as a relationship?

I was probably totally misunderstanding him.

I shook my head and turned back, resolving to get ready for my shift instead of worrying about what Riddick meant by *'I'll let you make that decision on your own.'*

Why did he make it sound like a test?

Like, if I chose wrong, he wouldn't train me?

Fuck!

I ran my hand down my face and let out an exasperated sigh.

Whatever. It's not like he would know if I beat off anyway. And I didn't need to right now, so there was no point worrying about it until it became an issue.

For now, all I needed to do was make it through my second shift and get as much sleep as possible before the enigma that was Riddick showed back up to confuse me even more.

CHAPTER
Eight

Finn

Predictably, Turtle wanted me to come back to the van after work. He'd invited Blake and her super hot friend, Quinn, to come 'chill,' which usually meant we were gonna try and get laid.

Quinn was a petite, tanned brunette with shiny hair and big green eyes. She was almost *exactly* my type. What made things worse was she was also super cool and really into surfing.

If we had met these girls on the East Coast, I would have been balls deep in Quinn before you could say *'hang loose.'*

But, I had promised Riddick I wouldn't fuck anyone, so I had to make up some excuse about having a stomach ache so I could head home.

I got a boner that night while showering and thinking of what could have happened with Quinn if I had stayed. Out of habit, I reached down to stoke myself when Riddick's piercing blue eyes suddenly cut across the forefront of my mind.

'It means exactly what you think it means.'

My dick throbbed in my hand, and I forced myself to stop stroking it, though I massaged my balls a little with my other hand, doing my best to quell the fire that had been building down there.

Fuck.

This was ridiculous.

He definitely didn't actually mean I couldn't beat off.

I closed my eyes and called Quinn's pretty face back up to the forefront of my mind and tugged on my dick again, pretending it was her puffy, gloss-covered lips wrapped around me instead of my own hand.

I got maybe two strokes in when my stupid mind started playing tricks on me.

Suddenly, I felt like someone was watching me. I blinked and found myself imagining that Riddick was in the bathroom with me, his blue eyes trained on my throbbing cock.

The expression on his face told me he wasn't impressed that I was in the shower touching myself, and I scowled.

Blinking again, I shook my head to rid myself of his image and tried to conjure Quinn back up, but I couldn't get back into it.

Why had I imagined Riddick in here, watching me?

My skin turned to gooseflesh, and my dick throbbed painfully at the thought of his eyes trained on my cock, watching me stroke myself.

I couldn't shake the feeling that he would be disappointed in me for failing his challenge on the first day... even though he had never confirmed that I actually shouldn't be beating off.

However, I was nothing if not competitive. Even if there was a slight chance that he actually *had* been challenging me not to jerk off, I couldn't let him win.

Especially not on the first night.

Shaking my head again, I released my still rock-hard cock and got out of the shower, hoping if I ignored my erection, it would die down soon.

CHAPTER

Nine

Finn

I woke up still hard.

"Fuuuuckkkk," I whined, rolling out of bed and stumbling into the bathroom to try and take a piss. It was difficult and hurt like a bitch, considering how hard I was. However, the effort seemed to help considerably with my little problem, and by the time Riddick strode into the shack like he lived here, my erection was gone.

Thank god.

His gaze slammed into mine while I was in mid-oatmeal scoop. My breath caught in my throat.

The memory of the weird fantasy I had the night before of him watching me in the shower swam across my mind, and I felt my cheeks flame.

What the fuck was going on with me?

"Is that all you're eating?" he asked abruptly, his face blank.

"Uhhh, it was gonna be, yeah."

"You need protein, too. Every day. Double your portion sizes. I want you to put on at least ten pounds before winter."

"Um, okay. No problem!" I agreed quickly. I would get Turtle to take me to get groceries after today's session.

"Let's go," he ordered before turning on his heel and stripping off his T-shirt on his way out.

"Fuck, um, okay." I shoveled the rest of my oatmeal into my cheeks and chased after him, trying to swallow down the bland, chunky porridge as I ran.

"Should I grab my board or…"

"No. Today, we're focusing on cardio and endurance."

I nodded eagerly. "Okay, great."

Riddick made his way to the shoreline, and I followed so close that I was nearly kissing his heels.

He stopped short before entering the water and spun to face me.

"You drink last night?" he asked abruptly. I frowned.

"No, I told you that I don't—"

"You smoke?"

"No, Riddick."

"Fuck?"

"No."

"You do anything else I should know about?" he asked, and my heart skipped a beat.

"What d'you mean?" I stammered, once again remembering the way I had imagined him watching me stroke my cock in the shower. His piercing, blue eyes pinning me with that devastating look of disappointment.

He didn't answer; he just stared at me with that stone-cold, blank expression he always wore.

"What do you mean?" I asked again, my voice quieter now. My heart was pounding so hard I was worried he could see my pulse jumping in my throat.

"I mean exactly what you think I mean, Finn," he replied, his voice low and quiet. I felt a rush of heat roll through me.

So he'd meant what I thought he meant yesterday? He didn't want me to beat off?

Was that weird?

Should I think that's weird?

Why did it feel hot instead of weird?

Was I... into that?

Was I into him? *Like... the same way I was into girls like Quinn?*

My mind couldn't even comprehend that thought.

I looked at Riddick... like, *really* looked at him.

Objectively, he was definitely hot as fuck. He was ripped and had one of those V-cut lines that disappeared into the waist of his shorts. My gaze slid down his chest and abs and landed between his legs, where I could make out the outline of his dick.

It was definitely a huge dick... If I was into him, what would I even *do* with a dick like that?

Fuck!

I totally just checked out his dick!

Did he notice?

I glanced up at him to find him still staring at me intently, waiting for me to answer his question.

I could have sworn the corner of his mouth twitched, but again, maybe I was imagining it.

"Uhm, well, I started to... you know, because I wasn't sure, but then I stopped because I thought that maybe if what I thought you said was *actually* what you meant, I didn't want to fail... especially on the first night. So, like, yeah, I kinda did, a little? But I didn't come!"

He just raised an eyebrow and continued to stare at me.

Oh god, why the fuck did I just tell him that?

My face was so hot, and I was definitely as red as a tomato.

I fidgeted under the weight of his gaze and wrung my fingers together. Why did I feel like I did something bad?

Was he disappointed in me?

Why the fuck did I care if this dude I just met was disappointed in me for *touching* myself?

Why had I even volunteered that information! I could have just lied.

What was worse was that I still wasn't even sure if that was *actually* what he had been asking me. Maybe he'd been asking if I'd told anyone about our arrangement? That would make way more sense!

Ohgodohgodohgod...

This was fucking humiliating.

"I—uhm—"

"You're going to give me an hour of high-intensity interval swimming," he said curtly.

The abrupt change in topics felt like he had dumped a cold bucket of water on me.

"Oh-o-okay..." I stammered, scanning his face for any indication at all that he thought I was insane for telling him I didn't come the night before. However, as always, his expression remained hard and impenetrable.

"You're going to give me five 100-meter sprints with 30-second rest, followed by a 500-meter relaxed swim."

He stepped closer to me as he said it, keeping his gaze locked on mine, and for some reason, my skin sheeted with goosebumps at his proximity.

I could feel the heat radiating off him, and I tilted my head back so I wouldn't be staring directly at his chiseled chest.

My dick twitched in my pants, and I swallowed.

"Yeah. Sure thing, Riddick, no problem."

We stood there, staring at each other, and I focused as hard as I could on not popping another boner.

Think of un-hot shit... think of grannies... dog poop, dead bugs!

"Finn." His voice rumbled through the short distance that separated us, competing with the crash of the waves as they rolled up on the shore.

I swallowed. "Um, yeah?"

"What are you waiting for?"

"Right, sorry…" I cleared my throat and turned to hit the water.

A strong hand wrapped around my bicep, jerking me back to face him.

I tripped and fell into him. Suddenly, my palm was flat against his warm chest as I tried to steady myself. My fingers grazed his nipple, and I watched in fascination as it hardened… just like a girl's nipple would.

My mouth watered, and I licked my lips before peeking back up at him.

He brushed his thumb against my bicep in what felt like a *very* intentional way and leaned down, pressing his mouth close to my ear.

"Don't drown," he whispered, and my scalp tingled as his hot breath caressed the side of my neck.

Then, without warning, he shoved me away from him, and I stumbled ungracefully into the water.

He watched me swim out with that same unreadable expression on his face, and I had never been so grateful to be in the ocean as I was at that moment.

As long as I was in here, the evidence of the strange effect he seemed to have on my body was just between me and the waves.

CHAPTER
Ten

Finn

After the first hour, when I showed no signs of tiring, he made me do another sixty minutes.

Then another.

Until I really *did* almost drown.

He had to come in and get me when my arms stopped working, and I could barely keep myself afloat.

I choked and spat out the seawater I'd swallowed as he dragged me unceremoniously back to the beach and tossed me effortlessly into the sand.

Pushing myself up on shaky arms, I coughed and winced at how exhausted I was.

"I feel like I'm going to die."

"Stop being so dramatic. You're not going to die."

"Dude, I just killed myself out there for three hours, and you still seem pissed with me or something!"

I peered up at him, squinting against the sun's blaring heat to try to make out his face as he towered over me.

"I just had to save you from drowning on day one, Finn. What did you think? I was going to give you a reward?"

I scowled at him, the first nips of anger finally starting to overtake me.

I shakily got to my feet, blinking away the dark spots swimming across my vision.

"I was doing high-intensity laps for *three hours,* Riddick! Anyone would have a hard time with that!"

His eyes flashed, but that was the only indication he gave that I'd pissed him off. If I was being honest, I'm pretty sure he was *already* pissed off. He was pissed at me before he even sent me out into the ocean.

A small, insecure part of me wondered if it was because I had admitted to touching myself, and this was some sort of weird punishment for disobeying his super vague order that I still wasn't even sure was actually an order.

Suddenly, he was crowding me. I took a few shaky steps back, but he cuffed my throat. He didn't squeeze as hard as he had the day before, and if I didn't know any better, I would say he was being careful not to aggravate the mild bruise that now marked my throat from the rough way he'd handled me in the shack.

"You think three hours is a lot?"

"Yeah! It *is* a fucking lot. I killed it today."

He chuckled, but there was no joy in the sound. It was actually scary, and I shivered despite the heat of the sun on my salt-slicked skin.

"Try two days, Finn."

"Wh-what? Why would I need to be able to swim sprints for *two days*?"

"Kai Kalani. Ever heard of him?"

I shook my head, and he stroked his thumb over the jumping pulse point in my neck the same way he'd done yesterday. The way he did it was strange. Like he was checking to make sure it was still there, and my heart was still beating.

"He was a buddy of mine. Kai had to tread water for nearly forty-eight hours in some of the roughest chop I've ever seen after we were stupid enough to ignore the warnings in Waimea. I thought for sure he was dead, but our pal, Jet, wouldn't let us give up until we at least had a body to take back with us."

My entire body rolled with goosebumps as he stroked his thumb over my pulse again. He didn't even seem to notice he was doing it. His eyes were burning with intense heat as if he were reliving some horrible memory and couldn't even see me standing right in front of him.

"We found him alive. It wasn't a *miracle* like the newspapers claimed. It was his dedication to his training mixed with pure *dumb fucking luck.*"

The rage in his voice was like a drug. It skated over my flushed cheeks, and I could feel each thump of my heart like the beat of a drum.

"So... that was really a lesson? You were trying to teach me how to survive if I get stuck in a situation where I'll need to swim that long to wait for help?"

"Everything I do to you will be a lesson, Finn."

I bit my lip at the dark way he said that, trying as hard as I could not to get hard again.

"So you weren't punishing me?"

His eyes dropped to my mouth, and his tender strokes on my neck came to an abrupt halt.

I held my breath as he leaned closer. I knew he was doing it to try and scare me, but honestly, it was just turning me the fuck on and confusing the shit out of me.

His lips were *right there.*

Why did I have this overwhelming desire for him to kiss me?

"Of course I'm punishing you, Finn."

He was angry. *So, so angry.* I searched his eyes, frowning.

"Why?"

He slid his hand up my neck and stroked his thumb over me one more time before letting me go. Only this time, he traced my jawline instead of my pulse, and I shuddered.

"You know why," he rumbled, then pulled away.

I nearly whimpered out loud as he stepped away from me. Losing his touch and his presence felt like this cataclysmic thing, and I didn't understand the sudden and very intense feelings that seemed to be consuming me.

"You're done for the day, Finn. Make sure you eat. I'll be back. Same time tomorrow. Rules still apply."

Then he walked away, leaving me standing alone on the beach, shaking, hard, and *so fucking confused.*

CHAPTER
Eleven

Finn

Alexa Play: Vienna by Ben Platt

My shift ended at eight that night, and as much as I wanted to avoid anything that might get my dick even *close* to hard, I agreed to hang out with Turtle for a bit.

He assured me that Blake wouldn't be coming over until her shift finished at 10, so I figured I could chill for a few hours without worrying about running into Quinn and those glossy lips of hers.

"How's training going?" Turtle asked as he deep-throated a joint, coating the papers with his saliva. We were crammed next to each other on the tiny couch he'd installed inside Shelly.

His laptop was propped up on a stool, and he had Point Break on. Both of us had seen it a thousand times, but after my weirdly sexual training session with Riddick, I was looking at everything a little differently.

Like... if I kept getting boners around Riddick, did that mean I was gay now?

I looked at young Keanu Reeves and tried to decipher whether or not I thought he was hot. He was definitely good-looking, but I wasn't getting the same pulse in my dick that I did around Riddick.

Turtle slurped on his joint again, and I cocked my head to the side, wondering if I would get turned on by him basically giving his spliff a blow job, but... nothing.

I felt the same way I always did while hanging out with my best friend—who, if I was being honest, was also objectively hot—but it wasn't doing anything for me.

I felt a little relieved, as I wasn't in the mood to try to sleep with another rager and not be able to beat off, but it also just made me feel more confused.

If I was attracted to Riddick... shouldn't I be attracted to all hot guys?

I guess I wasn't attracted to all hot girls... Was I bisexual?

Ugh. My head hurts.

"Yo! Earth to the Finn Man! I asked you a question!"

I snapped out of my potentially gay—or bisexual—awakening and muttered an unattractive 'uhhhhhh' until Turtle took pity on me and repeated his question.

"How was training?"

I knew I couldn't tell Turtle I was training with Riddick to ride Leviathans, but I had to tell him that I was training to up my game in general. He already knew I planned to ride those waves, and if I didn't give him some excuse, he was going to wonder why I wasn't shredding the pipelines on the main beach with him every day.

I shrugged. "It was good. Kicked my own ass with swim sprints."

Turtle nodded, finally lighting up the joint he'd just thoroughly pleasured with his mouth.

"Gnarly."

"Yeah."

We fell into an amicable silence, Turtle puffing away while we watched Keanu and Patrick Swayze do some seriously unrealistic surf stunts.

"Hey, can I ask you something?" I finally burst out, turning to face my friend. He looked at me with hooded, red eyes, his usual goofy smile curling on his face.

"Always, brother."

I didn't hesitate. If I could talk to anyone about something like this, it would be Turtle.

"You ever pop a boner over a dude?"

My question didn't really phase him. He just took a big toke and screwed his face up in thought as if he were trying to wrack his brain for an occasion where he might have.

"No, I don't think so," he finally replied, and disappointment brewed in my gut.

"But there was this one time where I got a major stiffy watching a show with Tom Selleck in it," he said abruptly, taking another inhale of his joint.

This caught my attention.

"Really!?" I asked, trying not to sound as excited as I was to hear that I wasn't the only one popping boners over older men.

"Hell ya, bro. It was that show he used to star in... what's it called..." he trailed off, smoking and thinking again.

I waited for him to get there. This was how he earned his nickname, after all. He was quick like lightning in the water but slow as a turtle on land. *Especially* when he was getting high. I didn't mind, though. I liked that he took the time to gather his thoughts before he spoke. It was something I never seemed to manage to do.

"Magnum P.I.!" He snapped his fingers in excitement as the name came to him. "He was always wearing these little shorts and showing off his chest hair. I dunno, man, something about that did it for Turtle Jr., if you're catching my wave, bro," he said, gesturing lazily to his crotch.

I nodded in understanding.

"Yeah, I could see that."

"Right?" he said, grinning at me. "Man, that's what I told my buddy Riko at the time. He gave me shit for it, and I was like, 'Brother, you telling me if Tom fucking Selleck asked you to take a mustache ride, you would say *no?*'"

He snorted and ashed his joint, his eyes nearly fully closed now, as he giggled at the memory. "I told him he was full of shit. Everyone thinks Tom's hot, man; it's like science."

"Do you think that makes you, you know… gay?" I asked, and Turtle shrugged.

"Probably not, man. I love pussy too much to be gay."

"But you would fuck Tom Selleck if you could."

Turtle somehow managed to give me a *'what a stupid question'* look, even with his eyes basically closed.

"Get real, bro. 'Aint no one fucking Tom Selleck. Tom Selleck does the fucking.'"

And I wasn't sure if it was a contact high or just the way Turtle had a way of making literally *everything* feel unserious, but I burst into hysterical laughter and couldn't seem to stop for a ridiculous amount of time.

We spent the rest of the night watching the movie and arguing over whether or not Johnny Utah and Bohdi were secretly kind of into each other, and that was the reason for their spicy rivalry in the film.

By the time I left to head home, I'd decided I wasn't going to worry too much about whether I was gay or not.

I was clearly attracted to Riddick, and I definitely was still attracted to Quinn. The only trouble was that I knew Quinn was into me, and she would hook up with me if I initiated something.

Could I say the same for Riddick?

Probably not.

Was he even gay, or into dudes, or whatever? Were the intense feelings that had started brewing in my chest completely one-sided?

Also, if they weren't, what was I supposed to do about that?

'Tom Selleck does the fucking.'

My eyes widened at the realization that Riddick was definitely the Tom Selleck in this situation out of the two of us.

If he was into me... would I want him to fuck me?

My dick twitched in my shorts at the thought, and I swallowed.

Oh-no...

I was in trouble.

And this wasn't the kind of trouble my dimples could get me out of.

CHAPTER
Twelve

Finn

When Blake showed up, she offered to drive me back home since I needed to call it an early night.

"So, Turtle tells me you're officially training for your suicide mission," she deadpanned as she drove.

I shot her a devilish smirk and shrugged.

"Sure am, babe."

She sighed and shook her head. "I've seen you surf, Finn. You're good, but you're not *that* good."

"I'm not *that* good *yet*," I corrected her, and she let out a little annoyed huff.

She didn't respond, and it took me a moment to put together that she was a little angry at me for not listening to her.

"Listen, I'm not that Jake guy, okay?"

"No, you're not," she snapped, and I frowned.

"You know, I looked him up and couldn't really find anything. Not even an obituary. Do you know why that is?"

She glanced at me as she pulled onto the dirt road that led to my shack.

"Kai and Jet worked really hard to keep the accident from being sensationalized," she explained, and I nodded, recognizing the names from Riddick's story earlier.

"They were all friends then?"

"More than friends. They were basically brothers. They discovered Leviathans almost ten years ago now. They spent some time in Hawaii to get some experience on more well-known big wave beaches before tackling Leviathans since no one had surfed it before.

"While they were there, Kai almost died, and Riddick got cold feet. They almost didn't end up surfing Leviathans, but the boys talked him into it after a while. Now I'm sure they all wish they listened to him."

Fuck. I bet.

I frowned at her. "Where are the others now?"

"They did everything they could to keep Leviathans out of the media after the accident. They were hoping to prevent anyone else from finding the beach and losing their lives. After they were sure nothing about the accident was going to be printed, they left. I think Kai went back to Hawaii; I'm not sure."

We were in front of my shack now, and I moved to get out, but she stopped me, laying a dainty hand on my arm.

"I can see that your mind's made up, so this is the last time I'll say anything about it, Finn. But you being here is *exactly* what those guys were trying so hard to avoid."

I met her earnest, sapphire blue eyes and felt a flash of guilt. This girl was *really* worried about me. I felt a little bad about how much my decision seemed to be stressing her out.

Laying my hand over hers, I gave her fingers a comforting squeeze.

"I know. But I also need to do this. This is just who I am. Once I decide to go for something, I can't back down. Besides, even if Leviathans *does* kill me, at least I'll die doing something I love."

Her mouth twitched, and she shook her head and sighed.

"Spoken like a true adrenaline junkie."

I laughed and shrugged, popping the passenger door open.

"Hey. I'm here for a good time, not a long time, babe." I winked at her, noticing the way her cheeks blushed a light pink as I flashed her my dimples.

Softening slightly, I paused for a second before stepping out of the car.

"For what it's worth, Blake, I heard your warning. I'm just choosing to ignore it, and that's on me. If anything happens to me, it's not on you, okay? You did your best."

She gave me a sad chuckle and shook her head again as if she didn't know what to do with me.

"Goodnight, Finn," she said before throwing the car in reverse.

I waved as she drove off back to town and smiled.

She was wrong about me.

I *was* good enough to tame Leviathans. I would prove to everyone I could do it. *Especially* Riddick.

No wonder he was so against me training for this. He had been the one to try to talk his friends out of it in the first place.

CHAPTER
Thirteen

Finn

Alexa Play: Malibu by Miley Cyrus

I made sure to get up even earlier than usual so I had time to cook all the stuff I had bought at Riddick's request.

My dick was hard as a rock when I woke up, but I forced myself to ignore it. I hadn't beaten off the night before, and I almost felt like starting a tally of how many days in a row I could go without busting a nut.

Happily – ignoring it seemed to work, and soon, my morning wood faded away, and I forgot all about it.

When Riddick walked into my shack, I was tucking into a massive breakfast with eggs, pancakes, bacon, and sausage.

Suddenly, it felt like all the blood rushed to my groin again, and I nearly choked on a bite of fluffy, syrup-soaked pancakes as my gaze collided with his.

He felt larger than life, standing there in my little shack, staring at me with that piercing look he always had.

"Morning," I greeted him around the mouthful of food that I suddenly seemed to be having a hard time swallowing.

He didn't respond. Instead, he approached the table and critically examined the spread of food I had laid out in front of me.

I sat a little straighter, hoping he was happy with what I made, but he didn't comment.

He looked at me, his lips pursing into a hard line, and I fidgeted in my seat.

He was so fucking *intense.*

It was like I could *feel* the heat radiating off of him. After my chat with Turtle yesterday, I was more willing to admit that I was insanely attracted to him, and the idea of that fascinated me.

I'd never been attracted to a man before, so I found myself examining every inch of him, trying to decide what it was about him that turned me on so much.

Was it his broad shoulders? Or was it the memory of how he had effortlessly tossed me against the wall and wrapped one of those massive hands around my throat?

What would it feel like to kiss him? Would I like the roughness of his stubble against my skin? His hair was thick and shiny too, like a girl's hair. Would it feel just as good to thread my fingers in it while he—"

"Did you drink?" he asked, snapping me out of my fantasy.

"Uhm, no."

"Smoke?"

"No."

"Fuck?" The word shot through me like a lightning bolt, and suddenly I wanted to know more than anything what it would feel like to be fucked by Riddick. To have that large body spread out on top of me.

My dick swelled between my legs at the thought, and I was hella grateful he didn't have x-ray vision and could see through the table.

"No, Riddick," I breathed, unable to tear my gaze away from his burning blue eyes.

"You do anything else I should know about?" It was the same question he'd asked me yesterday, and again, I assumed he was asking me if I beat off, though I didn't make that quite as obvious this time.

"No," I replied honestly.

He stared at me for one more long moment as if waiting to see if he would catch me in a lie. After I passed his weird little lie detector test, he finally nodded curtly.

"How are you feeling?"

His question surprised me.

How was I feeling? Well, besides being *horny as fuck,* I was definitely feeling the effects of yesterday's workout, and I told him as much.

"Sore and stiff."

He bobbed his head in acknowledgment of my response.

"Finish eating and meet me outside."

"Yes, sir," I replied, and he tensed up, his blue eyes darkening briefly.

For a moment, I thought he would say something, but he didn't. He just turned on his heel, peeling off his white cotton T-shirt as he went.

I scarfed down the rest of my food as fast as I could and chased Riddick outside. I peeled off my own shirt as I stepped into the sunshine, expecting to find him waiting for me with our boards.

I was surprised to find that he'd set out a longboard on the sand, but I didn't think we would be using it to surf.

A yoga mat was rolled out on top of the board. I raised my eyebrows in surprise.

"We're doing yoga?"

He glanced at me and pursed his lips.

"*You're* doing yoga. Today, we'll do an active rest day before we get you into weight training tomorrow. If you're sore, I don't want you to push yourself too hard. It'll do more damage than good."

"Okay! Sounds smart." I grinned, genuinely excited. "I've never done yoga before, but I've always wanted to try it," I admitted, and his eyes widened in surprise.

"You've never done yoga before?"

I shook my head.

"Nuh-uh. Like, I have obviously seen people do it. I know all about doggy-style and nah-imma-stay in bed or whatever. Just yoga is expensive. Never really had the money to take a class."

"Downward dog."

"Huh?"

Riddick was staring at me, his eyes shining with what I could have sworn was amusement.

"The pose is called the downward dog. Not *doggy-style.*"

"Oooh. Gotcha!" I grinned, blushing a little at hearing him say *doggy-style.* The image of me on all fours and Riddick hammering into me from behind ripped across my vision, and I clenched.

Jesus. Would that even feel good?

I'd never had anything come remotely close to penetrating my ass before. I wasn't sure if I would like it, but my weird brain kept putting me in fantasies where it was happening.

Would it hurt?

It *must* feel somewhat good if gay guys did it. Right?

Riddick was staring at me again, and I watched him trace his tongue over his bottom lip, causing me to blush harder.

Fuck. I hope he couldn't read minds or something.

Shit! What if he could read minds!?

Riddick, if you can hear this, blink twice!

Okay, he didn't blink... He probably can't read minds.

Unless... he doesn't WANT YOU TO KNOW he can read minds!

The corner of Riddick's lip twitched as I fidgeted before him, and he gestured to the yoga mat.

"Get on the board. Sit with your legs crossed and your hands on your knees."

I scrambled to do as I was told, settling quickly into position.

"The most important thing you can do on this earth is breathe."

I peered up at him as he slowly walked in a wide circle around my board. He wasn't looking at me. He seemed to have slipped into the role of instructor.

"Close your eyes, Finn. Listen to my voice and follow my instructions."

"Okay, no problem. I can totally—"

"With*out* speaking. No talking, Finn. Pay attention."

I closed my mouth with a snap and nodded, slamming my eyes shut and doing my best to listen.

"As I was saying. Your breath. It's the most important thing. Not just in yoga but when you're in the water, too. Staying connected with your breath is the best way to ensure you're setting yourself up for success.

"Breathing properly means you're present.

"It means you're locked in. *Focused.*

"On a more physical note, breathing properly gives your body the correct amount of oxygen it needs to perform incredible tasks... because that's what you're doing, Finn. You're asking your body to do something incredible."

His words washed over me, and I found myself centering in an oddly peaceful way.

I focused on my breath, and the tension that sang through my muscles melted away. The sense of urgency that always plagued my mind seemed to fade into nothing.

That insistent voice that was always in my head screaming at me to *go, go, go,* quieted, and it was Riddick's voice that took over, freeing me from the oppressive cage of my own thoughts.

"Breathing, Finn, means that you're *alive.*"

He was closer to me now, his voice rumbling near my right ear.

"I want you to *feel* every inhale. Imagine the lungs in your chest filling with that life-giving oxygen. Feel that breath spread through your entire body. It's nourishing your blood cells, healing your muscle tissue, and giving you the ability to think. To live. To *exist.*"

My whole body was lighting up from the inside. Every inhale I took gave me a rush of energy, while every exhale relaxed me.

"Good, Finn," He whispered, his words of praise nearly lost in the distant crash of waves. I shivered and swallowed, doing my best not to let him see how much my body wanted to react to the praise.

I wanted *more.*

I wanted him to always think I was doing good.

"Get on your hands and knees." He hummed, and my eyes flew open. I peeked up at him, shocked by his demand. He met my gaze without flinching and raised an eyebrow.

Without looking away from him, I slowly unfolded myself and did what he said. My cock was swiftly filling with blood, and by the time I was on all fours, I was fully hard in my swim trunks. Thankfully, Riddick didn't seem to notice what was happening between my legs. He'd gone back to pacing slow circles around me as I waited for him to tell me what to do next.

"You're going to do a few rounds of cat and cow. On your next inhale, I want you to arch your back."

Jesus Christ... this was... Was this really what yoga was?!

"Inhale..."

I took a deep breath and arched, pretending I couldn't feel my ass cheeks separate from the movement.

I couldn't see him. He was standing directly behind me, and my cock throbbed.

Was he looking at me?

I twisted to look back at him, but he tutted his tongue.

"Face forward. Hold," he demanded, and I wasn't sure if he meant the position or my breath, so I did both.

"Good, Finn. Now exhale and release." Another rush of need rolled through my groin at the praise as I obeyed.

He told me to round my back and exhale, still standing directly be-hind me. After a few more rounds of this, he told me to get into 'down-ward dog.'

Trying to force down the furious blush that was burning my cheeks, I lifted my ass directly into the air, the way I'd seen people do in 'yoga on the beach' classes at home.

"Tilt your pelvis and press back into your heels," he instructed, and I struggled to do as I was told.

"No, like this," he said, and I almost moaned as I felt him press his warm palm on the small of my back.

His hand on my bare skin sent fireworks erupting through my body, and my already hard dick *throbbed* in my swim shorts. I knew I was leak-ing at this point, and the humiliating thought of what would happen when Riddick finally noticed was all I could think about.

He applied gentle pressure to my back, forcing me to press further into my heels, and this time, I moaned as I felt the stretch all the way up my hamstrings.

"Good, Finn. That's so good," he murmured, running his left hand down the back of my thigh, gently massaging the tight tendon.

Ohfuckohfuckohfuck!

What the fuck was he doing!?

"Relax your neck, let your head hang." His voice was a low, luxuri-ous growl. With the hand that wasn't stroking the back of my bare leg, he began massaging the back of my neck.

JesusfuckingChrist!

I was so turned on. I'd literally never been this turned on in my life. My cock throbbed again, and I had a moment of panic when it felt like I might spontaneously come in my shorts. Riddick's hot hand slid farther up my thigh, his fingers slipping under the hem of my shorts slightly, and I whimpered. I couldn't keep it in; what he was doing felt so *good* and so *fucking erotic.* I couldn't help myself.

"Fuck, Finn. You're so tight," he muttered, using his thumb to mas-sage my hamstring in a firm, circular motion.

Still cuffing the back of my neck while I hung in this precarious position, he moved on to apply the same treatment to my other leg before letting me go and stepping away.

I almost begged him to come back, to keep touching me, but he was already instructing me to move into a plank.

Riddick taught me how to do a flow, and when my hips pressed against the forgiving but *firm* yoga mat, an impossibly intense rush of pleasure shot through me.

Fuckfuckfuckfuckfuck!

Don't come, don't come, don't come!

My heart was pounding in my chest, and as I pressed back into what Riddick told me was a 'cobra' pose, it took everything I had not to hump the board beneath me until I blew my load.

He circled around the front of the board to face me as I held the position, and I met his serious, burning gaze.

"Press your shoulders back. Do you feel a stretch in your core?" he asked me, and I had to grit my teeth to keep myself from telling him I could feel it in my *dick.*

I glanced down at his crotch, praying to the sea gods that he was just as hard as I was.

Unfortunately, I couldn't tell if he was… Which meant he probably wasn't, and I was the only one who was getting off on this yoga session like some sort of perverted freak.

Fuck, why was I like this?

He frowned when I didn't answer, his blue eyes racking over my form. I watched him take in the way my ribs were expanding and contracting in quick, rapid pants as I worked against my own body to prevent myself from coming.

I was a hair trigger away from losing it, and it would be *mortifying* if he watched me explode all over myself when I was almost positive the attraction I was feeling was one-sided.

"Focus on your breath, Finn," he instructed, and I nodded, slamming my eyes shut and forcing myself to think about my breathing instead of the simmering pot of pleasure that was burning in my groin, just waiting to overflow.

"Deep breath in..."

I inhaled.

"Good... deep breath out."

I exhaled.

He coached me through a few more breaths, and by the time he was done, I had more of a grip on myself.

However, I was still hard as stone when he told me to stand up.

I hesitated, and he frowned again and cocked his head to the side.

"Get up, Finn," he repeated, and I nodded, biting my lower lip.

Maybe he wouldn't notice?

With shaking arms, I pushed myself back onto my knees and stood up.

My cock was tenting the shit out of my shorts, and I peeked up at him through my lashes, hating how much my cheeks were burning.

He *definitely* noticed.

I watched, completely mortified, as his eyes dropped down to the *very* obvious boner I was currently sporting like it was the newest fashion trend.

"Uhm..." I murmured, feeling like I needed to say something to explain myself.

His eyes flit back up to meet mine, and he cocked his head to the side, raising an eyebrow.

"I just... uhm. I haven't...*you know*, in a few days..." I muttered. It sounded like a weak excuse, even to my own ears.

"I didn't ask," Riddick replied, and I frowned.

"I know—I just—"

"Are you going to be able to continue? Or do we need to stop?" he asked, and for some reason, a flicker of anger licked the inside of my chest.

"I don't need to stop," I snapped. His expression didn't change, but somehow, his energy did. I couldn't put my finger on what changed, but the tension between us turned from confrontational to playful.

He stepped closer to me as if taking my tone as a challenge, and my traitorous dick throbbed again.

"Are you sure, Finn? If you can't handle it, there's no shame in admitting it. Not everyone is cut out for this."

"*I* am," I snarled. If he thought a little embarrassment was going to keep me from training for Leviathans, he didn't know me *at all.*

So what if I had a boner? I would do his stupid yoga class hard. What did I care?

"You're sweating," he pointed out, and again, he dragged his gaze down my naked chest. I could literally *feel* it when he settled on the tent in my shorts.

"It's hot."

A smirk.

Riddick smirked!

"It sure is."

What did that *mean!? Was he flirting with me?*

"Now, step back into a lunge. Don't forget to focus on your breath. Inhale, and raise your arms. Reach for the sun like you want to pluck it out of the sky…"

And just like that, the whisper of flirty Riddick was gone, and the stone-cold, professional surf instructor was back.

I forced myself not to outwardly groan in frustration. This strange tension between us infuriated me, and it was only day two.

What had I gotten myself into?

CHAPTER
Fourteen

Finn

I finished the yoga session without busting in my shorts, but it was a challenge. Every time I thought I was finally starting to soften, Riddick would make me get into a downward dog again and massage me.

He asked me if I wanted him to stop, and though my mind screamed *'fuck yes, or I'm going to fucking come,'* I always told him no.

He asked in this strange, teasing tone. Like, if I asked him to stop, it would be proving I couldn't handle it or something.

So, I shook my head each time and just focused on my breathing, doing my best to keep the insanely strong need to come under control.

By the time he finally told me we were finished, I was a tense, sexually frustrated mess.

"You did good, Finn," he informed me, a small ghost of a smile on his face as he watched me roll up the yoga mat.

"Yeah. Thanks. I guess," I mumbled, and he chuckled.

"You earned an afternoon of surfing. Just take it easy. Don't strain yourself; tomorrow is going to be a rough day."

I glanced up at him, all my irritation with him melting away instantly at the thought of hitting the water.

"You gonna surf with me!?" I asked excitedly, and his almost smile slipped off his face.

"No."

"Awh, come on, Riddick. Stick around for a bit. Let's have some fun; not everything needs to be so serious all the time."

His expression darkened even further, and suddenly he looked angry.

"If you insist on surfing waves that will kill you, then yes, Finn. Everything *does* need to be serious. This is life or death. How do you not get that?"

I rolled my eyes, shooting him one of my most mischievous smirks.

"Okay, Mr. Grumpy Gills."

For a second, he looked completely taken aback, then, to my delight, the corner of his mouth twitched.

HA! Finally got a reaction out of him!

"Did you just quote '*Finding Nemo*' to me?" he asked, and I nodded, tucking the yoga mat under my arm. I moved to grab the longboard too, but Riddick brushed me off, picking it up himself and following me to the lean-to.

"Sure did."

"I suppose you *are* nearly as annoying as Dory."

I shot him another grin, impressed that he even knew who Dory was.

"I think you meant to say *endearing.*"

"I meant exactly what I said."

Rolling my eyes, I stashed the yoga mat next to the surf rack while Riddick put the longboard away.

"Whatever, we have more of a Gill and Nemo relationship anyway."

His lip twitched again, and I felt a warm buzz of pride that I'd been the one who almost made him smile.

He looked me critically up and down, that barely-there quirk to his lip still present.

God, he was so good-looking. An absolute *mountain* of a man. What would he look like if he actually smiled?

I imagined it would be the kind of smile that people would pay millions of dollars to put on the front page of a magazine.

"You *are* pretty small. Shark bait would be an appropriate nickname for you." His eyes twinkled. "If a shark ate you, they would definitely still be hungry after."

I allowed my mouth to drop in mock offense.

"Excuse *you*. I am not *small*. You're just ridiculously *big.*"

Suddenly, the light-hearted energy between us heated up, and my breath caught in my throat at the way he was looking at me now. He ran his tongue over his bottom lip, and his gaze flicked down to my dick again.

There was no way I was imagining this... was I?

"You have no idea, shark bait." He smirked, and I swear to god, the entire planet stopped spinning for a second.

OMG—HE DID A FLIRT! That was definitely a flirt! This was not all in my head... was it?!

GAH, WHAT SHOULD I DO?!

I laughed nervously, clearing my throat and rubbing the back of my neck. If he were a chick, I would have flirted back, but he wasn't. I wasn't sure if *either* of us were gay, and I didn't know what the protocol was in this situation.

What if I openly came onto him, and it turned out I'd entirely misread the situation? What if he was a super straight homophobe, and he punched me in the face and refused to come back to train me again?

I didn't think that was the case, but I didn't want to risk it. Instead, I changed the subject and focused on surfing.

Surfing was safe.

Surfing was comfortable.

Surfing was my *home.*

"Anyway, I really think you should stay and surf with me for a bit. That's the whole point of you training me, right? So you can use my beach?"

He chuckled and shook his head, his blue eyes shining with amusement.

"I thought we'd already established that I'll use your beach whether you want me to or not, Finn. I'm not doing this so I can 'use your beach.' I'm training you with the hope that you won't die this winter when you willingly feed your dumbass to the proverbial sharks."

"Tomato, potato." I grinned, waving my hand in the air as if his concerns were inconsequential.

He looked at me sharply, and for a moment, I thought he might actually give me a real smile or maybe even laugh.

"What?" I asked innocently, and his eyes shimmered with amusement.

"It's tuh-may-tow, tuh-mah-tow. Not tomato potato."

I gave him a dimple-popping grin and shrugged.

"I like potatoes better. Can't make a French fry with a tomato."

There it was again. That *almost* smile.

"Come on, Riddick. Please? I've been dying to learn how to hang ten, and you're, like, freakishly good at it."

I pulled out my pink shortboard and bent down to strap on my ankle tether. He watched me silently for a moment before letting out a defeated sigh.

"*Fine.* I'll stay. But only for an hour. Then I need to go, and you need to eat more."

An elated thrill ripped through me, and I did my best not to show him how excited I was that he was staying... and *failed miserably.*

"Really! *Sick!* Ahhh, I can't fucking wait! You have to give me all the tips! There's this girl at work, Blake, and she told me that I was *good* but not *that* good. Can you believe that!? Anyway, I need to prove her wrong. Next time I surf with her, I want to pull the sickest stunts. Just to rub it in her face, y'know? Not in a *mean way*, but in an *I told ya so* way. Know what I'm saying? Like, I like her and all, but the *audacity* she has to - "

"Finn?"

"Yeah?"

"Shut the fuck up."

CHAPTER

Fifteen

Finn

Alexa Play: Riptide by Vance Joy

The version of Riddick that was relaxed and screwing around in the water was a totally different person from Coach Riddick.

He still didn't smile, but he was softer somehow. Like the water was his safe place as much as it was mine. If I didn't know any better, I would almost say he was having *fun* teaching me silly tricks.

He stayed way longer than an hour, and the sun was setting by the time we caught our last waves of the day back to shore.

"Good work, shark bait," he said as we returned our boards to the lean-to.

Since our little *Finding Nemo* discussion, he'd taken to calling me that stupid nickname, and I'd be lying if it didn't make butterflies erupt in my gut every time he said it.

It made me feel special.

Connected to him in some way.

Like we shared some inside joke that was just between the two of us.

I smiled at him as he toweled off, sliding my board next to his on the rack.

He'd made me switch my shortboard out for a longboard, explaining it was easier to hang ten on something with a bigger counterweight.

With his direction, I had the trick down within a few hours, and I couldn't *wait* to show off to the rest of the surf rats after work tomorrow.

"Thanks, Riddick," I beamed at him. He pulled on his T-shirt, and his lip was curled at the corner.

"No need to thank me, Finn. You earned it."

Unable to contain my massive smile at his praise, I nodded jovially.

"You wanna stay for dinner? I was planning on making a feast, you know, so maybe I can graduate from shark bait to shark entree."

His eyebrows rose in surprise, and I swore he almost laughed. Disappointment swirled in my gut as he obviously repressed the urge to smile, but I didn't say anything about it.

"I've got food at home, but I'll help you cook," he replied easily, handing me his towel so I could dry off too.

His easy acceptance of my invitation surprised me, and I nodded, still grinning.

"Okay, great! I'm kind of a shit cook," I admitted, and Riddick frowned as he followed me into the shack.

"The breakfast you made looked good."

"Yeah, but anyone can make breakfast. It's just frying shit up in a pan. Anything more advanced than that, and I get all turned around and distracted," I admitted.

"Distracted?"

"Yeah. Focusing on stuff that doesn't interest me is, like, *really* hard. I usually need to make a game of it or something. My mom was really good at that. She's the one that taught me how to make breakfast, actually. She wasn't home for dinners much, so I was usually on my own and just made frozen shit. She died before she could teach me how to make anything good from scratch, which sucks. She was a really good cook; she just never had time for it. She was always working, trying to keep a roof over our heads," I rambled, and I opened my condo-sized fridge and pulled out a packet of chicken breasts.

Riddick pursed his lips as he considered what I'd said, then squeezed my shoulder.

"Give me those," he ordered, gently taking the chicken away from me. He placed the styrofoam package in the sink and scanned the kitchen before settling on a bowl filled with veggies I had purchased the day before.

"Do you know how to dice an onion?" he asked me, glancing over his shoulder. There was no snideness in his tone. He was genuinely asking me, which made me feel better about the fact that I wasn't really sure if I did.

"I *think* so? That's when you chop 'em real small, right?"

He nodded and tossed me an onion.

"Show me what you got."

I pulled out a cutting board and got to work. He stopped me almost immediately.

"If you cut it like that, your eyes are going to be leaking all night," he informed me. "This is the root, and it's where that chemical that makes you tear up lives. The trick is to avoid cutting the root right off. Here…"

He sliced the onion in half and laid it face down before cutting off the end opposite the root. Making quick work of the peel, he passed the knife into the flesh of the onion horizontally, then vertically, cutting a grid into it. He did this all while pointedly avoiding cutting too close to the root.

"Now, you slice it like you normally would, and look, it cuts apart into a perfect, even dice."

"Woah! That's sweet!" I said, genuinely impressed. He'd reduced half of the onion to tiny pieces so quickly and efficiently. Usually, when I cut up veggies, I just attacked them without any rhyme or reason.

"Now you try," he said, handing me the knife.

I nodded, taking the utensil from him and doing my best to mimic what he'd shown me. Everything was going well until I got to the part where I was supposed to slice.

"No, not like that; you're going to chop your fingers off!" He barked, a tinge of alarm coloring his usually calm, even tone.

"What? Then how—"

Suddenly, he was behind me, caging me in with his arms.

He lay each of his hands over mine, and I shivered as he rumbled instructions into my ear.

"Curl your fingers on your left hand… like this, so you don't accidentally cut yourself," he murmured, his hot breath sending sheets of goosebumps down the side of my neck.

"Now, run your knife through the onion; you don't even need to take the tip off the cutting board; just use a rocking motion…"

I had a sudden visual of me using a rocking motion while grinding on top of him, and my dick swelled between my legs again.

"Focus, Finn," he hummed in my ear, and I pretended not to notice the fact that he was so close that the tip of his nose was pressed into my hair.

I swallowed embarrassingly loudly, and I was sure he heard it. Powering forward, I tried to focus on the motion he was guiding my hand through.

"Good. Yeah, perfect. Just like that," he murmured as I diced through the onion, my movements becoming more steady and confident with each swipe of the knife.

God. Why was everything he said so fucking hot?

We were cutting an *onion,* for Christ's sake. It shouldn't be turning me on this much!

He told me to stop a few inches before the root and stepped away. I felt cold, suddenly, missing the way his warm, hard body had been pressed up against mine.

"There. Now you know how to properly dice an onion. Let's do a sweet pepper next, and then we'll season the chicken. Did you buy any rice?" he asked, completely unaffected by what had just happened.

"Uhm. Yeah. In the cupboard over there." I pointed, and he moved to retrieve it.

And this is how the rest of dinner prep went. Riddick teaching me new things while unintentionally turning me the fuck on.

Every time he touched me, my whole body reacted to him, and by the time we sat down at the table, I was *so tired* of being hard.

I could barely stand it anymore.

"So. How is it?" he asked as I took my first bite of chicken. We'd barbequed it on a tiny charcoal grill that Riddick found around the back of the shack.

He'd shown me how to season it with salt, pepper, onion, and garlic powder, and honestly, it was way better than any frozen chicken dinner I'd ever had.

I groaned in appreciation as the chicken melted in my mouth.

"*Fuck,* that's good."

Riddick watched me eat with his usual enigmatic expression, his gaze never straying from my face as I dug into my meal.

"You sure you don't want any?" I asked. "You must be starving. You haven't eaten all day."

"I told you. I have food at home. You work hard for your money. I don't need to eat all your groceries. Especially when you clearly need it more than I do."

I laughed. "You're going to make me fat."

"No. I'm going to make you strong, and hopefully, that'll be enough to save you."

I sighed, pushing my now empty plate away from me.

"You're always such a downer."

He was staring at the corner of my mouth with a small frown on his face.

"You have barbeque sauce right here," he said, tapping his finger against his lip.

I poked my tongue out of my mouth in an effort to lick it up, and his eyes followed the motion like a hawk.

My mouth flooded with the smokey-sweet taste of BBQ, and I drew my tongue back in.

"There. Did I get it?" I asked, and before I knew what was happening, he was reaching across the table and cupping the side of my cheek. He brushed his calloused thumb over my lips, wiping the sauce away and causing my breath to hitch in my chest.

Okay. That was definitely a flirt...

Dudes didn't wipe sauce off other dudes' mouths unless they were into said dude... did they?

"Riddick..." I murmured, my gaze darting back and forth between his eyes, trying my hardest to see if he was giving me *any* indication at all that these intense feelings I seemed to be developing for him weren't one-sided.

He pulled back, and for a split second, I thought he was going to suck the barbeque sauce off his thumb, but he didn't.

He wiped it off on a paper towel and stood up, grabbing my empty plate and striding over to the sink to rinse it.

"I've got to head out," he said gruffly.

"Wait, can we talk about—"

"Goodnight, Finn," he barked abruptly. The softness in his tone was gone, and he was hard and cold again as he made his way to the front door.

"Riddick—"

"I'll see you in the morning. Same rules apply."

Then, the door shut, and he was gone.

CHAPTER

Sixteen

Finn

*S*ame rules apply.

This was absolutely fucked up. Even though Riddick didn't seem interested in confirming that I wasn't supposed to be experiencing any sort of release, I *knew* that's what he meant.

He'd punished me the first day when I told him I'd touched myself a little. Then, today seemed to be a reward. He stretched me out, surfed with me, and kept me company while I made dinner.

It was nice.

I hadn't had a home-cooked meal for dinner in a really long time. The last time I got to sit at a real table and eat something homemade was with my mom. That happy memory cut me directly to my core, and I glanced at the picture of her that I had hung up on the wall next to Mark Foo.

She was laughing in the photo, and it was how I liked to remember her. Having her up in the shack made me feel less alone, though it obviously wasn't a good substitute for a real person.

Having Riddick stay over for dinner, even though he didn't eat with me, had made me feel for the first time like this place I'd bought for myself was more than just a house.

It was home.

I'd been so happy.

Until he left and dropped more mixed-ass signals on me.

Unintentionally or not, the dude had basically edged me all day. Showering and getting ready for bed was fucking *uncomfortable.*

My balls were literally *aching* with how many times I'd gotten hard with no release. Like, I'm not joking; they actually kinda hurt a little.

I crawled into bed, tugged up my charcoal grey duvet, and snuggled in. I contemplated just saying fuck it and jacking off for some relief. Eyeing up the bottle of lotion that had sat unused on my nightstand for the last two nights, I bit my lip.

Why was he doing this to me?

There had to be a reason. Remembering how pissed I had been with him for making me do three hours of swim sprints, only to find out there had been a legitimate reason for that level of intensity in his training, is what stopped me from reaching for the lotion.

What if this was some sort of mental training he was putting me through?

Like some Mr. Miyagi shit?

Yeah. That was probably it. This had to be some kind of super-specialized mental conditioning. There was no other explanation for it.

After the way he'd left, like touching my face had burned him or something, I wasn't under any illusions that he was actually into me.

Even if he *was* into me and this was all some weird way of flirting, I was still hella competitive at my core, and I couldn't let him win. If this was a challenge, I needed to come out on top. It's just who I was.

Forcing myself to ignore my painfully hard cock, I dug into my end table drawer and pulled out a bottle of over-the-counter sleep aids.

I didn't love taking them because they made me wake up all groggy, but I started taking them after my mom died. The memory of how she'd looked when I needed to identify her body had kept me up all night. So, for a while, these little sleepy skittles were the only way I could ever get any rest.

After taking the tiny white pill, I rolled onto my side and shut my eyes.

I could do this.

I wouldn't let him win.

CHAPTER
Seventeen

Riddick

Alexa Play: Sparky by Lights

I didn't know what brought me back to the shack in the middle of the night.

I *hated* that I kept ending up here. It felt like fate or some sort of magnetic attraction that kept bringing me back to the kid.

I almost didn't show up that morning. My plan was to just ghost him, but every time I thought of him paddling out to face Leviathans with his pitiful level of training, my entire body would ice over with terror.

If he went out there unprepared and died, the guilt would eat me *alive*. And after only two days of knowing this little shit, I knew he would do it with or without my help.

What was worse—he was clearly attracted to me.

I saw the way he looked at me... The heat in his eyes. To add even more insult to injury, his willingness to submit to me turned me the fuck on. When I gave him orders, he always became pliant and docile, which was a complete contrast to his usual spunky and fiery personality.

It had been a mistake to lean into it when he asked me if the rules included him jacking off.

At first, I thought the kid was straight, so I hadn't thought much of it. I'd been pissed with him for dropping in on my wave and wanted him to suffer a bit. So when he brought it up, I just kinda... let him believe what he wanted.

What I hadn't been expecting was the level of anger I'd felt toward him the next day when he told me he'd touched himself.

I couldn't really explain why it had made me so angry. Maybe because even though I'd only been half serious about it, I needed him to *listen* to me if he was going to survive.

His failure to do so had sent me into a tailspin.

I knew it hadn't been fair for me to work him almost to exhaustion, and I'd felt shit about it after the fact... Which is why I'd given him an active rest day today.

The only problem was I hadn't really considered just how sexually charged a yoga class would be.

I also wasn't expecting to be as affected by the kid as I was. Watching him arch his back for me on that mat had been... annoyingly arousing.

I'd needed to tuck my cock up in my waistband to keep him from seeing how hard I was.

Though, he hadn't thought to do the same and had completed the rest of the session with his cock tenting his shorts like a fucking spear.

All of this was very bad for so many reasons.

I couldn't be getting involved with him like that. If I was being serious, I didn't even want to be involved with him in a platonic way.

All I wanted was to be left alone.

So why was I walking up to his shack in the dead of night?

Why was I gently pressing the door in and turning the knob a quarter turn to disable the locking mechanism?

Why was I in his room, watching him sleep?

He was sleeping rather fitfully. We were moving into a California summer, and the shack was sweltering. There was no AC, so his room was a furnace, even with the window open.

He'd kicked off his duvet, giving me a full view of his sweat-slicked, lean body.

His little boxer shorts had tiny sharks on them and did nothing to hide how fucking hard he was, which didn't shock me.

I wasn't proud to admit that once I'd realized how attracted he was to me, I'd played up the yoga session a bit.

There was no excuse for it other than the fact that I was a fucking bad person, and I couldn't help myself. I hadn't touched anyone in *so* long, and here was this young, attractive man with beautiful skin, presenting his ass to me like he wanted me to split him in half.

It had started innocently enough; I really *had* just been trying to correct his positioning in downward dog. It was common practice with beginners to help maneuver them into position... But he'd made this tiny little *moaning* sound, and I temporarily lost my mind. I'd wanted to hear it again.

So, I'd taken every opportunity to massage him after that. I knew it was wrong, and I knew I was fucking with his head.

But again.

I was clearly a shitty person because here I was, breaking into his space and watching him sleep like a fucking creeper.

He frowned and made a small mewling sound in his sleep, and I noticed an open bottle of sleep aids on his bedside table.

Had he taken one of those?

His mop of dark blond hair was damp with sweat and plastered to his forehead. Feeling emboldened by the fact that I was sure he had taken a pill, I reached out and brushed the sweaty strands back, smoothing his frown out with my thumb as I did so.

I hated it when he frowned – though, I hadn't done a good job of making him smile.

Mostly because when he flashed those dimples at me, I tended to forget why I needed to stay far away from Finn Summers.

"Riddick..." he groaned, and I froze. My blood went cold. Maybe I had miscalculated? If he woke up, I had no idea how I was going to explain the fact that I was in his room in the middle of the damn night.

However, I needn't have worried. He was still very much asleep and clearly having a sexy dream.

A sexy dream about me.

Blood rushed to my cock, and my gaze fell to his hips, which were now rocking back and forth methodically.

His cock was so hard the tip of it was peeking out of the top of his waistband.

I licked my lips.

He'd been so good today.

He earned a bit of a reward.

Before I could stop myself, I reached out and brushed my fingers gently down his shaft over his soft, cotton boxers.

He moaned softly and rocked his hips again, dragging himself back and forth over the tips of my stationary fingers.

I knew he was hanging by a thread. I'd put him through a lot over the last two days, and like he said, he was twenty-one.

When I was twenty-one, I wasn't sure I could have endured what I put him through without some form of release.

His balls were probably sore.

I slid my fingers down his shaft and gently cupped him over his boxers.

He let out a sleepy whine, and a jolt of need shot straight through my dick.

"Fuck..." I hissed. His balls were stiff and drawn up tight. So full of cum, just waiting to be released...

With a flat palm, I rubbed him in a petting motion, enjoying the feeling of his hot cock beneath the soft cotton of his boxers. I alternated between rubbing down his length and carefully massaging his balls between my fingers. With my free hand, I gently tugged down his waistband a bit so I could see his fat, pink head more clearly.

Oh yeah. He was leaking like crazy.

"You need to come, don't you, you little imp?" I whispered, continuing my gentle but consistent strokes up and down his shaft.

He was frowning again, and his head was rocking back and forth as if he needed to come so bad it almost hurt.

A small smile quirked at the corner of my mouth as I felt his dick surge beneath my fingers. This wouldn't take long. I was barely touching him, and I could already tell he was close.

"Riddick..." he whined again in his sleep, humping up into my hand, chasing the feeling of my fingers.

A pleasant, warm sensation curled in my gut at the sound of my name escaping those puffy lips of his. Everything about him was just so...*suckable.* I wanted to bite and nip at those lips until he said my name again.

Instead, I just continued to gently stroke him.

"That's it, Finn. You did so good today. I'm going to make you come so you're not sore tomorrow." I licked my lips, staring at the glossy pink tip of his cock in anticipation.

My own dick was hard as fuck now, and I wanted to watch him shoot his load more than I had ever wanted anything.

"Be a good boy and come for me, Finn," I murmured, and even though his eyes never opened, he groaned like he heard me.

Then, his cock started pulsing in my hand, and I tugged his waistband down a little farther so his boxers wouldn't obstruct my view of his orgasm.

"*Fuck,* yes, Finn. That's so good. Look at you coming for me like a good boy," I murmured, my voice so rough and quiet I could barely hear it myself.

I continued to leisurely rub him as I watched cum spurt out of his tip in beautiful, thick lines.

It splattered up his stomach and under his jaw, and I nearly came in my own shorts at the sight of it.

The little breathy groans that puffed out of his lips with each pulse sounded so good I wished I could bottle them and swallow them.

When he was done, I gently slid his boxers back up to cover him and reached out to thumb some of his cum off his jaw.

I sucked it off the way I'd wanted to suck off that barbeque sauce earlier, and my eyes rolled back into my head as the heady taste exploded in my mouth.

Fuck.

He tasted so *fucking* good.

I wanted to *devour him.*

Reaching out and gently smearing his cum across his chest, I stared at his sleeping face.

He looked so much more peaceful now. He'd definitely needed that.

I felt a conflicting sense of guilt and satisfaction.

Guilt because it was my fault he'd been suffering in the first place.

Satisfaction because *I* had been the one to give him the release he needed... which was bad.

What I had just done was *so bad.*

I mean, *obviously*, it was bad. But I wasn't worried about it for the reasons you would think. Outside of the fact that it was obviously fucked up to stroke someone to completion while they were fully asleep, it was bad that I had even *wanted* to do it in the first place. I couldn't allow myself to get involved like this, and the fact that I already seemed to be unable to leave him alone was concerning.

It wasn't because he was a man. Finn was not the first man I'd been attracted to.

Jet and I used to hook up all the time.

The problem was that he was young, and he had his entire life ahead of him. Finn couldn't develop an attachment to me. I would *ruin* him, and as much as he was an annoying, cocky little prick, he deserved better than what I could offer him.

I liked him. He reminded me of a younger version of myself, and the last thing I wanted him to do was make the same mistakes I had and throw his whole life away over some stupid pipedream.

Brushing his damp hair back from his face again, I sighed.

"This can't happen again, shark bait. This was a one-time thing."

Even as the words left my mouth, I knew they were a lie.

I could feel it in my bones like some massive, predetermined timeline was snapping into place that I was helpless to stop.

Finn Summers had ended up here for a reason, and I was starting to think that it had something to do with me.

"I'm sorry, kid," I said softly, hoping his subconscious mind could hear me and understand how sincere I was.

"I'm so, so, sorry."

CHAPTER
Eighteen

Finn

I woke up feeling predictably groggy from the pill I'd taken the night before, but other than that, I was feeling *great*.

I basked in the dopey, sleepy euphoria for several long moments, wondering why I was feeling so good when I brushed my hand across my chest and froze.

"What the fuck?" I glanced down and gasped.

I was *covered* in cum.

Fuckfuckfuckfuck!

I had a wet dream! I hadn't had one of those since puberty...

Shit... was that against the rules?

No. It couldn't be. I had no control over that... though I wasn't convinced Riddick would see it that way.

Feeling anxious and unsure, I hopped in the shower and scrubbed the dried cum off my body before rushing to make myself a protein-heavy breakfast.

I was just tucking in when Riddick arrived.

I'd unlocked the door for him, and he strolled in looking as hot as he always did.

His white T-shirt clung to him like a second skin, and it was worn out and faded enough that I could see the shadows of his nipples through the cotton.

Averting my gaze, I took a big gulp of orange juice to distract myself from the wall of a man who had just walked into my space.

"Morning," I greeted him, trying to act natural.

He helped himself to the seat across from me and stared.

I eyed him warily, taking a bite of my eggs and waiting for him to say something. Of course, he didn't.

"Why are you looking at me like that?" I asked, and the corner of his mouth twitched.

"You drink?"

"No."

"Smoke?"

"No."

"Fuck?"

"Of course not, Riddick, Christ. Are we going to do this every damn day?"

His blue eyes twinkled with a playful sort of amusement, and I found myself beginning to grin despite myself.

"You do anything else I should know about?" he asked, completely ignoring my question.

Why was he smirking like that?

I narrowed my eyes at him, remembering how I woke up covered in cum.

I bit my lip nervously, and his gaze flicked down to my mouth before returning to meet my gaze.

Should I tell him?

I was sick of these head games he was playing with me. He was taunting me with that little smirk on his stupid, handsome face and his gorgeous, sparkling eyes.

He knew what he was doing.

I wasn't going to let him continue to gaslight me into thinking I was crazy. He was definitely vibing with me, too.

"I had a wet dream," I told him, studying his expression carefully so I could pick apart his reaction and examine it later.

"Did you now?" he asked, and my heart thumped.

"Yeah. I woke up covered in cum," I said, doing my *very* best to keep a straight face.

He licked his lips, and his eyes darkened.

"Do you feel better?"

I narrowed my eyes.

"What do you mean?"

He leaned forward, staring at me so intently I could feel his gaze burning holes into my retinas.

"Do you feel better now that you've come?"

He looked me up and down before leaning back in his seat and crossing his arms over his chest.

"Yeah. I do, actually. But I didn't do it on purpose." I frowned, hoping he wasn't implying that this meant I failed his little test.

"What was the dream about?" he asked, and my eyebrows raised in surprise.

"I don't remember."

The twinkle in his eyes suddenly seemed sinister.

"You don't remember?"

"Nope," I said, popping the 'p.'

"Well. I'm not surprised, but I *am* disappointed." He sighed, getting up.

Shock exploded through me, and I shot to my feet in outrage.

"What do you mean?! I can't help a wet dream!" I cried out, chasing him out of the shack, refusing to let myself get distracted by how ripped his back was as he peeled off his T-shirt.

"I really thought you had more self-control than that. Guess I was wrong," he lamented as he made his way to the lean-to and started sliding plates onto the bar stationed on the bench press.

"Self-control?! I was asleep! How was I supposed to control that?"

He just shrugged.

"This is *bullshit,* Riddick! I didn't fail your little test. I didn't jerk off! And frankly, I think it's fucking weird that you even made that rule! What does jerking off have to do with surfing!?"

This was it.

This was the Mr. Miyagi moment where he was going to tell me that by not beating off, I was teaching myself how to beat the waves off or some epic, deep shit like that...

He paused and examined me the way he always did. No one had ever stared at me with the intensity that Riddick did. It was like he was peeling the skin off my bones with his gaze.

"Who said it had anything to do with surfing?" he asked, his tone completely flat and unreadable.

"Wh-what?"

"You heard me, Finn. I won't repeat myself."

"If it doesn't have anything to do with surfing, why did you tell me I can't masturbate!?"

"I never told you that you couldn't masturbate, Finn. You're the one that said that."

"Yeah, but... you *just* told me you were disappointed in me for coming in my sleep! I'm sick of whatever these fucking head games are, Riddick. Are you into me or not? Because yesterday it sure as shit seemed like you were into me, and now you're gaslighting me into thinking that never happened."

There. I did it. I just straight up asked him.

His usual stone-cold expression shuttered, and a look of remorse passed across his features.

"You're right. I've been a dick."

I crossed my arms over my chest and nodded, pinning him with a glare. He wasn't getting off that easy. I wanted him to admit that he was attracted to me and that it wasn't just all in my head.

"So you *are* into me." I said it like it was fact, not a question.

He sighed and ran his hand down his face in frustration.

"It doesn't matter, Finn."

"It does! It does matter!" I protested, feeling panicked that he was somehow managing to sweep this all under the rug. "I'm not attracted to dudes, okay? Or... I never was before. These last two days have been really confusing for me, and if there's a chance it's not one-sided, I *need* to know, or I'm going to go crazy here, Riddick."

"Finn..."

I stepped closer to him, my eyes stinging with tears for some reason.

"Tell me you're not attracted to me, and I'll leave it alone. I'll never bring it up again," I challenged, and he swallowed.

His Adam's apple bobbed, and it was just *begging* me to run my tongue over it.

"Alright. Fine. I'm attracted to you. But I meant what I said. It doesn't matter. Nothing can come of it. I shouldn't have been playing with your head like that, and it stops now, okay? We need to focus on your training. No distractions, remember?"

Honestly, I stopped listening after he told me he was attracted to me.

"I knew it!" I bellowed, punching the air.

He chuckled in that subdued way of his.

"So you think I'm cute?" I beamed at him, and he shook his head, the corner of his mouth twitching dangerously close to a smile. "It's the dimples, isn't it? My mom always told me no one could resist the dimples."

"Don't push it, shark bait. Did you hear anything I just said?"

"Nope. All I heard was Finn is the hottest surfer in the world, and Riddick has a big gay crush on him."

"I didn't say any of that."

"You might as well have." I gave him my signature grin, popping my dimples as much as I could.

He sighed and pinched the bridge of his nose.

"Would you focus?"

"You wanted me so bad you made me save up my love juice for you!"

"Jesus Christ. Never call it that again."

"Well, what else should I call it?"

"Finn…"

"You want me to call my love juice *Finn?* I mean, we can; I just think it might get a little confusing."

"Finn!" His tone was suddenly dark, and my smile slipped at the serious look in his eyes. "I need you to listen to what I'm saying. Nothing can ever happen between us, okay?"

"Why not?"

"Way too many reasons to list."

"Give me five."

He glared at me but then held up his hand and started counting on his fingers.

"One: I'm your coach; it's inappropriate for a coach to have relations with his trainee. Two: The 'no fucking' rule still stands. Three: Sexual relationships are a distraction, and you need to focus on training if you're going to survive Leviathans. Four: You're too young for me—"

"What? Too young? I'm twenty-one. I know you call me a kid and whatever, but I'm an adult."

He gave me a stern look and pursed his lips.

"I'm seventeen years older than you, Finn. That's too much."

I pouted. "I don't think so. You don't look that old. Plus, age is just a number."

"The answer is no."

"What about number five?"

"What?"

"I told you to give me five reasons; that was only four."

"You're not ready to hear the fifth reason."

"That feels like a copout."

I could tell he was running out of patience with me, but I didn't care. It didn't make any sense to me why we couldn't explore this. We could be into each other and still train for Leviathans. And who cared if he was older? I was a full-fledged adult. I could make my own decisions. I didn't need him to make them for me. He was being overly cagey for no reason.

"The answer is *no,* Finn," he finally snapped. His tone was harsh enough that I knew he wasn't leaving me any room to argue. "You either accept that our relationship stays strictly professional, or I'm *done* helping you. What's it going to be?"

For the first time since I came here, I considered giving up Leviathans. If he wasn't my coach, would he be more willing to explore this thing between us? Though, the second the thought entered my head, I knew I couldn't do it. I remembered the day Blake had taken Turtle and me to see the beach. The way the water had called to some deep-seated part of my *soul.*

I couldn't give up Leviathans, no matter how badly I wanted Riddick to give me a chance.

My entire body felt like it was deflating with the reality of the situation.

I glanced up at him, feeling totally crushed, and my heart broke even further at the soft look on his face.

He was looking at me like he knew he'd just hurt me and he actually cared.

"Come on, shark bait. Don't look at me like that. You can do so much better than me. I'm just some washed-up old-timer. I'm sure you're going to have tons of young, cute chicks just begging for a chance to date you after you tame Leviathans... or dudes, if that's what you want."

That brightened me up.

Not the part about people begging for a chance to date. If I was being honest, that was already kind of the case. I'd never had a hard time pulling. I was cute as fuck, and I knew it.

What made my stomach rush with butterflies was how he'd said *when* I tamed Leviathans.

"You really think I can do it?" I asked, suddenly feeling happy and hopeful again.

He stared at me for a long moment, then gave me one slow nod.

"If you give me your all, then yes. I think you can do it," he said, though his expression was back to that cold, unreadable mask he always wore.

I nodded, clenching my fists in determination.

"Alright. Deal. I won't let you down, Riddick!" I promised, grinning at him so big that I knew my dimples were on full display.

"I know you won't, kid," he grunted, then got back to work loading up the bench press.

CHAPTER

Nineteen

Finn

Riddick stayed true to his word, and he stopped with the sexy mind games. Over the last few weeks, he refused to touch me, like, at all. He always kept a foot of space between us. It just made things worse, though. Not touching me just turned my massive crush on him into this throbbing, yearning ball of need.

Despite the lack of touch, he softened considerably in other aspects of our routine. He was always grumpy and dry, which was fine. I was spunky and animated enough for both of us. But he was also sweet and had this tendency to go out of his way to do things for me that felt special and intimate.

For example, since that first night when I told him my mom could never make it home for dinner because of work, he never missed a meal with me.

If I didn't have a shift at Sharkies, Riddick always stayed and helped me cook dinner. He taught me all kinds of things about nutrition and how to make healthy food taste good. I missed the way he'd wrapped himself around me that first night to teach me how to properly dice an onion, but I was becoming so obsessed with him that I would take what I could get.

He also learned that I absolutely *hated* waxing my board pretty early on in our training program.

We were gearing up for a surf day, and when I grabbed my board, he frowned.

"You need to wax that board, shark bait. There's barely anything left on it."

I wrinkled my nose at him.

"Nah, it's ok."

His frown deepened. "No, it's not. That board's a mess. When was the last time you waxed it?"

I screwed up my face thinking. I honestly couldn't remember.

"I dunno. A while ago."

"Clearly."

"It's fine. I don't need wax. I have sticky feet." I winked at him, and he growled, snatching the board away from me.

"If you think I'm going to let you surf Leviathans without a properly waxed board, you're even more delusional than I originally gave you credit for, Finn Summers."

My eyebrows rose, and my heart skipped a beat.

Fuck.

I loved it when he laid down the law.

So hot.

"Full naming me, damn. You mean business." I grinned at him, and his scowl darkened. In the beginning, I thought my dimples seemed to have the opposite effect on him than they did on most people, but it turned out it was all a ruse.

Scowling to Riddick was smiling to most people. The grumpier I made him, the more he seemed to come around. So I'd made it my mission to continue being as annoying as possible so he would never leave me.

"How the fuck have you stayed alive this long? Jesus," he grumbled, slapping my board down on the rickety wooden table next to the bench press. I assumed it was there for this purpose, not that I'd ever used it.

"I dunno. People kinda meet me, then realize that if they don't keep an eye on me, I'm a goner." I grinned. It was true. Even Turtle, despite his stoner ways, was usually subconsciously keeping an eye on me and making sure my ADHD ass didn't walk into traffic or some dumb shit.

He was always doing things to make sure I thrived, like making that points game up for dishes at work to keep me engaged, and I didn't know what I would do without him.

Riddick glanced up at me, and for a moment, I saw real fear in his eyes, and my heart squeezed in my chest.

"Why do you not want to wax your board?" he finally asked, and I tilted my head to the side, thinking about it.

No one had ever asked me *why* before, so it took a second for me to sort through my thoughts and pick out the reasons.

I only got distracted admiring how hot Riddick's forearms were twice.

"I think it's a sensory thing. I don't like the way the wax feels. It's all sticky and gritty, and even when I wash my hands after, I feel like it's stuck between my fingers for hours, and it makes my teeth hurt."

"It makes your teeth hurt?"

I nodded earnestly. "Yeah, it's weird, and I hate it. Also, it takes *forever*. Sometimes, when I think, okay, maybe I *should* really do it, I get too antsy and just want to get in the water. It feels like a waste of time."

His head snapped up at that, and he looked angry.

"Nothing that helps keep you safe is a *waste of time,* Finn," he said. His voice was low, and there was no amusement in his tone.

I laughed nervously and rubbed the back of my neck. "Wow, didn't know you cared," I said, grinning at him awkwardly.

His expression darkened further, and I felt a rush of pins and needles through my body. When he looked at me like that, the feelings I was always trying to repress around him tended to come flooding back to the surface. My skin suddenly felt hot, and it had nothing to do with the sun.

"Of course I care, Finn," he murmured, his voice so soft, it was almost drowned out by the distant crash of waves.

"You do?" I asked, my own voice suddenly small and shaky. His eyes were glued to mine, and the tension between us mounted.

His mouth parted, and for a second, I thought he was going to give me the affirmation I desperately craved, but he blinked, and suddenly, the moment was gone.

"I'll wax your boards for you if it's a sensory thing. I'll do it while you eat breakfast so you don't get antsy," he said gruffly and went back to work, leaving me feeling dizzy and off-center.

CHAPTER

Twenty

Finn

Alexa Play: The Wave by Colouring

I t was Wednesday, which was my favorite day of the week because it was always an active rest day. Every Wednesday, I would rush outside after breakfast to find Riddick waiting by my usual longboard/yoga mat combo, and he would coach me through a class. Yoga was always followed by freestyle surfing together, and it was always the closest I ever got to seeing him smile.

Though Riddick didn't touch me anymore during our yoga sessions, I still almost always ended up getting turned on. His deep, growly voice ordering me to move myself in all kinds of compromising positions was like the ultimate edging. It was almost hotter when he wasn't touching me because I could always feel his eyes on me the whole time I had my ass in the air.

It didn't help that he seemed incapable of not staring at my cock every time it inevitably got hard. The way he would lick his lips and shamelessly allow his gaze to rake over my body was so erotic that it almost made me angry.

He *clearly* wanted me as much as I wanted him, and seeing the evidence of that on his face felt like an insult for some reason.

However, I was too obsessed with him to say anything about it, and by the time we finished our surf sesh in the afternoon and spent the evening cooking together, that frustrated, angry feeling always seemed to melt away.

Also, I always seemed to wake up on Thursday mornings covered in my own cum. It was my fault, really. After yoga days, I knew I should really relieve myself in the shower before bed. But the little game Riddick had played with me in the beginning had given me a taste for delayed gratification.

Besides, I found that I almost always dreamed of Riddick if I didn't touch myself on active rest days. These dreams manifested every Wednesday night like clockwork, and they were always the same. He would stand over me in my room and leave feather-light touches on my cock until I came.

In my dreams, he always handled me with such care and whispered gentle words of praise that some deep, insecure part of me needed to desperately hear.

'You're such a sweet boy. Look at you, all hard and needy. Give me that sweet cum, beautiful.'

'Fuck, Finn. You're so gorgeous. You going to come for me, gorgeous?'

His imagined words would swirl through my mind the following day, leaving me feeling light and buzzing with dopamine. What I wouldn't give to hear him speak to me like that in real life.

Though, no matter how hard I tried to sway him, he kept up his stone-cold ruse under the pretense that he was doing it for my benefit. Which I hated.

However, today was different.

I burst out, ready for my weekly edging, I mean, *yoga* session, to find that there was no longboard/mat combo waiting for me.

Riddick was finishing up waxing one of my shortboards.

"No yoga today?" I asked, somehow feeling both weirdly relieved and disappointed. As much as I loved it, I was getting sick of it never amounting to anything.

Something needed to give soon, or I was going to snap.

"No. Today, we're doing something else."

I perked up at this, excited.

"What?"

"We're going to Leviathans."

Instantly, all my irritation with him disappeared, and I was so excited that I started to hiccup.

"What! You're ser-*hiccup* serious!?" I squealed, literally bouncing in place.

He wiped his hands off on the rough towel he used specifically for waxing and gave me an amused but quizzical look.

"Yeah. We're going to study the wave patterns, and then I'll coach you through some visualization techniques."

"Fuck YES!" *hiccup* Omg, omg, omg, I can't *hiccup* WAIT!"

Though he was smirking, he gave me a 'you're weird' look.

"Calm down, don't hurt yourself," he muttered, grabbing a water bottle and handing it to me – I assumed to help with the spontaneous bout of hiccups that seemed to have consumed me.

I chased after him as he made his way to my property line. He disappeared into the brush, and I hiccuped a few more times as I struggled to push through the thick palms and shrubs that he seemed to effortlessly be cutting through.

"Hey! Why are we going this way? It's like a four-minute walk down the street!" He shot an amused look over his shoulder, and before I knew it, the brush cleared away, and we were on a narrow dirt path, wide enough for a single person.

"This way is faster."

"Faster than *hiccup* *four* minutes?"

We walked for maybe a minute and a half, and suddenly, the palm trees opened up, and we were on the edge of a cliff, looking down at Leviathans.

On the opposite side of the coastline, I could see the precipice that Blake had taken Turtle and me when we first arrived in Stars Cove.

"Woah… it's been *right here* this whole time?"

Riddick's mouth tilted up, and he nodded.

"Leviathans is inside your property line. You technically own it."

My mouth dropped open, and my eyes grew so wide that my eyeballs were at risk of popping out of my skull.

*"Fuck, *hiccup* OFF!!"* I exclaimed.

He frowned at me and reached out, cuffing the back of my neck and applying pressure to each side of my spine.

I froze, my entire body lighting up at his touch.

He hadn't put his hands on me in *weeks,* and the casual, possessive way he'd just grabbed the back of my neck made my mind suddenly go blank with lust.

"Take a sip of your water," he said softly as he massaged the muscles on either side of my spine. I did as he said, too afraid to make a comment about how happy I was to have him touching me again. I didn't want him to stop.

I swallowed the cold water as he gently pinched my neck, and I felt a lump of air dislodge from deep in my chest and rise up as the water slid down. I let out a tiny burp, and his mouth tilted up in the corner.

"There… that's better." He hummed, and the way he said it felt like he should have been whispering those words to me in a dark bedroom instead of on the edge of a cliff.

I peered up at him with wide eyes, and he stared right back, the corner of his lips still lifted and his warm hand still cupping my neck.

"Are they gone now?" he asked softly, and I opened my mouth to respond, waiting for a hiccup to interrupt me, but it never came.

"Uhm. Yeah. I think so…" I replied, though I was whispering for some reason. He was no longer pinching my flesh but stroking it. His thumb brushed gently up and down the side of my throat. I leaned into his hand, wishing he would always touch me like this.

The moment I leaned into it, he ripped his hand away and cleared his throat, rubbing the back of his own neck instead.

"Let's get down there," he said abruptly, and my cheeks flushed with irritation.

I was getting so *sick of all these mixed signals.*

My earlier excitement was significantly dampened, and now I was in a decidedly bad mood.

I followed Riddick down a very steep and slippery natural stone pathway down the cliff to the small beach below.

Once we made it to the shore, I realized what had looked like black sand from the top of the cliff was actually a thick layer of dark pebbles.

It was a rock beach, and though everything had been worn smooth by the constant crash of water, it would still be uncomfortable to walk on it barefoot.

Down here, the waves were even more impressive.

Watching the water gather and swell into a massive wall of dark navy and gunmetal grey sent shivers and chills rushing down my spine.

It was now midsummer, so they weren't even close to as big as they would get in the winter, but they were still twice the size of the waves I'd been shredding on both my private beach and the pipelines in Stars Cove.

Riddick was staring at me, and I could feel the weight of his gaze buzzing on my skin like liquid sunshine, but I ignored him. I was still pissed at him, and honestly, the waves deserved my attention more than he did.

I was *itching* for a surfboard. If he wasn't here with me right now, I would've jet back to the shack to grab one and be in the water before you could say *'P. Sherman 42 Wallaby Way, Sydney.'*

"You have to promise never to come here without me," he said, his tone firm and serious. Finally, I tore my gaze away from the water and glared at him. I could still feel where he'd rubbed his thumb up the side of my neck, and that angry part of me that constantly felt rejected by him was getting the best of me.

"I'm not going to do that, Riddick. I'm an adult. I'll do what I want."

He narrowed his eyes at me, but I think he could tell I wasn't in the mood to fuck around today, so he let it go. Sighing, he turned to face the water again and pointed to the horizon.

"These waves are much smaller than what you're going to be facing in the winter, but they still show examples of some of the dangers you need to look out for," he explained.

"What makes this beach so tricky is that there are multiple factors that come into play to make the waves as large as they are, but these factors also tend to make the peaks unpredictable."

I pushed my irritation aside and listened. The information he was giving me was crucial, and I suddenly wished I'd brought a pen and notepad so I could write what he was saying down.

"Here, you need to *always* watch the horizon. Leviathans is not like the beach at Stars Cove, where you'll get consistent pipelines every time. Here, the peaks shift, making it difficult to know where to paddle out. This beach is also notorious for rogue waves that come out of nowhere. You could be waiting for a twenty-footer, only to have a fifty-foot behemoth roll in directly behind it out of nowhere and take you by surprise."

"*Fifty feet?*" I gasped. "I thought the biggest they got was twenty-five?"

Riddick shot me a dark look, his lips pursed.

"I've seen eighty-foot waves hit this beach," he told me, his voice hollow and haunted.

I swallowed.

"How do you think this beach got its name? These aren't waves, Finn. They're Leviathans. Sea demons sent to punish the men that try to tame them."

That was... *insane.*

"See where the water turns black right where the break hits?" he asked, and I followed the line of his arm, nodding at the strip of darkness that ran parallel with the wave lines.

"That's the reason for these massive swells. It's a deep water canyon that funnels these waves to shore, but it's also the reason ninety percent of these waves are susceptible to an unexpected break."

I scoffed.

"An unexpected break isn't that big a deal, Riddick. If I wipe out, I can just try again."

He rounded on me, his face white with fury, and for a second, I thought he was going to grab me.

I narrowed my eyes on him, challenging him with my stare.

Do it. Grab me.

He stopped himself and clenched his fists at his sides instead.

"These aren't those pussy swells you grew up surfing on the East Coast, Finn. An unexpected break when you find yourself on a rogue eighty-footer is a fucking death sentence. Do you know what happens to the human body when it hits the water after falling *eighty feet?*"

My confidence wavered slightly as I tried and failed to imagine just how tall eighty feet really was.

"Then, if by some miracle you *do* survive that fall, you could get pulled and trapped in the canyon beneath, rolling through the rip tide like a T-shirt in a fucking washing machine."

"I just meant—"

"*Then,* if you survive *that,* you may break the surface only to find yourself in the death zone." He pointed to the east side of the beach, where multiple wave sets converged and crashed relentlessly into the rocks, forming a deadly, choppy pool of white water. "People more skilled than you have *died* getting caught in two wave-hold downs in the death zone."

I blinked, and suddenly, his hands were wrapped around my shoulders. His face was inches from mine, and my eyes widened in surprise at his sudden proximity. I could feel the heat of his breath coasting across my lips, and I suddenly wasn't thinking about eighty-foot waves anymore. I was wondering if his lips would taste like saltwater and how the stubble on his chin would feel rubbing against me while we kissed.

"This beach could kill you a hundred different ways, Finn, but it only really needs one. *One* mistake. *One* fuck up. And you could lose your *life.*" His fingers were trembling against me, and his blue eyes were angry but also strangely glassy.

A tear slid down his cheek, and without thinking, I found myself cupping the side of his face and brushing the tear away with my thumb.

The roughness of his stubble felt *exactly* how I imagined it would.

"Riddick. I'm not going to die," I breathed, feeling like my heart was breaking for him. He was clearly hurting from the loss of his friend, and the thought of me dying the same way was eating him up more than I'd realized.

"But you *could,*" *he* gasped, shaking me roughly, his voice coming out strained and hoarse like he had a throat full of tears.

We were so close our chests were touching. I tilted my head back so I could look at him properly, marveling at the fact that he was still letting me stroke the side of his face.

"Shh. It's gonna be okay." I stood on my toes, brushing my lips against his so gently I barely felt it. His eyes fluttered closed, and another tear slipped free. His hands tightened on my shoulders, and I hovered there, keeping the tiniest sliver of space between us.

I wanted him to come to me. I *needed* him to initiate it.

The broken parts of me that had never really recovered from the abandonment of my father and the loss of my mother needed proof that he wanted me just as badly as I wanted him.

I needed to feel *wanted*.

"Finn..." His voice was feather soft, a whisper, and his lower lip moved against mine as he said my name.

Do it, Riddick. Kiss me...

I urged him as I continued gently stroking his cheek with my thumb, much like he'd done to the side of my neck earlier.

I parted my lips and turned my head to the side, giving him every opportunity to claim me, but it had the opposite effect. The slight movement seemed to snap him out of the moment.

He ripped away from me so abruptly I gasped, and I was left reeling and chilled from his absence.

The waves crashed against the shore with a sinister sort of violence, and for the first time, I wasn't enthralled by them.

They felt like a metaphor for the crash and break of the stupid, naive organ that was struggling to beat in my chest.

I was an *idiot.*

Why did I keep bothering to chase after this guy? He clearly didn't want me enough to pursue this.

The same hurt feeling I used to struggle with as a kid washed over me.

'Why doesn't he want us, Mommy? Why'd he leave us all alone?'

'You're not alone, sweet boy. I'm right here!'

But I didn't have her.

I *was* fucking alone.

And now, Riddick didn't want me either.

"I *told* you, we can't do this, Finn!" Riddick was shouting at me. His fingers were buried in his thick hair, and he looked like he wanted to tear it out at the roots.

But I didn't care.

I was so *done* with this.

"This is over, Riddick," I said, shocking myself with how cold and dead my own voice sounded. I felt numb.

"What?" he snapped.

"I'm done. I don't want to train with you anymore. In fact, I don't want to fucking *see* you anymore. Stay off my property."

He narrowed his eyes at me, and I could *feel* his rage like it was a living thing.

"We've been over this, kid," he growled.

"What, all of a sudden I'm *kid* again? It's like that?"

"Yeah. It's like that. I'll surf wherever the fuck I want, and if I want to surf your beach, I will."

I cut him a cool look and shrugged.

"Fine. I'll go then."

"What do you mean *you'll* go? Go where?"

"None of your business."

"Stop being ridiculous. You're not abandoning your own house just because you don't want to see me."

I was already making my way back to the cliff face.

"Watch me," I snapped.

"Finn!" He called after me, but I kept walking, and he didn't chase me.

Once I made it back to the shack, I packed a duffle with some clothes and sent a text to Turtle, asking him to come pick me up.

I'll admit I packed a little slower than necessary. Some small pathetic part of me couldn't help but hope Riddick would show up and beg me to stay. To prove that it wasn't all in my head and that he really *did* care about me.

But he never came, and by the time Turtle showed up with Shelly, my mood had soured even further.

Turtle helped me load up my fish board and my shortboard, which had both been recently waxed for me by the man I was leaving behind.

I tried not to let that fact sway me as we strapped the boards to the roof of the van.

I watched my shack get smaller and smaller in Shelly's side mirror, and even when the silhouette of a tall, broad-shouldered man appeared next to it, I didn't tell Turtle to stop.

I'd learned all I needed to know from Riddick to surf Leviathans.

I would do the rest of my training alone.

CHAPTER
Twenty-One

Finn

"Dude. You're such a buzzkill lately," Turtle complained, flopping down in the lawn chair next to me.

I glanced away from the campfire I'd started in the firepit on Shelly's lot. Every lot on Stars Cove's campsite had one, and I'd spent the last hour tossing rolled-up bits of *The Stars Cove Gazette* into it.

The big black and white photo of Mayor Tully's face was now missing a forehead due to my nervous picking and fidgeting.

"Am not," I grumbled. My friend frowned at me, looking uncharacteristically worried.

"You are too, man. You've been down in the dumps since you made me come get you. What happened anyway?"

It'd been three days since I left my shack. I hadn't gone back once and hadn't heard from Riddick... which made sense since I was pretty sure he didn't even own a cell phone.

That didn't stop me from constantly checking my phone to see if he'd somehow messaged me anyway.

"Nothing happened," I replied. I wasn't sure why I hadn't told Turtle about Riddick. I didn't owe him anything, and since he wasn't my coach anymore, the rules no longer applied.

I could drink, smoke, and fuck anyone I wanted, though the thought of doing any of those things just made me more miserable.

It didn't help that I'd walked in on Blake and Turtle fucking enough times that they were starting to feel bad for me. They kept pushing me to hook up with Quinn, who had become increasingly clingy at work over the last few days. So, I suspected they were telling her to hook up with me, too.

It was annoying, and I had no way of explaining to them that I was going through what felt an awful lot like a break-up... even though we hadn't actually *been* anything.

I hadn't even had any dreams of Riddick, which I guess was a good thing. Jizzing all over Turtle's tiny couch was the last thing I wanted to do... Especially since he'd hung a Magnum PI poster up since our last conversation, and I always felt like Tom Selleck was staring at me... It was creepy... but somehow, it also reminded me of another man with a hairy chest and kind eyes...

I missed him.

I missed Riddick *so fucking much,* it was insane.

I missed making dinner with him and the way his eyes would sparkle when I made some stupid joke or got overly excited about things.

I missed how he would wax my board for me every morning because he knew I didn't like how the wax got stuck between my fingers.

There had been this strange sense of *home* that had been growing in that shack... a feeling I hadn't had since my mom was alive, and now that it was gone, I couldn't remember how I had ever been happy living in this van with Turtle.

It felt lonely, even though Turtle and I were basically living on top of each other.

"Something definitely happened, dude. You're acting the way you do when..." he trailed off, running his hand through his long hair.

"The way I do when *what?*" I snapped, already knowing the answer.

He gave me a very *un*-Turtle look and sighed.

"You're acting the way you do around the anniversary of her death, dude."

I swallowed.

"No way. It can't be that bad."

"It's pretty bad, brother. You may not be fully horizontal under the covers, but there's no light in your eyes. Someone hurt you. Bad."

"I don't want to talk about it." I sighed, and he looked at me like I was crazy.

"See! This is what I mean. You *always* wanna talk about stuff. We shoulda named you Motormouth Mike!"

My lip twitched, and I tossed one of my tiny paper balls at him.

"That's a terrible name."

Turtle laughed and shrugged.

"Terrible but accurate, bro."

"Whatever." I sighed.

"Why don't you come to the beach party tonight?" he asked, and I was already shaking my head before he even finished speaking.

"Come on, man. You don't have to drink or anything. Just come hang out. Quinn will be there. I don't know who put you in this funk, and you don't have to tell me if you don't want to, but maybe you just need someone to fuck her out of your system."

The '*her*' threw me for a loop for a second until I remembered Turtle still thought I was exclusively into girls.

To cover up my weird reaction to what he'd said, I just sighed again. "Fine."

"Dope!" He clapped me on the shoulder jovially. "We're gonna have a fucking blast, bro! This party is going to be a *rager!*"

CHAPTER
Twenty-Two

Finn

The party *was* a rager. Almost all the staff for Sharkies showed up, and even some people from the neighboring town.

I only knew, like, a handful of people, and I more or less stuck as close to Turtle and Blake as I could.

Stars Cove Beach had a tiki bar they staffed for these events, and there was a line of three people deep trying to get drinks.

A DJ was bumping top forty hits, and as the sky got darker and the crowd got tipsier, people started to kick off their shoes and dance.

I was nursing a rootbeer, half listening to Turtle tell Blake all about some douchebag customer he'd needed to deal with at Sharkies, when some preppy dude in a polo and beige cargo shorts appeared.

"Hey, it's the Turtle Man, how's it hanging?" Preppy Boy grinned, flashing freakishly perfect teeth.

Like, they were *so* perfect. I wondered vaguely if they were veneers. Dude looked like a ventriloquist dummy.

"Tully, my *man*, what's going onnnnnn?" Turtle grinned in his usual good-natured way, clapping hands with the guy in a friendly manner. I didn't know this guy, but his name sounded familiar.

"Nothing much, nothing much, just figured I would come and mingle with the common folk," the guy, *Tully*, said.

I narrowed my eyes.

That was kind of an asshole thing to say.

Turtle didn't seem perturbed; he just nodded, still smiling.

"Right on, brother."

"Who's this?" Toothtastic Tully asked, jerking his head to me but talking to Turtle like I wasn't even here.

I wrinkled my nose.

This guy was giving me the serious ick.

"This is my best bro, Finn Summers."

Tully's eyes flashed, and his creepy, fun-land smile turned mean.

"Ah, yes. I heard about you. Quinn talks about you a lot."

"Oh yeah?" I deadpanned, not even bothering to pretend I was interested in this conversation.

"Yeah. She says you have some dumbass dream of riding Leviathans. You know that's only for the pros, right?"

He said it like he was implying that *he* was the pro in question.

"Whatever, man," I replied mildly, already scanning the crowd to see if I could come up with an excuse to get away from this dickwad.

"Hey, I see Blake. I'll be right back," Turtle said suddenly, disappearing from my side.

I almost shouted after him not to leave me alone with this douchebag, but by the time I opened my mouth, he was already gone.

Turtle, my ass. Dude was fast as fuck.

"Anyway, that's why my dad is opening up Leviathans for an annual surf competition. He says it'll bring loads of money into the town. I've already been training for *months.*"

It was like someone turned the sound off, and all of a sudden, all my attention zoned in on Chip fucking Skylark's stupid face.

"He can't do that, man," I said dumbly, knowing that Riddick would absolutely *lose his mind* if something like that happened.

The guy scoffed, taking a giant swig of his beer. "Of course he can. My dad's the mayor of Stars Cove. He can do whatever he wants."

That's when it clicked. *Tully.* That must be this kid's last name. He was Mayor Tully's son.

I glared at him, shaking my head.

"Nah, man. Leviathans is on *my* property. I bought Jake Whittling's old place. There's no way I would let him do that." Feeling pleased with myself, I took another swig of my rootbeer.

Tully just started laughing. "God, you're dumber than I gave you credit for. Leviathans falls under the Public Trust Doctrine. Even if it's technically on your land, it's still owned by the state and is open for public use. You think my dad would start putting something like this together without checking all his boxes?"

I scowled.

What the fuck? What was even the point of buying land if everyone could just do whatever the fuck they wanted on my property anyway?

I rubbed my temple, suddenly feeling like I was getting a headache.

"Is Kyle bothering you?" I glanced up to find Quinn standing there with her hands on her hips and a scowl on her pretty face.

"Quinn, baby. I was just teaching this jerk off the basics of California property law," he said, puffing out his chest like that made him cool instead of a complete dweeb.

"Ew, Kyle. I'm not your baby. Why don't you crawl back under whatever rock you scuttled out of?"

His expression changed from amused to violent so quickly that I had to blink to keep up.

Suddenly, he was grabbing Quinn's arms so hard she cried out in pain, and he was snarling in her face.

"You think you can talk to me like that, you stupid bitch?" he spat.

My mouth dropped open in surprise. What the *fuck!?* I'd gotten the feeling this guy was a piece of shit, but I wasn't expecting this level of depravity.

Quinn didn't look surprised, but she didn't cower either. She turned her angry green eyes on him and *spat* directly in his face.

"You *cunt*!" he bellowed and tossed her down into the sand like she was a rag doll. He pulled his foot back, and I suddenly realized that he was planning to *kick* her.

"Oh, *hell* no!" I snapped.

I kicked out his knee on the leg that he'd put all his weight on, and he collapsed into the sand next to Quinn.

I was on him in a second.

"You like to hit girls?" I snarled, cocking my fist back and slamming it into his nose so hard blood gushed out. "Why don't you try fucking with someone who hits back, huh?" I slammed my fist into his stupid, ugly teeth and grunted as I split a knuckle open on his veneers.

"Finn! Stop!" Quinn was shouting and pulling me off the little douchebag, who was now sputtering and spitting blood into the sand.

"You're gonna pay for that!" Kyle yelled at me as he got to his feet.

I lunged for him again, but he turned tail and ran like the little bitch he was. He was lucky Quinn was holding me back, or I would have given him a black eye to go with his broken nose.

"What a fucking asshole," I growled, and Quinn gently took my throbbing hand in hers and held it up to examine the damage.

"You shouldn't have done that, Finn." She sighed.

I scoffed, finally tearing my gaze away from Kyle's retreating form to look down at her.

"He was going to hurt you. Right in front of me! What was I supposed to do? Watch him beat the shit out of you? Fuck that."

She looked up at me with those pretty eyes surrounded by dark lashes, and for a moment, it looked like she might cry. Her dark hair was so thick and healthy that it reflected the warm orange flicker of the flames in the tiki torches that lit up the beach.

She really was gorgeous. In a different life, I would have chased her down in a heartbeat. As it was, even after putting three days of distance between us, I was still chasing Riddick.

"No one's ever done something like that for me before," she said softly, and I frowned.

"Then you need to hang out with better people, Quinn. That was fucked up. Is that the first time he tried to hurt you?"

She shook her head and dropped her gaze. Her shame was so great I could feel it roll across my skin like a living thing.

"Hey," I said, tilting her head up so she would look at me again. "There's nothing to be ashamed of. *You* didn't do anything wrong."

"I basically called him a cockroach... and I spat on him." She pointed out, and I burst out laughing.

It was the first time I'd laughed since I left the shack. It felt really good.

"*True.* But I mean, if the antennae fit."

She giggled. "Did you see how he scuttled away after you beat his ass?"

I nodded in mock seriousness.

"Serious cockroach behavior."

She giggled again, and I felt another surge of sadness that I wasn't into her. She deserved someone to take care of her the way Riddick took care of me.

Or, I guess, the way he *had* been taking care of me before I left him on that beach.

"I used to date him. Believe it or not, he was really nice to me at first. Charming. Then, after we were together for a while, he started to change. I broke up with him after he hit me the first time, but he's been obsessed with me ever since."

I was starting to understand why he'd seemed to hate me on sight. He thought I was after Quinn, who he seemed to think belonged to him.

I fucking *hated* dudes like him. I should've hit him harder.

"He's not going to let this go, you know," she said, gesturing to my now swollen and bleeding hand.

I snorted. "I'm not afraid of him, babe."

"You should be. His dad's the mayor, Finn. They could make your life here very complicated if they wanted to."

I shrugged.

My life here was *already* complicated, and it had nothing to do with bitch-ass Kyle Tully.

"I like it when you call me that, you know?"

"Huh?" I asked, shaking my head to snap myself out of my thoughts of Riddick.

"*Babe,*" *she* said, her cheeks blushing, and my chest flooded with guilt.

Ah fuck.

The last thing I wanted to do was lead her on. Riddick had done that to me for weeks, and it felt like shit. I wasn't down to do that to someone else. Especially not someone as cool as Quinn.

"Listen, Quinn. I think you're rad and all, but it's not like that," I said, and she frowned.

"It's not?"

"Nah. I know Turtle's been pushing for us to hook up, but I'm not looking for a relationship right now."

"Why not? Is it me? Is it something I did?" she asked, and I could see the anxiety in her features. Something told me that Kyle guy hadn't just hit her. He'd damaged her self-esteem. Someone who looked and acted like Quinn shouldn't be this insecure.

"No, babe. It's not you. You're gorgeous and funny and smart, and you deserve way better than that douchebag Kyle. I'm just... into someone else."

Her face lit up at that, and I immediately regretted saying anything.

"Really? Who?! Do I know her?" My cheeks flushed, and I shook my head.

"Nah. Probably not," I muttered.

"Well, she's very lucky. Whoever she is."

I huffed out a painful laugh, shrugging. I doubted Riddick would agree that he was *lucky* to be the object of my affections. He couldn't push me away fast enough.

She reached out and placed her hand on mine gently, smiling up at me.

"Thanks again, Finn," she whispered, and I grinned down at her.

"Of course, Quinn."

Suddenly, a deep, angry voice ripped through the balmy California night, causing me to jerk away from Quinn in surprise.

"And *what,* exactly, is going on here?"

My head whipped to the side, and Riddick was there, barely a foot away from us.

And he looked *pissed.*

CHAPTER

Twenty-Three

Finn

"What are *you* doing here?" I scowled, and Riddick narrowed his eyes at me. I didn't miss the way his gaze dropped to where Quinn's hand was still resting on top of mine.

Quinn glanced at me, then over to where Riddick stood, her brow creasing in concern.

"What's going on?" she asked, sounding confused.

"Nothing, let's go get a drink," I said, turning away from Riddick.

"So you're drinking now?"

"That's none of your business," I snapped, and Quinn looked even more concerned. Her gaze darted back and forth between us like she was afraid I was going to get into another fistfight.

"You fucking her too?"

"Again. None of your goddamn business, Riddick!" I snarled, abandoning my plan to take Quinn to get a drink. I turned to face him and leveled him with the hardest look I could muster.

"Finn," Quinn said. Her voice was shaky, and she was talking to me like I was some rabid animal that was going to lose control at any second. "Maybe we should—"

"Go find Turtle, Quinn," I snapped.

Quinn hesitated and bit her lip. She kept glancing between the two of us. We were glaring at each other so hard I knew she probably thought we were going to kill each other.

"I don't think I should leave…" she whispered, and I glared at her.

"I said *go,* Quinn!"

Her frown deepened, and finally, she nodded before hurrying away.

"I want you to come home," Riddick said the second she was gone.

My blood rushed in my ears at the way he said *home.* Like it was *our* home. I shook my head. No. I wouldn't let him do this to me again—make me hope with all these tiny little morsels of implied commitment and affection.

I deserved better than that.

"I don't really give a fuck what you want, Riddick."

"That wasn't a *request,* Finn," he growled, and I shuddered. Some deep-seated part of me ached to submit to him and obey, but I couldn't. I couldn't go back to days of mind games and never-ending sexual tension. I was going to go crazy.

"The answer is *no,*" I hissed, spitting his own words back at him. He visibly flinched.

I turned to walk away, but what he said next stopped me in my tracks.

"I'm *sorry,* okay? Please come home."

I glanced over my shoulder, and the way he was looking at me made my heart ache. There was this deep, yawning sadness in his eyes that I hadn't noticed before.

"Why should I?"

He glanced around the party, and I followed his gaze. We were getting some weird looks, and a growl rolled through my chest in frustration.

Fucking nosy assholes.

"Not here... Can we talk? In private? Please?" he asked, and I swear to God it was the *please* that got me. I was so used to him bossing me around that hearing him beg made my spine tingle with the strangeness of it.

I glanced around at our steadily growing audience and sighed.

I was shit at holding grudges. Although I wasn't ready to fully forgive him, I could admit to myself that I obviously still wanted him. If he wanted to talk, I would hear him out.

"Alright. Fine. Let me go find Turtle to let him know I'm leaving. I'll meet you at ho—I mean, the shack."

"Alright." He nodded. "I'll be waiting."

"Fine," I snapped, then went off to find my friend.

I FOUND TURTLE CHILLING WITH BLAKE BY ONE OF THE BONFIRES. He grinned at me as I approached and held his fist out to bump.

"Hey man, what's been going on?"

"Not much. Hey, any chance you can drive me home?"

"No can do, Finn Man. I've had a couple crispy boys if you're catching my wave."

I felt myself deflate. The walk wasn't impossible, but it was a bit of a hike.

"Here, you can take my car; just bring it to Sharkies tomorrow for our shift," Blake said, handing me her keys. I grinned at the faux lucky rabbit's foot keychain she had attached to it.

"Thanks, Blake."

"Don't mention it." She winked at me.

"Hey, have you seen Quinn?" I asked, and she shook her head. "No, not yet."

"Make sure you check on her. She's had a bit of a rough night," I said, and Blake nodded.

"Okay. Noted. Thanks!"

"No worries," I called over my shoulder as I trotted away, suddenly more anxious than I'd ever been in my life to get home.

What could he possibly want to talk about?

Was he finally going to admit to wanting to be with me?

By the time I pulled up in my driveway, my heart was pounding in my chest.

Fuck, why was I so nervous?!

My slides crunched on my gravel driveway as I approached the front door to my beach shack. I wondered how long I would need to wait for him as I unlocked the front door and stepped inside.

"Hey."

"Jesus Christ!" I yelped, accidentally sending my keys flying.

Riddick was standing in my kitchen with his hands in his pockets and a miserable expression on his face.

I'd forgotten how built he was. It hadn't been as obvious out in the open, on the beach.

In here, with all my condo-sized furniture and low ceilings, I felt dwarfed next to him.

I wasn't sure when my tastes had changed from the small, dainty features that girls like Quinn wore so well to this towering wall of sheer *man* that stood before me, but there was no denying it.

He just *did it* for me, and it was taking all my self-control not to just melt into a submissive puddle of goo at his feet.

"Sorry, I didn't mean to startle you."

"How'd you get here so fast? On second thought, how'd you get *in* here? I locked the door when I left."

His mouth tilted in that classic Riddick smirk, and he shrugged.

"Magic fingers," he replied, and I narrowed my eyes.

"More like felony fingers," I grumbled, and his lips twitched again. Then, his gaze fell to my hand, which was swollen and bleeding from punching Nigel Thornberry in the face so many times.

"What the fuck happened?" he growled, rushing forward, reaching for my hand like he wanted to inspect it closer.

I jerked away from him and took a step back. "Nothing. The mayor's douchey son tried to hurt Quinn, so I kicked his ass."

Riddick's nostrils flared with rage. "Did he hurt you?"

"What? No. He couldn't even land a hit on me."

Riddick was clenching and unclenching his fists at his sides, his gaze still trained on my bleeding hand.

Suddenly, I felt tired. *So tired* of all his fucking mind games and mixed signals. Maybe coming back here was a mistake.

"Why am I here, Riddick? Say what you need to say so I can go." I sighed, and he bit his lip, his small smile disappearing.

"I wanted to apologize."

"Yeah? For what?"

He remained silent, and I scoffed.

"That's what I thought; you don't even know what you're apologizing for."

"For hurting you."

I growled. All this was doing was pissing me off even more.

"Well, I don't forgive you. Now kindly fuck off."

"Finn..."

"No! You're either in this or you're not. If you're not into me, then that's fine, but fuck off then and leave me alone. I've made it clear how I feel about you, and I'm sorry, but I don't want to train every day with someone who clearly doesn't want me back."

Suddenly, he was crowding me, and my back was pressed against the door. He was cupping my face in his large hands, and he rubbed the tip of his nose intimately against mine.

"You think I don't want you, Finn?" he murmured against my lips.

"I—"

"I want you so fucking bad I could have killed that silly little girl for putting her hands on what's mine."

What's...mine?

My whole body was suddenly on fire. His lips were so close to mine that he was practically swallowing each one of my breaths.

"I'm not *yours,* Riddick. You've made that perfectly clear."

A low, animalistic growl built in his chest, and he pressed me more firmly into the door.

"I'm trying to *protect you*, Finn. Can't you just trust me on that?"

"Protect me from *what!?*"

"From me! I'm not *good* for you. It doesn't matter that I want you so badly that you're all I can think about. Because it's not about *me*. It's about *you* and what you deserve."

He was telling me all the things I'd been dying to hear, but it still wasn't enough. I needed more than pretty words. I needed *him.*

"And what do you think I deserve, Riddick?" I asked, though my voice was a whisper. He rested his forehead on mine and closed his eyes, both thumbs stroking my cheeks tenderly like I was something precious to be worshiped and treasured.

"Everything... *Anything*, Finn. You deserve anything you want in the world, and I'm sorry if I made you feel like you don't."

"What I *want* is you."

He pulled away slightly so he could search my eyes. I stared back at him, holding my breath as I watched his resolve crumble.

"You're still going to try to ride Leviathans, even without my help, aren't you?" he choked, and I nodded.

"You know I am."

He stroked my cheeks again, and I watched his Adam's apple bob as he made a decision that would change my life forever.

"If I give in... If we explore this... *thing*, will you come home?"

Still unable to breathe, I nodded once.

"Say it. I need to hear you promise me you'll come home and let me help you."

I let out the breath I'd been holding in a rush and nodded again.

"Yes, Riddick. I'll come home if you agree to give this a chance."

The longest second of my life ticked by as my words hung between us, and then he wrapped his large palms around the backs of my thighs and hoisted me up, forcing me to wrap my legs around his waist.

"I hope you can forgive me one day, Finn... I fucking tried. I really tried," he murmured, his voice rough. My heart was slamming in my chest, and for a moment, I thought he was going to refuse me again. I shivered as he turned his beautiful but horribly sad blue eyes on me, and I watched him break.

"But I'm too fucking weak to fight this anymore." He grabbed me roughly by the jaw and held me firmly in place while he massaged my hip with the other. "You deserve so much better than what I'm about to give you, Finn."

I whimpered as he pressed me further back into the wall, digging his fingers into me hard enough to bruise.

"But I'm a shitty fucking person, and I'm going to give it to you anyway."

Then, he slammed his lips into mine.

TRUCK UP FM
PACIFICO

CHAPTER
Twenty-Four

Finn

Alexa Play: The Space Between by Dave Matthews Band

Riddick tasted just as I imagined he would. Sea salt with a touch of something more earthy and masculine. It was like nothing I'd ever had before, and my entire body lit up as he forced his hot tongue into my mouth.

I moaned, and my body arched into him instinctively, which caused him to growl and pin me more firmly into the wall with his hips.

His fingers curled into my hair, and he controlled the movements of my head as he devoured my mouth. I'd never been dominated like this before. The girls I'd hooked up with had always been so shy and submissive.

This was a completely different experience, and now that I'd had a taste of what it felt like to be owned by Riddick, I didn't think I could ever go back.

I gasped as he sucked my entire tongue into his mouth, pulsing on it with a wet, slurping sound before releasing me and doing the same thing to my bottom lip and then the top.

He nipped and bit at my mouth each time I whined, as if the sounds he was forcing out of me were little sweet treats that he'd earned for himself.

"Riddick..." I gasped, rocking my hips in an attempt to grind my *painfully* hard cock against his abdomen. "I need..."

He pulled his mouth away but increased the pressure of his hold on my hair and my hip, keeping me completely still and at his mercy.

"I know what you need, baby boy."

With very little effort, he dropped the hand that had been controlling my head to my hip and pulled me off the wall.

I placed my hands on his shoulders to steady myself as he walked us toward my bedroom.

Oh fuck.

It was happening... Was he going to fuck me?

I hadn't really thought that far ahead. I'd just wanted him to admit that he wanted me. Was I ready to fully commit to this?

I wasn't sure I could back out now, not after the scene I'd made. Besides, my dick was so fucking hard I was sure I was leaking in my shorts. The last thing I wanted to do was say anything that might scare him off.

With his massive hands cupping each side of my ass, he gently squeezed me and pulled me apart as he walked. I felt my cheeks spread, and even fully clothed, it was insanely erotic and nerve-wracking.

"Do you have any idea how badly I've wanted to split this fucking ass in two?" he growled, kicking the door to my room open and dropping me down on the bed.

I whimpered, but he leaned over me, pressing me back onto my elbows and dropping more kisses over my swollen lips.

"Watching you push your little ass in the air every fucking week has been *torture*," he murmured against me, and I could have fucking cried with relief. The confirmation that it had been just as difficult for him as it had been for me was so vindicating. It was everything I'd been desperate to hear.

He deftly undid the string of my shorts and tugged them off of me before sliding flat palms over the hot skin of my abdomen under my surf tank.

I instinctively raised my arms over my head to make it easier for him to take that off, too. Once I was lying there in nothing but my boxers, he stood up, towering over me by the side of the bed.

He peeled his white T-shirt off, discarding it on the floor without a second thought, and I stared up at his ripped chest and chiseled abs with hungry eyes. He was dusted in coarse, golden hair, and I wondered what it would feel like to finally be able to run my hands over him.

"Take off my shorts," he ordered, and I rushed to fumble with the ties to his swim trunks. I was so nervous I kept dropping the strings, and he grew impatient, batting my hands away and pulling them off himself.

I gasped as his cock popped out and bobbed in the air before me.

It was fucking *massive.* I wasn't sure what I'd expected. A man of his size would obviously have a giant cock. It only made sense, but seeing it was extremely humbling.

Was he going to try and put that thing inside me?

I couldn't tell if the thought of that excited me or terrified me. Maybe both.

He wrapped his hand around his monster cock and shamelessly stroked it while he watched me eye fuck him.

With his free hand, he reached over and palmed me over my boxers, and the contact sent an electric shock of need all the way up my spine.

He stroked me just the way he did in my dreams, and I was whining his name when he slid his hand between my legs and toyed with my crack over my boxers.

Ohfuckohfuckohfuck...

"Has anyone ever been in here?" he asked, his voice husky and dark. I shook my head, unable to form words. I was panting and sweating with anticipation as he stroked his finger up and down the crease of my ass, tickling the underside of my balls.

He gave me a look of pure lust and possession before grunting.

"*Good.* That's good, Finn. Take off your boxers," he ordered, and I hesitated, staring at his massive dick, which was so hard it was pointing straight up at his face.

"Is it going to hurt?" I whispered, and his expression softened slightly. He leaned forward, cupping the side of my face gently and kissing me again. This time, slow and deep. His tongue tangled with mine, and I whimpered as he licked and sucked me into oblivion.

When he finally pulled away, I felt lust-drunk and relaxed again.

"It might sting a little at first, but I'm going to make sure you're nice and opened up before I fuck you. Once your body adjusts to me, it's going to feel so fucking good, Finn. I promise."

"O-Okay," I whispered, deciding I trusted him not to hurt me.

He seemed pleased with my response, and he dropped another wet kiss on my mouth.

"You'll be a good boy and take it for me, won't you?"

I forced down my apprehension and nodded.

His lip curled up, and then, he *smiled.*

A.

Full.

Blown.

Smile.

My heart felt like it was going to explode in my chest at the sight of it. He looked younger when he smiled. Less burdened by the trauma of Jake's death and the guilt that I knew haunted him to his core.

When Riddick smiled, it felt like everything was right in the world, and I would never be touched by darkness again.

"My brave, beautiful boy. You're gonna make me so proud, aren't you?"

I was dizzy with emotion and endorphins, and I could barely manage a head nod as he tugged at the waistband of my boxers gently.

"Take these off, baby. Let me finally take a look at that tight, sweet little hole."

Baby.

Fuck.

For some reason, my throat closed up, and I felt like I might burst into tears. Riddick calling me baby felt like the most intimate thing in the world. Even more intimate than the physical act we were about to commit to together.

I wanted him to always call me that.

Needing to please him, I wiggled and squirmed my way out of the final barrier between us, kicking my boxers off and shivering with barely contained anticipation.

Even though my room was a furnace, my skin was so hot and flushed that I felt chilled and feverish.

He stood there for a moment, leisurely pumping his cock and just staring at me with those impossibly blue eyes. The fat, pink tip of his cock was glistening in the sliver of moonlight pouring in through my window, and I suddenly wanted to put it in my mouth more than I'd ever wanted anything.

I sat up to do just that, but he stopped me.

"No, sweet boy. There'll be time for that later. Lie on your back and spread your legs for me. I want to look at you."

My cheeks flushed with the thought of spreading myself open like that. It was so intimate... so...*vulnerable.*

I'd never done anything like this with someone before. I don't think any of the girls I'd fucked had even seen my ass, let alone my asshole.

The longer I hesitated, the more stern Riddick's expression became.

"You know how I feel about repeating myself, Finn," he growled, and I swallowed. Wanting to please him more than I cared about being embarrassed, I did what he said.

"That's a good boy..." he cooed as I pulled my knees into my chest. "Fuck, Finn. You're so fucking gorgeous, look at you..."

I could feel his gaze burning between my legs. Tingles shot up and down my cock as I lay there, and I felt my balls tighten.

How he could affect me like this without even *touching* me was insane. Swallowing nervously, I averted my gaze and stared at the ceiling while he took his time looking at me.

I felt the bed dip as he crawled onto it, and he kneeled between my legs.

A whimper escaped my lips, and he made gentle, soothing sounds as he whispered a few more words of praise. Then he laid his forearm across my knees, pressing me back to expose me to him even further.

'Shhh. You're doing so good, baby.'

'You're so beautiful.'

'Look at that tight, perfect little hole, just waiting to get fucked.'

I felt him reach over to the bedside table, and the telltale sound of lotion being pumped into his palm filled the room. My cock pulsed between my spread legs, and a rush of pre-cum escaped my tip and dripped across my abdomen.

With his right arm pressing my knees back, he positioned himself between my legs and leaned over me so his face was hovering over mine.

Gently, he used his left hand to feather the lotion over my crack. He was barely touching me. It was just enough to notify me of what he intended to do, and I took a deep breath, squeezing my eyes shut and tensing.

"Hey. Look at me, baby. Open your eyes," he ordered softly, and I did. My gaze slammed into his, and I was met with the most tender yet somehow lust-filled look I'd ever seen on his face.

"We're going to go slow, okay? I need you to relax. I'm going to coach you through each step so there won't be any surprises."

I nodded, and he smiled again.

"Tell me you understand, baby."

"I-I understand," I whispered, stumbling over my words as his lubed fingers continued to hover.

"Alright. I'm just going to rub you first. Get you nice and ready for me, okay?"

I nodded, and he closed the distance, sliding his fingers directly over my puckered hole.

The lotion made his touch slippery and soft, and when he started rubbing me in firm, tight circles, I let out an embarrassingly loud and shaky moan.

"See? That feels good, doesn't it?" he asked, and I shivered beneath him. "Tell me it feels good, baby."

"It-it f-feels, g-good..." My mind was literal mush. I would have told him the sky was purple if he asked me to. My entire universe was now just Riddick and what he was doing to me with his fingers.

"I'm going to put a finger inside you. You need to bear down. Remember what I taught you about your breath? Give me a deep inhale..."

I took a long, shaky breath and held it in.

"Exhale..."

As I let out my breath, I felt him apply pressure to my hole. There was a stinging sensation and a *pop,* and the next thing I knew, he was knuckle-deep inside me. I felt it everywhere. In my balls, in my dick, in my chest... just *everywhere.*

"Fuck, Finn." His voice was dripping with lust, and I felt him rock his hips as he wiggled his finger deeper. "I knew you were going to be tight but, *Jesus.* "

I whimpered and strained against his hold on my knees, arching into the new sensation as my body adjusted to accommodate him.

"How does it feel, baby? Does it feel okay?" he asked as he began to slide his finger in and out of me. There was a wet, squelching sound that accompanied each thrust. My cock let out another rush of pre-cum, and I whimpered a shaky *'yes.'*

"More, Riddick, please. I want more..." I begged, and he chuckled as he continued to work his finger in and out of me.

"Baby boy wants more?" he cooed, and I nodded frantically. I crushed my eyes shut so I could focus better on the new feelings he was subjecting me to.

"Alright, gorgeous. We're going to work up to three fingers before we go any further. Are you ready for the next one?"

"Yes, Riddick... please. I need... I need to come." Somehow I knew he wasn't going to let me come until he fit that huge dick of his inside me, and the need was growing more and more urgent with every second that passed.

My balls were aching again, and I think he knew it.

"I know. I know you do, but you need to earn it, my gorgeous, gorgeous boy. Here comes finger number two. Breathe for me again, baby."

I obeyed, slowly inhaling and exhaling, breathing through it each time he slid another finger deep inside me.

The third one stung the most, and I was mewling uncontrollably as he forced it past the tight ring of muscle.

"Shh, shh, you're okay. You're okay. It'll only sting for a second..."

I focused on my breath, and just as the burn subsided, he curled all three fingers and brushed a spot inside me that made my eyes fly open, and an unexpected gasp burst out of my mouth.

He chuckled and leaned down to kiss me. He licked my lips with a flat tongue and nipped me gently.

"Feel that, baby? That's your special spot. I wonder... If I were to keep stroking you here, would you come for me hands-free?"

He ran his fingers over it again, and I cried out, my hips suddenly rocking on their own accord, chasing the intense feeling.

"Riddick..." I whined. "Riddick, *please...*"

I couldn't think; I didn't even know what I was asking for. I just needed him to never stop. To *keep* touching me. I was a writhing ball of heat and need, and I was worried I might die from fucking pleasure.

"Oh yeah. I think I could definitely make you come just like this." He sounded so pleased with himself as he continued to roll over that spot again and again.

How could anything feel this good? How was this possible?

"Keep begging, baby, and I'll give you what you need."

He was smiling at me again, clearly loving how he'd reduced me to a submissive puddle of pure want and desire.

"I need to come, Riddick. So bad. I need to come so bad!" I panted as he continued to torture me.

My balls were throbbing, and I could feel my orgasm building fast. I was about to fucking blow, and he wasn't even touching my dick...

Then, he pulled his hand away abruptly, and I hissed in frustration, only to find him chuckling again.

"*Bad,* Finn," he scolded, though he sounded amused. "No coming until I say."

"*Riddick! Please!*" I whined, but he was pulling away from me, and my legs unfolded with the release of his weight.

"Stand up," he ordered, and I frowned, my lust-drunk mind confused. I didn't think I could stand even if I wanted to. My hips were stiff from having my legs folded back for so long, and my knees felt like they were made of jelly.

"Wh-what?"

"You heard me, stand up."

I forced myself to do as he said, rolling off the bed, feeling like a mess of loose limbs held together by elastic bands. He pumped more lotion into his hand and smeared it over his thick, veiny cock, before sitting on the edge of the bed.

"Come here, straddle me."

Oh fuck. It was happening. He was going to fuck me. I was really going to let a man fuck me! Holy fucking shit.

Feeling like I was in a dream, I did what he said, placing my knees on either side of his thighs.

He steadied me with one hand on my hip and the other on his cock. He pushed his slippery cockhead between my cheeks and rubbed it against my thoroughly prepped asshole before meeting my gaze.

"I'm going to let you control the first thrust, okay baby? Take your time. I'll take over again once I'm inside you."

"O-okay..."

He gave me an encouraging smile and asked me to breathe again as he notched the tip inside my asshole.

OhfuckJesusChristfucccckkk!

There was that stinging sensation again. He was so much thicker than even his three fingers had been, and for a second, I thought I was going to come just from the thought of his dick being slightly in my ass.

"Remember to breathe, baby," he whispered, wrapping his large hands against my naked hips. He stroked my hip bones with his thumbs, and I slowly lowered myself down onto him.

"Jesus, Finn. Your ass is fucking choking me," he grunted, his voice thick as honey. "I've never been inside someone so tight... You're so fucking perfect, baby. Look at how well you're doing, taking my big cock in your tiny little hole."

"It...feels... so *intense...*" I whined, squeezing his shoulders, and I wiggled my ass down on him another inch.

"I know. You're doing so good, gorgeous, you're halfway there. You can do this."

I felt his cock drag past that magical fucking spot again just as my ass hit his thighs. I clenched around him, loving the strangled groan that escaped his lips as my hole fluttered around his dick.

"*Good fucking boy.* Fuck, Finn. *Good boy.*"

His praise lit me up, and I rocked on his lap in response, practically purring with ecstasy at the feel of him fully seated inside me.

Instinctively, I dropped my hand down from his shoulder to stroke myself, but he batted my arm away with an angry growl.

"No touching. I want to make you come just from fucking you."

I stared at him with wide eyes.

Was that even possible?

"I'm going to move now. Are you ready?"

I nodded frantically.

"Yes, Riddick, *please!"*

He was already lying back on the bed and pulling me down with him. He braced one hand on my shoulder and the other on my hip, holding me in place as he lifted his hips.

I screamed as he pulled out almost to the tip and slammed into me for the first time. My cock bobbed between us, and I felt it somehow get even harder.

"That's it, take my fucking cock, you beautiful, gorgeous boy. Is this what you wanted, baby? You wanted me to fuck you senseless?" He was speaking through gritted teeth, and I could feel his cock surging inside me, telling me he was just as close to coming as I was.

"Yes, Riddick. *Please* don't stop. You're making me feel so good." I was sobbing now, tears literally streaming down my cheeks, and he continued to fuck up into me.

"Such a needy boy. Look at your greedy little ass swallowing me whole. Does my baby boy need to come?"

"Yes, yes, please, fuck, *yes!"*

"I'm going to fill you up, and I want you to drench me with your sweet cum. Can you do that for me, gorgeous?"

I wasn't even saying words anymore. My entire body was just pleasure, and when my cock started pulsing on its own, I felt my asshole clench with each spurt of cum that shot out of me.

"Holy fuck..." I moaned. "Fuck, I'm *coming!"*

"Yes, baby. Fucking give it to me. *Drown* me in it."

I painted him with cum. I watched as it coated his chest and throat, and I whimpered and cried as he continued to force my hips down onto his cock as he came inside me, too.

I could feel his cock pulsing as he emptied his load deep in my asshole, and I shook and trembled in his unforgiving grip as he held me in place.

"That's my good boy. Take it. Take it all, baby. I want you full and fucking dripping with me," he murmured, his eyes trained on the point where our bodies were connected.

"Riddick..."

I whimpered, my entire body going limp as I reached the end of my climax.

"I know, I know, baby," he soothed, allowing my body to slowly lower on top of him. His abs and chest were slick with sweat and cum, but I didn't care. I collapsed on top of him, and he wrapped his arms around me, holding me tight and kissing the side of my head and neck over and over again.

"You did so good, sweet boy. I'm so fucking proud of you," he whispered, rubbing my back as I shivered on top of him. He was still inside me, and I never wanted him to pull out.

"Riddick..." I whined again, not even knowing what I was trying to say, but just wanting him to keep holding me and telling me he was proud of me.

"Shh, shh. Just rest now. We can talk more in the morning."

A shot of panic ripped through me, and I struggled to sit up so I could face him, but he just tightened his grip on me.

"Please don't leave—stay with me," I begged, not caring how pathetic I sounded. If I woke up and he was gone, I didn't know what I would do...

He kissed the side of my head again, not seeming to care at all that my hair was damp with sweat and cum.

"I'm not going anywhere, baby. Rest now. You're safe; everything is fine. I won't leave you. I promise."

Feeling reassured, I allowed myself to lean into the bone-aching exhaustion that was suddenly taking over my body.

I'd never been this tired before, not even after a full day of surfing. Riddick rubbed my back as I snuggled into him, inhaling his clean, masculine scent.

'I'm going to take care of you,' he whispered as I drifted, and I fell asleep on his chest with him still fully inside me.

CHAPTER
Twenty-Five

Riddick

waited for Finn to completely pass out before I slowly rolled him off of me. I shuddered as my dick slid out of his ass, and once I had him lying on his stomach on the bed, I gently spread his cheeks so I could watch my cum drip out of him.

Fuck, that looked good.

His tight little hole was still gaping and open from how hard I'd fucked him, and watching my milky white cum leak out of him made my dick swell up again.

Jesus.

I'd never been this turned on by someone before. Usually, it took me a couple hours to get hard again after coming. The fact that I was already ready for round two was fucking cruel.

Whoever was in charge of this bullshit universe was a sick fuck, and I hated them.

Finn let out an adorably soft little snore, and I smiled down at him. He'd really done amazing for his first time. I'd been worried he wouldn't be able to take all of me.

Even Jet, who was considerably more experienced, had struggled to handle me the first few times we slept together.

I got up and made my way to the tiny bathroom, where I wet a washcloth with warm water. Finn's cum was already drying and making my chest hair clump together in thick, sticky patches, but I would worry about that later.

Right now, I needed to take care of my baby.

The thought cut through my mind, and I winced.

My baby.

Fuck, this was so fucking bad.

I was already thinking of him as mine... which was impossible.

He could never be mine. Not really.

When he found out the truth...

I ran my hand down my face in frustration.

He couldn't find out the truth. Not until I made sure he successfully achieved his ill-advised goal of riding Leviathans.

I couldn't risk him refusing to train with me again and dying on that beach. As fucked up as it was, I was his best chance at survival, and I wouldn't trust his safety with anyone else at this point.

Especially not now that I... was *feeling* whatever the fuck these feelings were. So, for now, he would need to be kept in the dark.

I would tell him once I had made sure he made it through the winter alive.

Fuck. I was going to break his fucking heart.

The thought of hurting Finn in *any* way was starting to become unbearable to me, and I cursed the universe again for putting me in this situation.

Making my way back to his bedroom, I gently spread him back open and used the cloth to clean him up.

I dabbed around his quickly swelling hole and carefully checked to make sure there was no tearing or blood.

Once I was sure I hadn't hurt him, I let out a sigh of relief. He was fine; he would just be a little sore when he woke up.

Nudging him until he rolled onto his back, I wiped the cum off his stomach and chest next. He smiled in his sleep and reached for me lazily, half waking up due to my ministrations.

"Whaddruuuu doinngg?" he mumbled, causing me to smile.

He was so fucking adorable and sweet. As much as I knew this was wrong, I was so happy I'd claimed him.

Even if he couldn't be mine forever, he was mine for now, and I was going to take care of him while he was.

"Just cleaning you up, baby; go back to sleep," I whispered, and his eyes fluttered shut, though that goofy smile stayed plastered on his puffy pink lips.

"I like it when you call me that," he whispered, making my stomach flip.

"Oh yeah?" I asked, leaning over him and kissing him gently on the lips.

"Mhmmmmm," he murmured, and I chuckled.

"Then I'll make sure to call you that all the time," I promised, brushing his damp hair out of his perfect face.

I stood up, and he frowned, barely opening his eyes.

"Whereareuuu going? Please don't leave me..." he begged, and my heart cracked.

"I'm just going to shower, sweet boy, then I'll be right back. I promise I'm not leaving you," I assured him, stroking his hair again to soothe him back to sleep.

"Promise? Everyone always leaves me..."

I opened my mouth to respond, but he was already snoring softly again, and I cursed under my breath as I went to take my shower.

Everyone always leaves me.

I was so fucking fucked.

CHAPTER
Twenty-Six

Finn

I woke up to an empty bed and immediately panicked.

No. No, no, no, no!

He promised he wouldn't leave! I shot up and was about to bolt out the door when he appeared, holding a plate full of eggs and bacon and a cup of coffee.

"Ah, you're up." He beamed at me, and I was struck again by the fact that he was *smiling*.

Like a *real* smile, one that reached all the way to his eyes.

Had I done that?

"Yeah, uhm." I cleared my throat, doing my best to calm my still frantically beating heart. Rubbing the back of my neck awkwardly, I gave him a sheepish grin.

"I thought you left."

He frowned. "I told you I wouldn't leave you, and I meant it. I was just making you breakfast."

He came and sat on the bed, handing me the plate and putting the coffee down next to the bottle of lotion he'd used last night.

My cheeks flushed at the memory.

"Eat," he ordered, and my stomach growled as if on cue. He chuckled as my eyes widened, and I realized suddenly that I was fucking *starving.*

Without waiting to be told again, I dug in, shoving the eggs into my mouth in giant forkfuls, groaning at how perfectly cooked they were.

"Worked up quite the appetite, I see." He was grinning at me, his eyes twinkling with mischief. I nodded, swallowing, before taking a big sip of coffee and moving on to the bacon.

"You'll get used to it. The first couple of times will take a bit of a toll," he said, and my heart skipped a beat in my chest.

I blinked at him, feeling a rush of excitement as he casually poked a finger into one of my dimples.

"You mean... we're going to do that again?" I asked eagerly, though my asshole throbbed in protest as I said the words.

Fuck I was sore...

I munched happily on my last piece of bacon, and he took the empty plate out of my lap. He placed it on the end table before pitching my chin between his fingers.

"Oh yes, Finn. We're going to be doing that again."

"Now!?" I gasped, and he chuckled, the dark, dominating sound rolling over my flesh and making me shiver.

"That depends. Let's see how you're recovering. On your stomach, please. Push your ass up for me."

"What, why?"

"Don't question me, do as you're told, or you won't get your reward."

My cheeks heated, but I did what he said. In the light of day and without any foreplay, it felt strange exposing myself to him like this.

I was still naked, so when he slid his hands over my bare cheeks and spread me open, I gasped.

"Hmm. Still a little swollen. Are you sore?" he asked, and I nodded, my face burning so hot I was scared the pillows were going to catch on fire.

"I brought you something." He hummed, and I watched him open the drawer to the end side table and pull out a small, blue tin. He popped it open to show me it was full of a thick white cream.

"Found this in your cabinet. It must have been left over from before. This is a zinc balm; it should help with the pain," he informed me before dipping his fingers into the tin and applying the cool ointment directly to my sore asshole.

"Oh...*fuck,*" I groaned. It immediately cooled the sting, and I wiggled my hips happily as he rubbed it in for me.

"Good boy," he praised me, gently smacking my ass when he was done and putting the lid back on the tin.

"We'll see how you're feeling tonight. If you're up for it, we'll go again." He winked at me, gathering my dirty dishes and heading back to the kitchen.

"Where are you going now?" I asked, sitting up and leaping out of bed to follow him. I stumbled into my swim trunks as I chased after him.

"I'm going to do the dishes, then we're going to continue the rest of your training. If I'm not mistaken, you have a shift tonight as well," he said matter-of-factly, and I watched him bustle about my kitchen with wide eyes.

Was this actually happening right now?

He was acting like... like we were a real couple.

I pinched myself to make sure I wasn't dreaming and this was real.

"I wrote a list of supplies we're going to need." He jerked his head to the counter, where a piece of paper sat with a bunch of notes scribbled on it.

"Think you can pick that stuff up on your way home from work? I would, but I have some things I need to do."

"Uhm, sure. What kind of stuff is it?" I asked, assuming the list was surf-related.

"If I'm going to be fucking you regularly, there are some things you're going to need to do to prevent injury... among other things. If you can grab everything, I'll teach you how to use it all and make sure you stay on top of everything."

"O-oh... yeah, okay. No problem," I agreed, glancing down at the list, feeling my eyes widen further as I absorbed words like *anal douche* and *Astroglide.*

I glanced up at Riddick to find him smirking to himself as he washed my plate, and suddenly, I was grinning, too.

Fuck, YES!

I *knew* I would win him over.

My mom had been right.

No one could resist my dimples. After I'd conquered Leviathans, maybe I would use my dimple powers for evil and try to take over the whole damn world.

Bwahahahahahaha!

"Quit staring at me with that evil little smile and get outside. I want three sets of forty burpees before we hit the beach. Get going; we're burning daylight."

"Yes, sir!" I chirped, and his eyes immediately darkened.

"Don't call me 'sir' unless you're ready to get fucked again." He gave me a devastatingly sinister smile that made my stomach erupt with butterflies. "Now get out of my sight before I lose what little control I have left and claim your ass before it's ready."

"Eeep! Okay, okay!" I laughed, darting out of the shack to do the burpees he'd ordered.

I grinned like a fucking lunatic through all three sets.

CHAPTER
Twenty-Seven

Finn

"**Y**ou're in a better mood, brother." Turtle grinned at me as he helped me clear dishes off a party table.

I shot him one of my more mischievous grins.

"I don't know what you're talking about. I'm always in a good mood."

Turtle chuckled and shook his head, tossing a handful of dirty cutlery into his bus bin.

"Whatever, man... Hey, what happened last night anyway? Quinn found us after you left, and she was pretty freaked out."

"Yeah, I told you, she had a rough night. You know that Tully guy? He's bad news, bro. Apparently, she used to date him, and he got violent."

"No way, what the shiz?"

"Yeah, man. He, like, threw her on the ground and tried to *kick* her right in front of me."

Turtle dropped the plate he was holding, his mouth hanging open in shock.

"Fuck off, you're joking?"

"Nuh-uh." I shook my head and held up my injured hand to show him. Riddick had helped me wrap it up before work, and the memory of him leaving gentle kisses on each of my fingertips as he bandaged me up made my cheeks heat slightly.

"Yeah, bro. I beat the shit out of him. Pretty sure I broke his nose."

"Fuuuck, bro. That's some heavy shit. You know he's the mayor's son, right?"

I shrugged. "Doesn't give him the right to whale on Quinn like that."

"No doubt, no doubt. I would have done the same thing just... *damn.*"

"Yeah, pretty fucked up... Wait, Quinn didn't already tell you all this?"

"Nah, man, she was going on about something else. Saying you had a big blow-up. She kept going on and on about some dude named Rid-dick. She seemed pretty freaked out. I wasn't really following."

I frowned. My little argument with Riddick was way less dramatic than what had happened with Tully. Though Riddick had made it clear he didn't want me to tell people we were training together, I was start-ing to think his history with the locals went deeper than what he was telling me.

I remembered how people at the party had been staring at us while we argued. It had been weird that they seemed more invested in a heated discussion between me and Riddick than they had in me literally beating the shit out of the mayor's son.

Lost in thought, I gathered up my full bus bin and headed to the dish pit to unload, leaving Turtle to clear the last few things.

"Oh, hey Finn."

I glanced up to see Quinn filling up a tray of fountain sodas for one of her tables. Her dark hair was in a glossy, high pony, and her bright red Sharkies shorts made her long, tanned legs look like they went on for days.

I smiled at her.

"Hey babe, how was the rest of your night?"

She gave me a strange look, then shrugged.

"Not bad... Uhm. How're you feeling?" she asked, and I mimicked her shrug.

"Pretty good, all patched up," I said, flashing my bandaged hand at her, and she pursed her lips but nodded.

"Oh... that's good."

"Yeah. I gotta drop these in the pit, I'll see you around, yeah?" I said, not wanting her to get the wrong idea and think I was flirting with her again.

The jealousy I'd heard in Riddick's voice when he'd told me about seeing her put her hands on me made me weirdly shivery and happy.

The rest of my shift went by without anything eventful happening, though I did notice I was getting more loaded looks than normal from the Sharkies staff. I caught a few people whispering to each other at one of the service stations and staring as I bused a table nearby.

However, when I asked what they were whispering about, they pretended like they didn't know what I was talking about.

I brushed it off and resolved to grill Riddick about it when I got home.

CHAPTER
Twenty-Eight

Finn

The next few months went by in a blur.

I'd bought the supplies Riddick asked me to pick up, and he'd spent that same afternoon teaching me how to properly prep myself for sex with him.

It took some getting used to, and the first time I um... *cleaned* myself was... an experience. However, like anything, once I'd done it a few times and knew what to expect, it just became my new norm.

Having proper lube was a game-changer as well. Because of what that first night meant to me, I would still consider it one of the best nights of my life, but damn.

Jergens aint got shit on Astroglide when it comes to butt stuff. Let me tell ya.

Bless the lube gods because once we ripped off the bandaid and took that first leap, Riddick became *insatiable.*

Don't get me wrong, I wasn't complaining. But I hadn't expected him to be as obsessed with me as he was.

Apparently, he'd been seriously repressing his feelings for me, and now that everything was out in the open, I couldn't believe I ever doubted how much he'd wanted me.

He couldn't keep his hands off me. When I was working out, he was constantly touching me, and I usually ended up bent over the bench press by the time I finished my set.

Don't even get me started on Wednesday yoga. The first time he put me in a downward dog after we hooked up, I was in the pose for less than a breath when my shorts were suddenly ripped down to my ankles, and Riddick was balls deep in my ass.

Fuck. It was hot. The way he acted like he might literally *die* if he wasn't touching me was intense but also addicting. I couldn't get enough of him, and he clearly couldn't get enough of me, either.

It wasn't just the sex, and believe me, there was *a lot* of sex.

He did everyday things for me that no one, not even my mother, had ever done. He took care of me to the point where I sometimes needed to ask him to relax a little.

For example, I came home from Sharkies once, totally *stuffed* from a plate of nachos that management had comped to congratulate us on a particularly grueling Friday night. Riddick had been *appalled.*

'Nachos, Finn? Really? Do you know how many trans fats are in that disgusting squeeze cheese? Those are all empty calories and clogged arteries just waiting to happen! I need you healthy, baby... Next time, just come home. I'll make you something better."

He was obsessed with my health and safety, which I was learning extended to things like my nutrition and hygiene practices.

He'd sort of unofficially moved in and always made me perfectly balanced meals. He made sure I took care of myself, and after we had sex, he always insisted on being the one to clean me up and take care of me.

'Roll over, show me that beautiful ass... Are you sore? Do I need to apply some cream for you?'

'No, Riddick, I'm fine. Besides, if I need cream, I can apply it myself.'

SMACK!

'This ass is mine, shark bait, and I take care of things that are precious to me.'

It was both hot and sweet as fuck.

At first, I'd been a little nervous that our insane chemistry and attraction to each other were going to negatively affect my training, but it did the opposite.

I confided in him that I'd been diagnosed with ADHD as a child, but we'd never had any money for treatment, so I worked really hard to manage it by working with my symptoms instead of against them.

A few weeks later, I found him reading an article on my phone—I'd been right; the boomer didn't even own a phone. The article had been titled: *My Partner Has ADHD. How Can I Help Them Thrive?*

When I'd asked him about it, he'd smirked at me and told me he'd just learned that reward-based worked wonders for people who have trouble manufacturing an appropriate amount of dopamine, and he couldn't wait to put me on a reward-based training regime.

Spoiler alert: The rewards were orgasms.

Tee hee!

I was a hell of a lot more motivated to push myself past my limits when I knew that if I impressed Riddick, he would suck and fuck me until I saw stars.

It was the *fucking best.*

The only thing that I hated about our relationship was that he still wouldn't let me talk to anyone about him.

I'd asked Riddick why people had seemed so freaked out when he came to the beach to find me that night, but his mood had immediately soured.

'This town and I have a history. If you survive Leviathans, I'll tell you the whole story. But until then, can you keep the fact that I'm here just between us?'

It bothered me, but the look on his face had been so full of pain that I agreed and hadn't brought it up again. The weird looks and whispers stopped after a couple days anyway, and most people seemed to forget about that night as time went on.

The only person who remained a thorn in my side was Kyle Tully. He'd tried to press charges, but Quinn backed my story when I told the cops I didn't know what the hell he was talking about. When they asked about my hand, I told them I cut it on some reef while surfing.

It also helped that Tully wasn't generally well-liked. A few other witnesses took my side as well, so the charges were eventually dropped.

This only seemed to piss Kyle off more. Since then, every time I surfed Stars Cove with Turtle, Tully had a bad habit of turning up and trying to one-up me on every fucking wave.

It was more than annoying; it was starting to get dangerous.

Whenever I had a particularly sick run, he would aggressively attempt to surf a better one—at the expense of literally *everyone* else surfing.

He'd butt to the front of the line-up and even drop in on someone else's wave in an attempt to show me up.

He was responsible for several wipeouts at this point. One kid sliced their head open on the reef and needed to get stitches. It was *seriously* getting out of hand.

What was making it worse was with Riddick's coaching and my new diet, I was getting like... *really* fucking good.

Better than I really ever thought I would be.

I was quickly becoming a bit of a town celebrity, and one girl even asked me for my autograph once, which cracked Turtle the hell up.

By the end of the summer, every time I hit up Stars Cove to surf, I seemed to attract a little gaggle of both girls and guys who were self-proclaimed *Finnatics.*

They would gather on the beach and watch me ride for hours.

It was actually bananas.

We were surfing with Blake one balmy September afternoon when I absolutely *cooked* a pipe. My little fan club lost their minds so bad I could hear them all the way out at the line-up.

I accepted high fives and congratulations from some fellow Sharkies surfers as I paddled to the back of the line, feeling pretty good about myself.

"Bro, what the fuck are you *eating* man?" Turtle was grinning at me, his smile nearly tickling his ears. "That was fucking *awesome,* dude, like, you should try out for competitions. Plus, you're looking *jacked* lately. Share your secrets with the Turtle Man, brother. I wanna be you when I grow up!"

I beamed at him, blushing as I shook the water out of my hair.

"Nah, man. That was nothing. Practice makes perfect."

Blake was looking at me like she'd just seen a ghost, and my smile faltered a bit.

"What?" I asked, and she chewed her bottom lip, frowning.

"Nothing, just... your style reminds me of Riddick's a lot. That's all." She looked sad, and I wanted more than *anything* to ask her if she knew him well, but then that would be talking about Riddick, which was against the rules.

"Uhh..."

Not knowing how to respond to that at all, I sat there on my board awkwardly for a moment and was eternally grateful that Turtle just bulldozed over Blake's comment, yammering on about how I should be looking into getting sponsored or some dumb shit like that.

I could feel Blake's eyes on me for every run after that, though, and I couldn't shake the strange feeling I got every time we made eye contact.

I didn't understand the fear swirling in her eyes, and frankly, it unnerved me.

That night, when I got back to the shack, I asked Riddick if he knew Blake and told him about our strange interaction.

He'd pursed his lips and cupped the side of my face, kissing me softly.

"Survive Leviathans, and I'll tell you everything, Finn. I promise."

CHAPTER
Twenty-Nine

Riddick

Alexa Play: Young & Sad by Noah Cyrus

It was early November when I noticed the change in Finn. It was gradual, but I first noticed the light dying from his eyes on the first of the month.

Initially, I thought it was all in my head, but as the days went by, he seemed to get worse. I'd read everything I could possibly find online about ADHD, and I knew it could sometimes be misdiagnosed as depression, though that was more common in women.

So, when I asked Finn about his change in mood, and he brushed me off, I tried to give him the benefit of the doubt.

However, on the morning of November 15th, when I couldn't get him out of bed, I started to panic.

"Baby... you need to talk to me. If you don't tell me what's wrong, I can't help you," I whispered into his ear, brushing his soft, golden hair back from his normally sparkling, excited eyes.

Today, they were empty and dull. There was no life in his face, and I could barely get him to respond to me at all.

I didn't know what the fuck to do.

He wouldn't eat anything.

He wouldn't talk to me.

He hadn't even gotten up to take a piss.

I was truly on the verge of a full-blown panic attack when his phone buzzed on his end table, and I saw it was a message from Turtle.

"Baby, it's your friend. You gonna answer that?" I asked hopefully.

No response.

"I'm just gonna see what he said, okay?"

Nothing.

Grinding my teeth together, I snatched up his phone to see what Turtle was messaging him about. Maybe he knew what was wrong with him...

My heart sank as I read the text.

The Turtle Man:

Hey, brother. I know today is a rough day, just wanted 2 let u kno I'm thinking of u. I kno it's tough, but try 2 remember ur mom wouldn't want u 2 b sad, bro. She loved u so much, man. Try not 2 stay in bed all day.

The Turtle Man:

I'll swing by in a bit 2 check in on u

It felt like all my blood had turned to ice.

Today must be the anniversary of his mom's death. We'd talked about her, but he'd never told me when she'd died.

Fuck.

I glanced at Finn's lifeless form, and the amount of *pain* that I felt because *he* was in pain was not normal or healthy.

I wanted to reach into his chest and take his hurt away and carry it for him. Finn was everything I wasn't. He was light, energetic, and positive. But right now, my little impish ball of sunshine was completely unresponsive because he was hurting so bad he couldn't even communicate it to me.

I knew it was wrong, but I didn't care. The last thing I wanted was Turtle coming by when I needed to be here to take care of Finn. So, without a second thought, I fired a text back to Turtle from Finn's phone.

Finn:

Hey, man! I'm actually doing really great! I'm not even home right now; I'm out on a jog. No need to come by. I'll catch up with you tomorrow.

Turtle:

Woah, no way, dude. That's dope! Happy 2 hear. Have a good run; holler at me later, brother. Let's shred the cove tomorrow *hang loose emoji*

Finn:

hang loose emoji

I tossed the phone back on the table and crawled into bed with Finn. Slipping under the covers with him, I lay down, positioning my head directly in his line of sight.

"Hey, baby boy..." I murmured softly, brushing his hair away from his face again. It'd become a bad habit of mine. Any excuse to touch him, really.

I loved his hair so much. It was so soft, and I imagined it was liquid sunshine every time I ran my fingers through it.

"I didn't realize today was the anniversary of your mom's death," I whispered, and his empty expression sharpened slightly.

He winced, and my heart cracked. Seeing him in pain felt like a punch to my gut.

"Shh, it's okay, baby; we don't have to talk about it. If you want to lie here all day, I'll lie with you."

His eyes finally locked with mine, and I watched as they filled with tears, somehow making them look even bigger and more expressive than normal.

"She... she used to tell me that I wasn't alone because I had her." He hiccupped, his voice cracking over his words like tiny shards of glass.

"Oh, baby... come here..." I whispered, wrapping my arms around him and tugging him into my chest.

He broke down and sobbed, curling his hands in my T-shirt like he was a drowning man and I was his life raft.

"I'm here, Finn. I've got you. You're not alone," I whispered to him, rocking him gently as he continued to cry. Even as I said the words, guilt curled in my gut and I hated myself for saying them when they weren't promises I could keep. When the time came, I would have to let him go. He couldn't stay with me. He deserved more than a secret relationship born in a closet full of skeletons.

He deserved to be loved in the sun by someone who still knew how to find joy in life.

And I could never give him that.

But... for right now, he needed to feel like he wasn't alone, and he wasn't. He had me. I was here. I was with him.

I would go to war against the universe itself if it tried to make me leave him when he so clearly needed me here to hold him.

His tears soaked through the cotton of my shirt, and in that moment, if I could have traded places with his mother and given her back to him, I would have done it in a heartbeat... but that's not real life, and real life is shit.

So, instead, I just held him until his sobs turned into sniffles, and his sniffles turned into tiny, gentle snores.

I don't know how long we laid there, but the sun went down, and the moon came up by the time he finally woke up.

CHAPTER

Thirty

Finn

Alexa Play: Chew On My Heart - Piano & Voice by James Bay

I woke up to find Riddick still lying next to me, gently stroking my hair. My eyelids were swollen and puffy from all the crying, and my limbs felt like they were made of lead.

"Hey, sweet boy," Riddick whispered as my eyes fluttered open. It was dark now, and I was *so* relieved he'd stayed with me. "How are you feeling?"

I swallowed thickly and sighed.

"Really sad," I answered honestly, and the look he was giving me wasn't one of pity but of understanding. I realized that he'd suffered a loss recently too, and he was clearly just as fucked up over the death of his friend as I was over losing my mom.

The realization came as a surprise. I'd never met anyone who'd had a death in their family like I had.

Turtle even still had all his grandparents.

To have someone to talk to about my grief that didn't just listen but *understood* was a gift. One I didn't even realize had been sitting right in front of me.

"Does it ever stop hurting?" I asked, my voice so quiet it was almost a whisper.

He reached out and brushed his thumb over my cheek, and I closed my eyes, leaning into his comforting touch.

"No, baby. It'll always hurt. But it will hurt less as time goes on." He answered honestly.

If I asked that question to anyone else, they probably would have lied to me. This was what I loved about Riddick. I could always trust him to be real with me. He never lied, even if I didn't want to hear the truth.

"As you get older, you'll find things that make you happy, and they'll be beacons of light that you can cling to when the times of sadness get too hard."

"What do you cling to?" I asked him, and he laced his fingers in my hair while continuing to stroke my temple with his thumb.

He gave me a sad smile and pressed a gentle kiss against my lips.

"Lately, it's been you."

I frowned, and he leaned forward to kiss away the crease in my brow.

"Me?" I whispered.

"Yeah, Finn. You."

"What do you mean?"

For a second, he hesitated, and I could see the conflict in his eyes. Whatever secret he was keeping... whatever had kept him from admitting his feelings for me for so long was holding him back again. I pressed myself flush against his chest and left delicate kisses up his throat, enjoying the rough feeling of his stubble rubbing against my lips.

"Please, tell me," I begged, my voice cracking.

"After the accident... I... I was lost, Finn. I was floating alone in a sea of darkness. There was no one... no one who saw me. No one who..."

It was his turn for his voice to crack, and I pulled back to look at him and found that he had tears in his eyes, too.

"Until you." He let out a strangled chuckle, and the sight of his smile made me feel lighter.

"You barreled right up to me and gave me shit for trying to surf on your beach, and you were just so... so full of *life* and fire. You made me feel when I thought I would never feel again. You *saw* me when I thought no one would ever see me again, and I just... I'm so grateful for you, Finn. You've given me something that's worth looking forward to when, for a long time, all that stood before me were endless, empty days filled with nothing but bad memories and regrets."

"Riddick..." I whispered, reaching out and brushing one of his tears away as he did the same for me.

He was staring at me like I was this precious thing that he couldn't live without, and suddenly, I couldn't breathe.

I was always so excited to see him. Every time I opened my eyes in the morning to find him lying there, next to me... my heart would flutter, and my pulse would quicken.

He was always thinking of me, doing things for me, and he was *always* worried about me. Even now, he'd spent the entire day in bed with me because he knew I needed him.

Tears gathered in the corners of my eyes, and I suddenly needed to feel him. I leaned in and kissed his lips, shuddering as his warm mouth moved against mine, gently coaxing the tension out of my body.

He made me feel safe.

He made me feel like I wasn't *alone.* My feelings for Riddick were *so* strong. *Too* strong. They had the potential to sweep me away and absolutely ruin me... but they also felt *so good.*

He felt *so good.*

I wanted to tell him.

My mouth was moving before I could stop myself, and before I knew what was happening, I was saying three words that I'd never said to anyone before... except maybe my mom.

"Riddick, I love you," I whispered, and he froze.

I watched his face crumble in slow motion. It was like I could literally see his heart, and it was breaking before my eyes.

I didn't understand why, but what I'd just said devastated him so badly, and I wished I could take it back.

"I'm sorry..." I choked as my stomach bottomed out. "You don't have to say it back."

He pressed a finger against my lips, and another tear slid down his cheek, disappearing into the pillows.

"Don't be sorry for that, baby. I just wish..." his voice broke, and he cleared his throat. "I just wish things were different. I wish we'd met under different circumstances. But it has nothing to do with you, sweet boy. You're perfect, Finn. You deserve *everything,* and I'm so sorry that I'll never be able to be what you deserve."

He cupped my face and pulled me into him, his warm lips connecting with mine, and he kissed me like it was the last time we would ever kiss again.

"I'm so, so sorry..."

I didn't want his apologies. I just wanted to forget and pretend that everything was okay. I wanted him to take my pain away, even if it was just for a little bit.

"Riddick..." I breathed into him, "Help me forget," I begged, and he nodded, nipping at my bottom lip hard enough that I whimpered. "Make me feel good. Please? I don't want to be sad anymore."

"Are you sure you want this right now, baby?" He hummed against my lips, though he didn't stop kissing and sucking at them. His hands were wandering now, and I felt his calloused palms slide under my shirt and scrape against my ribs.

"Yes. Please. I need you, Riddick."

"Alright, baby. Take this off."

He helped me slide out of my shirt before rolling me on my back and tugging my boxers down. I was already hard and weeping for him as he sat back on his heels to peel off his own shirt.

He kicked off his shorts next, and I groaned as he lay back on top of me, our naked bodies rubbing against each other in a desperate rhythm.

He claimed my mouth again, possessing me with his tongue and showing me with each stroke that I belonged to him and only him.

I whined when he reached between us and wrapped his hand around both our cocks at the same time.

"Fuck," I gasped, glancing down between us so I could watch him stroke us in unison.

"Look how good we are together," he murmured, and I moaned as he swiped his thumb over our crowns.

"We belong together," I said, nipping at his lips again, my need for him to be inside me growing by the second.

"Fuck, Finn... I'm a fucking monster for doing this to you." He said it so quietly I barely heard him, but before I could argue, he was kissing down my throat and then my chest. He paused briefly to suck and play with each of my nipples, biting and pinching them until they were hard.

"Riddick, just... please, I need you inside me," I begged, but he ignored me and kissed lower and lower down my body.

He worshiped every inch of flesh with his mouth, running his tongue up each line in my abdomen before finally turning his attention to my dick.

"Fuck, baby... you're leaking for me already," he whispered, wrapping his massive hand around my shaft and lining my tip up with his mouth. He licked the cum off of the head of my cock with a flat, wet tongue, and I groaned, thrusting my hips into his hand.

My whole body felt hot, and tiny explosions of pleasure were firing off in my balls, causing them to tighten into a sensitive, plump bundle of need.

He fondled me while he slurped my tip into his scorching hot mouth. The dopamine centers in my brain exploded as he slid me in deeper and *sucked.*

"F-fuck... Riddick, that feels so fucking good." I whined as he bobbed on my dick. He forced me down his tight throat like it was nothing, all the while rubbing and massaging my balls until I was wound so tight I was worried I would snap.

"I could suck you all day, baby. You taste like fucking heaven." He murmured before sliding my cock back down his throat again. My fingers were in his hair, and I was fucking up into his mouth without shame.

For a second, I was worried he was going to make me come like this, but abruptly, he popped off and then crouched even further down between my legs.

"Riddick, what are you..."

He slid his hands under my legs and bent my knees, spreading me open before gently feathering his tongue over my hole.

"Riddick!" I cried out as he lightly flicked his tongue against me again. His soft mouth moved in slow, languid strokes around my rim, and I writhed against him. He gripped my thighs firmly, holding me in place as he licked and kissed and sucked me until I was literally in tears.

"Fuck... *ohmygod.*" My words were garbled, and my mouth opened and closed as his warm tongue continued to massage me gently and...

So.

Very.

Deliberately.

"You're so damn beautiful, baby," he whispered, kissing me again directly on my sensitive hole. "I'll never get enough of you."

I was panting now, lost in the cacophony of sensations. His lips, his tongue, even his teeth as he ate my ass like he was a dying man and I was all he needed to come back to life.

"Riddick..." I whined, and in response, he pressed the tip of his tongue into me.

I began to shake.

His hold on my thighs tightened, and he smoothed his palms up and down the backs of my legs. A low mewl bubbled out of my throat as he slowly pushed his tongue deeper inside me.

"You taste so sweet, baby…" he rasped, sliding his tongue out of me before slowly spearing it back in.

"You like that?" His voice was pure gravel, and I was blinded by the stars that were shooting across my vision. "You like having my tongue in your tight little hole?"

"*Yes*, Jesus… I didn't know… it could feel…like this…" I gasped, my eyes rolling back into my skull with each lick.

He reached for my cock and leisurely stroked it while he continued to suck and fuck me with his tongue. I moaned as my orgasm began to build—*fast*.

"Stop, stop, stop—I want you inside me. I don't want to finish like this," I begged, and he immediately let go of my cock, allowing me to get a hold of myself before I lost all control.

He looked up at me through my spread legs, and my throat closed with emotion at the expression on his face.

He hadn't said the words back, but it was there in his eyes.

He loved me.

I thought I knew what sex was, but I clearly had no idea. Sex before Riddick had never been like this. This combination of physical sensation and all-consuming *emotion*.

"*Please*, Riddick. I need you," I begged again, and he crawled up my body, kissing me gently on the lips and tracing his nose down the side of my face and into the crook of my neck.

Without another word, he reached for the bottle of lube I now kept on the end table and squirted a generous amount on his fingers. He braced himself over my chest while positioning his hips between my spread legs. Reaching down between us, he coated my hole.

He looked me in the eyes as he worked his fingers into me, scissoring them until I was soft and pliant.

"You want me inside you, baby?" he murmured, his own voice sounding strained and tight with emotion, and I nodded desperately.

"Yes. *Always.* I always want you inside me, Riddick."

He notched his cock against my hole and rested his forehead against mine.

"Breathe for me, baby. You're so beautiful when you *breathe.*"

I gasped as he slipped his fat cockhead past my tight ring of muscle, and we both groaned as he sank all the way in to the hilt.

He shuddered and closed his eyes as he settled deep inside me. He was literally *quivering* between my thighs, like the feeling of being inside me was so good he could barely control himself.

"I'll *never* get enough of this," he told me as he slowly began to rock his hips, dragging his cock in and out of me in a torturously slow, steady rhythm. "It's never been like this with anyone else, Finn. I've never felt like this with anyone else…"

With the hand he wasn't using to hold himself up, he traced my cheekbone delicately as he kissed me over and over again.

"You're so important to me, Finn."

He held my head in place so he could stare at me while he rocked his hips, his thick cock filling me up so much I felt like I might burst.

Each thrust was punctuated with a deep, emotionally charged kiss, and he whispered some of the most beautiful things to me in between each kiss.

"You're so beautiful, Finn. You feel so fucking good, baby. Every time I'm with you, it feels like the first time."

I slid my hands into his hair and curled my fingers into fists. I held on for dear life as he rolled against my prostate over and over again, building that burning hot need in my groin again.

"Touch me…" I pleaded, and he reached between us, running his fingers up and down my cock. His touch was so light and soft it drove me fucking wild.

"*Touch me!* Really touch me, *please.*"

Giving me exactly what I asked for, he wrapped his hand around me and stroked. He was still slippery from the lube, and his hand glided effortlessly up and down my shaft, driving me closer and closer to climax with each pass.

"I want to... fuck you hard..." he whispered, his pupils so large the blue of his eyes were gone.

"*Yes*," I whimpered, fighting off my orgasm with everything I had. "Do it, Riddick. Fuck me hard..."

Tears gathered in the corners of his eyes, and he pressed his forehead against mine, swallowing thickly.

"I love you, too, Finn. I'll always love you," he murmured before pulling out and slamming himself back into me harder than he ever had before.

I choked and gasped as he hit that spot deep inside me that made my entire body convulse with pleasure.

"Riddick... It's so *much*... I'm feeling so *much*..." I was sobbing softly as he slammed in and out of me, stroking my cock in gentle contrast with each thrust.

"I know, sweet boy. I know. You'll feel better after you come... Can you do that for me, baby? Show me how beautiful you are when you fall apart."

He rutted into me, pegging my prostate head-on as I shivered and writhed beneath him. He gently twisted my cock on his next stroke, and I *exploded.*

"Uuunnnghh, *FUCK!*" I screamed as the first wave of pleasure erupted through me, and my cock started throbbing sporadically in his hand. "Riddick, I'm coming!"

"Yeah you are, baby," he cooed as he continued to stroke me through it. "Let it out...give it to me. I want all of you...every last drop."

I came and came and came, Riddick's body and hand riding me through the entire ordeal. I was still spurting when I felt him shudder above me and grunt as his own cock started throbbing inside me.

"Fuck, Finn... you feel so good...when you come...on my cock..." He groaned, pumping out the rest of his release into me.

He collapsed on top of me, showering me with kisses as I gasped and quivered beneath him.

"I love you," he whispered in between each kiss, making my heart race and my eyes well with tears.

"I love you, I love you, I love you, Finn Summers."

I wrapped my arms around him and buried my face in his shoulder, unsure why words that should make me feel so happy were making me want to break down and cry.

CHAPTER
Thirty-One

Finn

As we moved into a California winter, my already intense training ramped up. We rarely surfed my private beach anymore. Riddick gradually eased me into surfing Leviathans in the early season so I could familiarize myself with how the water behaved before the waves reached their full potential.

By early December, the waves were still only reaching ten to fifteen feet. However, the second Riddick had me first dip my toes in, I could immediately feel the difference.

The rip tide alone was terrifying. Even just ankle deep, when the water pulled out, it was clear that this beach was out for blood.

The water was colder now, and I'd needed to purchase a wetsuit to keep my lips from turning blue each time we hit the waves, but I didn't care.

I.

Fucking.

Loved it.

The first time I surfed a baby Leviathan, I almost fucking came from excitement. The *high* I felt as I cut through the belly of the beast was like nothing I'd ever felt before.

I was immediately addicted.

Outside of the horrible way my mother died, there was a reason I didn't drink or smoke. I avoided substances like the plague because I was a dopamine chaser.

The second my ADHD-starved reward and pleasure centers received a *drop* of dopamine, I tended to get hooked.

This was no exception.

Adrenaline was my drug of choice, and I couldn't give it up if I wanted to, even though I knew it could one day kill me.

The water here was darker – more sinister than the crystalline blue waters of Stars Cove, and the rush of excitement combined with the exhilaration I felt as I rode through the dark, hollow barrel of each bloodthirsty monster wave was so fucking good... I couldn't get enough.

Riddick became a drill sergeant when we surfed these beasts.

"Eyes on the horizon!"

"Focus, Finn! You have doubles coming in!"

"What did I fucking tell you!? When in doubt, don't paddle out!"

I tried not to allow myself to get too annoyed with him. I could see the terror in his eyes the entire time we were in the water. His intensity increased when he was worried about my safety, and I knew it was coming from a good place.

But it was hard for me to take things as seriously as he wanted me to when I was having the time of my *fucking life.*

Surfing Stars Cove after Leviathans just didn't hit the same after a while, and before I knew it, I couldn't think of anything else.

Nothing held my interest but those cold, vicious waters.

I couldn't hear people when they talked to me anymore. My hyperfocus had been activated. When I wasn't actively surfing Leviathans, I was thinking about surfing Leviathans.

Imagining it.

Dreaming about it.

"Finn! Baby! Where'd you go?"

Snap, snap, snap.

I blinked to find Riddick snapping his fingers at me again to get my attention.

"Huh? Oh. Sorry. I was daydreaming again."

He didn't look amused.

We were finishing up for the day and were both dripping in seawater as we hiked across the pebble beach toward the natural stone steps that led up the cliffside back to the shack. We each had our shortboards slung under our arms as we walked, and I was already itching to get back in the water, even though we'd just surfed for, like, six hours.

"Come on, don't look at me like that. I can't help it. You know it's my cute lil' neurodivergent brain. The hyperfocus is *real.*"

"Yeah, well... why couldn't you hyperfocus on knitting or something less *deadly...*" he grumbled, and I pouted, shoving out my lower lip as far as it would go.

"But I want to play in the water Riidddickkk... knitting is for sweet little grannies and people more mentally stable than me."

His gaze locked on my lip, and he let out one of his dominant, hot-guy growls that always made my dick all tingly.

"Put that lip away before I bite it."

I winked at him, taking special care to give him an extra-cute dimple pop.

"What if I want you to bite it?"

"You're insatiable."

"Pretty rich coming from you, big guy. You fucked me twice yesterday."

"Are you complaining?"

"Only that you didn't try for round three. I put that special cream on my hole for you and everything."

"That's *my* job, shark bait!" He snarled, gripping my shoulder and spinning me to face him. I grinned up at him. I'd perfected the art of getting Riddick all riled up, and usually, if I could push his buttons just right, I ended up bent over with his dick in my ass.

It was the fucking *best.*

"What are you going to do about it?" I taunted, giving him my best evil smirk.

His eyes were dark and burning with something dangerous.

Oh yeah. I was in trouble. Hehehehe.

"Maybe I'll punish you, you little imp. You've been spoiled lately. Maybe we go back to how it was when we first met, hmm? Just as easily as I can give you orgasms, I can take them away."

My eyes widened, and I gasped.

"You *wouldn't!*"

"I would, baby." He stepped closer to me, sliding his hand around the back of my neck and brushing his lips against mine. "I love watching you come, but I also loved watching you get all hot and bothered. Maybe I'll keep you hard and needy for *days* before I let you come again?"

He traced his hand down my chest and skated his fingers over my groin, and I immediately hardened.

I whimpered, already wanting him to suck the cum right out of my dick.

"Riddick, *please.* Don't tease me like that."

"You didn't like that, baby? Was it tough for you when you weren't allowed to come?"

His eyes were dancing with a feral sort of mischief, and I shivered as he rubbed my now *very* hard cock over my wetsuit.

"I had wet dreams like, *weekly.* I'm not built for edging, Riddick. My poor balls get so sore, I can't handle it."

He chuckled and cupped the balls in question, his lips curling into an evil smile as he left gentle kisses over my mouth and cheeks.

"Those weren't wet dreams, baby. Those were rewards, too. I've been in control of your pleasure since the day we met."

"Wait, what?"

"You heard me..." he murmured, sliding his other hand down the front of my wetsuit, unzipping it as he went. He slid his hand in between the tight material and wrapped his hand around my thick, hard shaft. I gasped.

His hand was freezing from being in the water, and my dick was already so hot and full. The contrast in temperature was *sublime.*

"You... you were *actually* touching me? Those weren't dreams?"

"Mhmm..." he murmured, stroking me firmly as my mind reeled.

"So you always wanted me?" I choked, and he paused, pulling back to frown at me. Pulling his hand out of my suit, he placed it back around the back of my neck, resting his forehead against mine.

"Yes, Finn. I've always wanted you, and I always will. No matter what happens."

My lip trembled, and he chuckled, dropping a wet kiss on my mouth before spinning me back around to face the steps.

"Get going, shark bait," he said, slapping my ass playfully. "If you're good, maybe I'll fuck you after dinner."

CHAPTER
Thirty-Two

Finn

We were playfully jostling each other as we walked through the brush on the way back to the shack when suddenly, Riddick grabbed me by my wetsuit and jerked me back away from the tree line.

"Riddick, what?"

"Shh!" he hissed, and I followed his line of sight to find two men walking up my driveway, clearly heading toward the shack.

They were around Riddick's age, and they both had tawny skin and dark hair.

The guy on the left was leaner, with a short mop of hair and a serious frown. The guy on the right was roughly the same height but a little more built. His black hair was long and fell to his shoulders. He'd pulled the top half back in a half ponytail, and his features were prettier than his friend's.

"What the fuck are they doing here!?" Riddick hissed, but I could tell he wasn't actually asking me.

"Who are they?" I whispered, and he glanced at me. He looked... *worried.*

"Kai and Jet."

"Your old surf buddies?" I asked, suddenly feeling excited. Riddick took one look at my excited grin and grew even more tense.

He glanced down at my still-open wetsuit and snatched up the zipper, ripping it back up.

"Cover up," he snapped, and I frowned, cocking my head to the side.

"Why? They kinda gay, too?" I joked, but Riddick didn't seem to find it funny.

"Jet is," he grunted, and I raised my eyebrows, feeling the familiar twinges of mischief brewing in my belly.

"Ooooooh, I love it when you get all growly and jealous," I teased in a low whisper.

"I'm not *jealous!*" he hissed back, and I chuckled.

"Well, if you're not jealous, let's go say hi. Why are we hiding in the bushes like a couple of creeps?" I asked, though I made sure to stay quiet. If he didn't want them to see us, I wasn't going to draw attention to us until he was ready.

"I can't," he said, his voice sounding strained and full of pain. He glanced at me, and suddenly I wasn't laughing anymore. He looked genuinely upset. Like the kind of upset you got when someone you loved died or your life as you knew it was about to change forever.

"Okay... you want me to tell them to go away?" I asked, and he stared at me for a long moment before swallowing.

"Just... stay here. They'll leave on their own when no one answers," he muttered, though I could tell he was still worried.

"Okay," I agreed and settled in to watch and wait.

They banged on my door and waited for longer than most people would to see if someone would answer. Then, finally, after a while, they gave up and headed back down the drive to a car that was waiting for them.

I narrowed my eyes as I watched them climb in, realizing that it was *Blake's* car.

What the fuck?

I glanced at Riddick, whose jaw was clenched so tightly I could see the muscles in his cheek fluttering.

"Hey, they're gone," I whispered, reaching up to stroke his face. He jumped at my touch as if he'd forgotten for a moment that I was standing there. When he looked at me, my heart skipped a beat.

"Riddick... Are you going to tell me what's going on?" I asked, and he closed his eyes, pinching the bridge of his nose in exasperation.

"I think... my time is up."

CHAPTER
Thirty-Three

Riddick

was torn. Half of me wanted to just wrap myself up in Finn and savor every *fucking* second with him, while the other half felt like it might be better to just end things now.

He peppered me with questions all night as I made him dinner. When it came time to go to bed, he tried to initiate sex, but I just couldn't fucking do it.

It felt *wrong*.

It felt like I was lying to him.

And I was... *lying* to him.

I had been this whole time.

I thought I would have had more time to finish training him and then tell him on my own. On *my* terms. But now that Kai and Jet were here, I knew the truth would come out one way or another. I was honestly really lucky it hadn't already.

Almost every time he came back from a shift at Sharkies, I waited on pins and needles to see if someone had mentioned my name in relation to Jake's.

Every time Finn walked in and smiled at me – popping those dimples the same way he always did – I knew I'd been gifted another day in the warmth of his love. It always felt like a weight was being lifted off my chest.

The relief was short-lived, however, as I knew it was only a matter of time.

I *knew* it would be better coming from me... but...

Whenever I tried to work up the courage to tell him, the words died on my tongue.

Once I told him, it would be over.

And despite knowing it made me a weak, pathetic piece of shit... I wasn't *ready* for it to be over.

So, instead of telling him, I held him and stroked his hair until he fell asleep, basking in the warmth of his soft skin and his thick, silky hair.

"I love you. I love you, baby, and I'm so, so sorry," I whispered into his sleeping ears, hoping he would carry those words with him long after he'd left me.

CHAPTER
Thirty-Four

Finn

Riddick had been weird all night after his old buddies had come by our place. He wouldn't talk to me, and it left me feeling really uneasy. What made things worse was he wasn't in the house when I woke up the next morning.

Had to run out to take care of some things.

See you when you get home from work xx

I frowned. Riddick rarely ran out to *'take care of things.'* If we needed stuff, he usually sent me since he had a huge aversion to going into town. I didn't even know where he'd been living before we got together. Whenever I asked him about it, he'd always give me some stupid, flirty answer.

'Was living in purgatory 'till I met you, baby boy.'

'What do you mean? I've always been here, waiting for you.' Wink.

It hadn't bothered me at the time, but now I was starting to get freaked out. Something weird was going on, and the amount of nausea I was dealing with over it was *not* fucking cool.

I went through the motions of my morning workout on my own, hoping the exercise would help with the strange churning sensation I was experiencing in my gut.

It didn't.

I texted Turtle to see if he wanted to meet up to kill some time before my shift, and he came to pick me up in Blake's car, which just put me in a shittier mood.

"What's got you looking like someone dropped in on your wave, brother?" he asked, getting out of the car to greet me. I shrugged.

"I don't know; just having a weird couple of days."

"Yeah, man, I feel ya. The weather's turning. Wanna hit Stars Cove up before work? Maybe your fan club will cheer you up." He winked at me, and I grinned back.

"Yeah, alright. Let's do it."

"Load up your board, brother. Surf's up!"

THE WAVES WERE NICE BUT SORT OF BORING AFTER ALL THE TIME I'd been spending at Leviathans.

I shredded some easy pipes with Turtle, and by the seventh or eighth run, I was starting to feel more relaxed.

Turtle had been right. Surfing was my happy place, and it was definitely working as a way to get my mind off how weird Riddick was being.

Or it *was* until Jet and Kai showed up.

I had just finished a run, so I assumed the cheers coming from the beach were from my fan club. However, when I went to wave to them, I noticed they weren't cheering for me.

My Finnatics were all crowded around two dark figures that I immediately recognized as the guys who had come and knocked on my door the other day.

They both had their boards with them and wetsuits on, which told me they were coming to surf.

My heart was suddenly *racing* in my chest.

I didn't know what to do.

Riddick hadn't wanted to interact with them at all. I had to assume that meant he didn't want *me* to interact with them, either.

But...

Riddick was keeping secrets from me, and I was starting to get sick of being kept in the dark. Why didn't he want to talk to these guys?

Why were they even *here?*

I paddled back to meet Turtle in the lineup, and we both bobbed on our boards, watching as the two newcomers paddled out to join us.

"Heyyy, brothers, how's it hanging? Sick waves today," Turtle greeted them in his friendly Turtle way.

The guy with the long hair gave him a half smile while the dude with the shorter hair just glowered at us.

"Hey man, yeah. Nice day," Long-hair said. He had a full sleeve of what looked like traditional Hawaiian tattoos and a shark-tooth necklace.

"I'm Turtle, and this is my best bro, Finn."

As soon as Turtle said my name, both of their eyes flashed.

"Hey. I'm Jet, and this is Kai," Long-hair said, gesturing to him and his very pissed-off-looking friend. "Nice to meet you."

"Likewise," Turtle replied. I remained silent, but both of them were staring at me now.

"Blake told us a lot about you, Finn. Sounds like you've become a bit of a local celebrity. She says you're planning on riding Leviathans."

"Uhm. Yeah. I mean, I've already surfed there a bunch, but the waves should pick up next week. I'm hoping to hit my first twenty-footer then," I answered honestly.

Kai looked furious. "Oh yeah? Do we have you to thank for the fucking surf competition Blake told us about?"

I frowned. "What? No. I don't even know what you're talking about."

Jet studied me carefully, as if trying to decide if he believed me or not. "Blake tracked me down to let me know she'd heard some rumors from the mayor's son that he was organizing one. We came to see if it was true, and sure enough, they just printed an announcement this morning in the Gazette."

My eyes widened in surprise. That bitch Kyle had mentioned it at that party in the summer, but I hadn't heard anything about it since.

Kai narrowed his eyes on me.

"Cut the act, kid. Blake told us all about how you've been running around town telling everyone you're training for Leviathans. Do you know how dangerous that is? You're sensationalizing that beach! You're going to get people *killed!*"

"Hey, Kai, relax." Jet put his hand on his friend's shoulder. "He clearly had nothing to do with the surf competition. He's just one dude. This has Tully written all over it."

Kai just grew angrier. "My friend fucking died on that beach, and we've done *everything* we could to keep idiots like you from doing the same shit," he snapped. "And now look at what's happening! There's going to be headlines bringing surfers in from all over the world. I hope you're happy."

"Kai!" Jet snapped, his tone dark and authoritative. Kai glared at him and shook his hand off his shoulder, turning his board to face the shore.

"Fuck this. I'm not in the mood to surf with dumbass kids that have a death wish," he growled before paddling back to the beach.

Turtle looked thoroughly confused. He scratched his head as he watched Kai paddle away, and I raised an eyebrow at Jet.

Jet sighed and shook his head. "You'll have to excuse him. He's a little... *triggered* right now. That wasn't about you. He's a really great guy; you're just not meeting him under great circumstances."

I shrugged and rolled my eyes.

"I don't really care, dude. I'm just here to surf. How about you mind your business, and I'll mind mine, yeah?"

We moved up a few spaces in the lineup, but Jet didn't seem interested in backing off. He was staring at me intently, clearly curious about me.

Unlike Kai, Jet's interest in me didn't feel hostile, just cautious and wary.

"Blake says you're really good. She says you remind her of Riddick."

I froze, my heart literally stopping in its tracks at the sound of Riddick's name coming out of Jet's mouth.

"She says it feels like some sort of divine tragedy that someone with a surfing style so similar to Riddick's shows up out of nowhere, dying to rip up Leviathans."

I glanced at him, feeling my skin roll with goosebumps under my wetsuit. I had no idea what he was talking about, but the way he was staring at me was making my hair stand on end.

"We came by your place yesterday," he continued, and I nodded.

"I know."

"Why didn't you answer?"

"Why didn't I answer the door for two strange dudes I'd never met before? I'm Gen Z, bro. I ain't answering the door for anyone who doesn't text first."

Jet's handsome face split into a genuine grin, and he chuckled.

"Fair enough."

He glanced over my shoulder, and his grin widened.

"Looks like you're up, surf star," he said, jerking his head to indicate that we were now at the head of the line. "Let's see if you're as good as Blake says."

CHAPTER
Thirty-Five

Finn

Jet surfed with us the rest of the afternoon, and after a few runs, it was clear that he was just as good as Riddick, maybe even a little better.

His style was just... *cool as fuck.*

When he surfed, it was like the board was an extension of his body. I swear he was controlling it with his mind like some sort of surfing Jedi. Watching him was inspiring.

He was sick enough that when it became clear he was impressed with what I could do, I got a warm, fuzzy, accomplished feeling in my tummy.

He watched me intently every time I was up, and he even offered me a few words of congratulations after a particularly epic run.

When the three of us turned in for the day, the Finnatics were losing their minds. Both Jet and I were asked for autographs, much to Turtle's delight. However, whereas I obliged, Jet grew considerably more reserved than he'd been in the water and refused, telling us he would catch up with us later.

Turtle was yammering my ear off excitedly as we strapped our boards to Blake's car and headed into work. Since Sharkies was right on the beach, it was just a short walk.

I wasn't really listening to Turtle as we got changed in the staff room before punching in for our shift. My mind was running a mile a minute with everything Jet had said.

I was also *pissed* about the surf competition. Riddick was going to be in such a shit mood when I told him about it. I really wasn't looking forward to dealing with one of his grumpy ass moods when I got home.

It was a weeknight, so the restaurant was relatively slow. I went through the motions of clearing tables as the sun went down when I noticed one table had a copy of the Stars Cove Gazette left on it.

Remembering what Kai had said about there being an article about the surf competition, I snatched it up.

Right there, on the front page, in big, bold letters, read:

MAYOR TULLY LAUNCHING THE FIRST ANNUAL STARS COVE SURF COMPETITION: TAMING LEVIATHANS

Anger simmered in my gut as I read the article. He must have been working behind the scenes on this all year, as the competition date was already set, and it was a few weeks away. Of course, Kyle was listed as one of the contestants, along with several other relatively well-known names in big wave surfing.

The entire event was going to be televised and would last a whole weekend. My eyes skimmed the page, and I blinked in confusion when I saw Riddick's name mentioned.

In memory of Stars Cove's own surfing legend,

Jake Whittling, Mayor Tully has announced the first place award to be titled 'The Riddick' award. This is meant to be a tribute to Whittling in recognition of his contribution to Stars Cove.

'Without Jake, we might have never discovered Leviathans,' Tully explains. 'And though his passing is a tragedy, I have to believe he would look down on this competition with pride, knowing that his legacy lives on.'

Then, there, beneath Mayor Tully's *bullshit* fucking quote, was a black and white photo of Kai, Jet, and *Riddick* holding shortboards on Leviathans Beach. The caption read:

The Founders of Leviathans
Featured Left to right: *Kai Kalani, Makoa 'Jet' Kealoha, and Jake 'Riddick' Whittling*

I blinked again, trying to clear my eyes because clearly, my mind was playing fucking tricks on me... but no.

This was real. I ran my thumb over the face of the man I had spent the last seven months training with... living with, *sleeping* with as he stared up at me with that same smile he now gave me so freely.

My hands began shaking so violently I couldn't read the rest of the article. My breathing became choppy, and dark spots danced across my vision.

I couldn't breathe...

Fuck, fuck fuck...I COULDN'T FUCKING BREATHE!

CHAPTER
Thirty-Six

Finn

Alexa Play: Fire In The Water by Feist

I didn't tell anyone I was leaving.

I couldn't. I felt like I was underwater. I kept losing time as my mind tried to process what I'd read, and suddenly, I found myself walking alone down the dark street toward my shack, clutching the copy of the gazette I'd found to my chest like it could protect me from the truth.

This couldn't be happening... It couldn't be real. Riddick wasn't... He couldn't be *dead?*

It was a trick! He'd tricked everyone, faked his own death for some unknown reason...

I would ask him about it when I got home, and he would laugh and tell me it was just a coincidence. Or a misprint. Some sort of crazy misunderstanding that would feel obvious once he explained it all away...

With each step I took, I forced myself to focus on my breathing, the way Riddick taught me to do.

Inhale...

One, two, three...

Exhale...

One, two, three...

Rinse. Repeat.

It was over an hour's walk from town to the shack, and my phone had started blowing up about ten minutes in. I turned it off and continued on my slow, dazed journey home.

By the time I made it to my front door, I'd gotten a handle on myself. I was no longer worried I would die from a panic attack, but my heart was beating so hard you would think I'd just run a marathon.

I stared at the door for a long time before I finally turned the knob and walked in.

Riddick was home, sitting at the kitchen table with a plate of food for me like he always did, and his head snapped to me as I walked in.

"Hey, baby boy," he said, giving me his usual smile.

When I didn't respond, the smile slipped off his face, and immediately, I knew... I knew he wasn't going to explain it all away.

My entire world was about to implode... *Again.*

"You found out," he whispered. It was a statement, not a question. He said it like he'd been waiting for this day, and it had only been a matter of time before everything came crashing down.

Swallowing back my tears, I tossed the newspaper on the table in front of him.

I held out a violently shaking finger and forced a single word out past the painful lump in my throat.

"Explain."

He glanced at the paper, and I watched his heart break as he took in the photo that labeled him as Jake *fucking* Whittling. The man who'd died long before I even showed up in Stars Cove.

"What is there to explain, Finn? The truth is right here, staring up at you," he said, gesturing to the newspaper.

"It's not possible! What, did you fake your death? Is that why you won't go into town?" My mind was racing. I knew that wasn't the case because he *had* gone into town, and everyone had seen him that night on the beach. Wouldn't that have been a bigger deal if everyone thought he was dead?

He couldn't even look at me.

"I didn't fake my death, Finn."

"You must have! You can't be... you can't be... you're *right here!*" I cried out, my voice finally cracking on my tears. I rushed forward and grabbed him, digging my fingers into his flesh to confirm that he was *here* and he was *real.*

"I'm dead, Finn. I'm sorry you found out like this. I wanted to tell you, I just... I didn't know *how.*"

"No..." I was shaking again. I backed away, feeling like I could literally die from the horror of what he was telling me.

He stood up and came after me, looking just as miserable as I felt.

"Baby, I'm sorry-"

"Don't you *fucking* baby me!" I screamed at him. "I fucking *loved you!* You made me *love you,* and you're not even fucking real? Am I crazy? Am I having a mental fucking breakdown?"

My whole body was cold, and I was shaking so hard that my teeth were chattering.

"Of course, I'm real, Finn. I don't know how, but I am. You need to breathe, bab—Finn. You're going into shock."

He tried to pull me into him, but I jerked away.

"Don't *fucking touch me!*" I screamed, unable to get a grip on myself.

I was replaying every interaction over the last few months in my head.

When Blake had first mentioned those guys in her car, she'd said Jake and Riddick separately, and I'd assumed they were two different dudes... but no, she was just calling him by his nickname...

At the beach party... could no one else see him? Was that why everyone had been looking at me so strangely? Was that why Quinn had been treating me like some kind of rabid animal after?

I must have looked *insane* yelling at nothing on the beach like that...

His flirty answers to where he lived before he moved in here with me...

'Was living in purgatory 'till I met you, baby boy.'

'What do you mean? I've always been here, waiting for you.'

This was *his* shack. Jake's shack. He'd always been here... fucking *haunting* it!

Then, the thing that sent me screaming over the edge of my own sanity was the memory of what he'd told me on the anniversary of my mom's death.

'You made me feel when I thought I would never feel again. You saw me when I thought no one would ever see *me again, and I just... I'm so grateful for you, Finn. You've given me something that's worth looking forward to when, for a long time, all that stood before me were endless, empty days filled with nothing but bad memories and regrets.'*

An inhuman wail escaped me, and I collapsed into a boneless mass of grief on the floor.

Riddick didn't try to speak. He dropped to his knees and crawled to me. Gathering me up in his big, firm, very *real* arms, he tugged me into his lap.

"I'm so sorry, Finn," he whispered as he held me, rocking me back and forth as I sobbed wordlessly into his chest.

"I'm *so*, fucking sorry..."

CHAPTER
Thirty-Seven

Riddick

Finn cried himself to sleep in my arms. I knew there was nothing I could say to make the reality of our situation okay. I was probably the last person he wanted to be holding him in that moment, but there was no one else.

Just me.

The dead man that'd been haunting the beach that had killed him.

Once Finn had passed out, I carried him to bed and tucked him in. His cheeks were puffy, and his eyes were swollen from all the tears, and my heart *broke* seeing him like this.

On reflex, I moved to take his clothes off but stopped myself.

'Don't you baby me!'

'Don't fucking touch me!'

I winced. The privilege of seeing Finn's body had been revoked. Even if he would sleep more comfortably in his boxers, I didn't think he would want me to be the one to strip him down.

Not anymore.

A painful lump formed in my throat, and I forced back tears as I tucked him in, fully clothed, before wandering outside to get some fresh air.

Not that I needed air to exist, but breathing had been a tough habit to crack. I found the act of it still relaxed me.

It gave me the illusion that I was still alive, and it was a small comfort in the endless, lonely existence that is death.

I wasn't quite sure why I was stuck here, but after I drowned, something prevented me from following the light that had been calling my name.

I'd had this overwhelming feeling of regret and an insanely strong need to stay and ensure that the beach that had killed me didn't take any more lives, and I think for that reason, I missed my one-way ticket to wherever I had been supposed to go.

Instead, I found myself bound to my property, unable to move on, but also unable to exist.

I could move objects within the boundaries of my property, but I had learned that if I left and went into Stars Cove, I became less corporeal.

No one could see or hear me, not even within the perimeter of my land, and I certainly couldn't touch anyone.

Until Finn.

I'd heard him calling me that day we met, but I had assumed he was talking to someone else. Someone *alive*. When it became clear he'd been talking to *me*, I was so shocked I could barely respond.

Then, imagine my surprise when he reached out and *touched me*.

It was like his touch turned my normally transparent flesh real.

He'd been so warm and strong and... *alive*.

He was everything I'd taken for granted in life. At first, the fact that he could see and touch me felt like a cruel joke. Like dangling a carrot in front of a starved animal.

There was no future between me and someone who was alive. I shouldn't even be here to begin with.

Then, when I learned that he was here to surf the beach that had cursed me with an eternity of solitude, I'd been furious and terrified and *desperate* to keep him from suffering the same fate.

It was around that time that I began to wonder if this was some sort of divine intervention.

Was there a reason Finn was here and was the only one I could see and touch?

Was I *supposed* to help him survive Leviathans?

Or was this all just a cruel game the universe was playing for its own amusement?

Right now, it felt like the latter.

Because despite how hard I'd tried to avoid the inevitable... I had fallen in love with Finn Summers, and he'd fallen in love with me.

It was a fucking *tragedy,* and I knew it.

We were never supposed to be together because he needed to live, and my life was already over.

I pinched the bridge of my nose and sighed.

What a fucking mess.

Headlights lit up the driveway, and I turned to face the sound of tires crunching gravel.

It was Blake's car, but once again, she wasn't the one driving it. It was Makoa or *Jet.* Kai and I had given him that nickname after he pulled off an insane flip over a jetski when we were teenagers.

What the fuck was he doing here?

My eyes narrowed as he made his way up to the shack, his hair pulled back in a half pony and black dri-fit shorts.

He walked right past me because, of course, he couldn't see me and knocked on Finn's door.

"Hey! Kid! I know you're in there; I saw you walking up the road. Blake and everyone's freaking out 'cause you abandoned your shift or something."

"He's sleeping!" I snarled uselessly at my friend.

Of course, Jet didn't hear me and kept pounding away on Finn's door.

I wanted to throttle him. Finn was going through something insanely traumatic, and he needed to rest. I hated that I couldn't intervene. I'd felt similar when he'd told me that little twat, Kyle Tully, had given him a hard time at the beach party.

If I'd been alive, I would have beaten that kid within an inch of his life for fucking with my man. As it was, I couldn't even go to the store to buy fucking *lube,* let alone fight some little asshole.

"Dude! Open the door!" Jet bellowed, banging even harder with his fist, until finally, Finn swung the door open, looking furious.

"What the *fuck* do you want!?" He snarled in a very *un*-Finn way.

Jet shot him a classic 'Jet' grin, the kind of smile he used to give *me* back in the day. If I had blood, it would be fucking *boiling.*

"Hey, surf star. Knew you were hiding in there," Jet said easily, pushing Finn aside and stepping into the shack.

Finn looked shocked at Jet's brazenness, then his eyes found mine, and his expression darkened further.

I swallowed.

"Do you want me to stay out here?" I asked softly, not knowing where we stood now.

He glanced back and forth between me and where I assumed Jet was likely making himself at home in the shack. For a moment, I really thought Finn was going to slam the door shut on me, but he seemed to deflate after a moment and jerked his head, indicating that I should come back inside.

Guilt swirled in my gut at how tired he looked.

It was *my* fault he looked like that.

This wasn't like on the anniversary of his mother's death when I'd been able to comfort him when he'd been breaking. This time, I was the reason he was breaking, and I was terrified of doing the wrong thing and hurting him further.

Finn watched me warily as I stepped into the shack, his lips pursing as Jet clearly didn't acknowledge my presence.

I went and sat on the couch, feeling extremely on edge.

I didn't like that Jet was here. Not because I didn't think that Jet was a good guy. He was one of my closest friends growing up... I was uncomfortable because I knew how charming and attractive he was... and Finn was *just* his type, especially now that he'd put on so much muscle from all the training I'd put him through.

Finn wasn't the slight, lean boy he'd been when we met. His shoulders had broadened, and his muscles, which were already defined, had filled out and were now hard mounds of pure sex.

He was fucking gorgeous, and because the change had been so gradual for me, I hadn't really noticed until right this moment... but I was noticing now.

Because Jet had noticed too, and it was making me feel sick to my stomach.

Jet leaned casually against the counter, crossing his legs out in front of him and eyeing Finn up and down with that half-cocked grin of his.

"You look like you've seen a ghost, surf star; everything alright?"

Finn just gave him a tired look and rubbed the back of his neck, sighing.

"What are you doing here, man?"

"I told you. All your friends are worried about you. Blake said you left in the middle of your shift without telling anyone."

"That doesn't explain why they sent *you*. I don't know you at all."

He shrugged, though his grin widened.

"I wouldn't say that, surf star. I thought we got along pretty well today, shredding the cove."

My fists clenched on my lap.

"You surfed with him today?" I growled. Finn's eyes darted to me, then back to Jet, who was still looking at him like he wanted to know what he tasted like.

Finn didn't answer me. Instead, he pinched the bridge of his nose and sighed again.

"Look—Jet, right?"

"Sure, but I let my close friends call me Makoa," he said easily, and I grit my teeth together.

He was fucking flirting with him!

Finn, happily, seemed either unaware or uninterested. "Listen, I'm having a pretty shit night. I'm not in the mood to entertain some random dude I barely know. So if you don't have a reason for being here, then I'd appreciate it if you—"

"Blake was right; you *do* surf like him," Jet interrupted.

Finn glanced at me again, but it was brief enough that I don't think Jet noticed.

Jet pushed up off the counter and took a few steps closer to Finn, who was frowning now.

"I'll admit, I kinda jumped at the chance to come check on you when Blake messaged me freaking out. Seeing you surf today was... Let's just say I'm intrigued."

"Intrigued?" Finn breathed, and Jet continued to close the distance between them.

"Yeah. *Intrigued.* You're good, surf star. Like, *really* good. Do you have anyone coaching you?"

Finn's gaze darted to me again, and my heart sank as his normally bright eyes turned flat and dead.

"Not anymore," he whispered, and my stomach bottomed out.

Jet's grin widened.

"Cool. So the position's open, then?"

Finn met his gaze, and there was a long beat of silence that made me want to tear my fucking hair out before, finally, he nodded.

"Yeah. I guess it is."

"Dope." Jet grinned, and I watched in horror as he *reached out and touched Finn's chin.*

He literally *touched his fucking face.*

Like he had a *right* to.

"See you tomorrow, surf star. I'll be here bright and early. Can't wait to see what you've got on the real shit." He winked, then left the shack, spinning Blake's car keys in his hand as he went.

CHAPTER
Thirty-Eight

Finn

I felt like shit. My body was heavy, and getting out of bed was hard. It was very similar to how I felt after I'd learned my mom died. The difference was that I didn't have the luxury of lying in bed and wishing for death to take me too.

We were only a few weeks out from the surf competition, and I wanted to be ready to surf a true Leviathan before the beach was flooded with news and paparazzi.

I didn't have any interest in the competition, but I *did* want to prove to myself that I could survive this beach before any of those other assholes did it.

So, when Jet started pounding on my door, I pushed through the heavy blanket of depression that was threatening to pull me under and got up.

Riddick was waiting in the living room. He'd made me breakfast like he always did but hadn't tried to crawl in bed with me the night before.

I was grateful. I could barely look at him. I wasn't even angry with him. I was just… *heartbroken.*

I thought I knew what heartache was, but I'd been wrong. This wound in my chest was all-consuming.

I felt the pain *everywhere.* The grief of losing Riddick was a living thing. It crouched on my shoulders—a feathered scavenger that preyed on things already halfway dead.

What made the grief cut even deeper was the fact that he was gone… but somehow also still *right there.*

I could *see* him.

I could smell him.

And I knew, if I allowed myself to, I could touch him.

How was it possible? Was he really a spirit, or was I having a full-blown psychotic break?

I wasn't sure, but all I knew was he was so real to me, and knowing that he wasn't an actual tangible, breathing human being was so fucked up I couldn't begin to process what was happening.

"Morning ba—Finn," he whispered, and my already tense shoulders shot up to my ears. I didn't respond; I simply made my way to the door to let Jet in.

I wasn't sure how I felt about the guy, but I was grateful that fate seemed to have dropped an alternative to Riddick directly in my lap.

I knew I would have to talk to Riddick and decide what I was going to do about our relationship at some point. I just needed a second to work through what I was feeling.

I also still needed to train, and I didn't think there was any way I could continue training with Riddick while feeling the way I was at the moment.

So, Jet, with his playful smile and easy attitude, would have to do for now.

I think if I wasn't using every scrap of energy I had to just stay upright, I might have liked Jet. As it was, I could barely put one foot in front of the other, let alone put any effort into a new friendship.

I opened the door to find Jet leaning against the frame with a pair of charcoal Oakleys and a plain black T-shirt.

He gave me one of those handsome, easy grins and snapped the gum he was chewing as he straightened.

"Morning, surf star. You're looking rested." He smirked, giving me an up and down over the rims of his shades as he brushed past me.

"Ah, you made breakfast, dope," he said, slipping into one of my kitchen chairs and digging into the pancakes Riddick had made me.

"Uh. Yeah, help yourself," I mumbled, though Jet's mouth was already full. He patted the chair next to me, indicating that he wanted me to join him.

"Eat up. Gotta get these carbs in and digest a bit before we hit the waves."

I slid into the chair next to him, ignoring the angry burn of Riddick's eyes on me from where he was sitting silently in the living room.

"So, how'd you hear about Leviathans in the first place?" Jet asked me casually, taking a big gulp from a cup of orange juice Riddick had poured for me.

"I was surfing with Turtle on the East Coast, and someone said they heard a rumor that you could hit up twenty footers here, so we came to check it out."

Jet raised an eyebrow at me and put his fork down, turning to face me.

His knee brushed against mine, and I noticed he didn't make any move to pull away. I frowned, wondering if that was intentional or if I was just imagining it.

I was still staring at where his knee was pressed against mine when he spoke.

"The waves at Leviathans get way higher than that. It's late enough in the season that we might catch some twenties today. Over the next few weeks, they're going to get even bigger."

I nodded, sliding my chair back slightly so I could sit next to him without touching him.

"I know."

He was watching me carefully, and I felt weirdly exposed.

"How do you *know*? Only Kai, Riddick, and I really know Leviathan's patterns. Or that *was* the case before Kai and I left. As far as I know, no one has tried to surf the beach since Jake died."

This easy flip back and forth from Riddick to Jake triggered me for some reason. This was how I'd ended up so fucking blindsided.

"Call him Jake or Riddick. Fucking pick one," I snapped and immediately regretted my outburst. Jet looked surprised for a minute, then nodded.

"Alright. Jake then. His fans called him Riddick, but the people closest to him always knew him as Jake."

"Why Riddick? Where'd that name come from?"

A sad smile spread across Jet's face, and he leaned back in his chair, sliding down slightly. His knee brushed mine again, but I didn't think he even noticed. He had this far-away look like he was remembering something that somehow both made him happy and sad at the same time.

"When we were kids, it was pretty clear early on that Jake wasn't like the rest of us. He was a natural."

"I've seen you surf. You're incredible," I said, remembering how Jet looked the other day riding the waves like he was a part of the ocean. He almost seemed like he belonged in the water more than he did on land.

"Yeah, I've got years of practice and experience under my belt. I worked my ass off to stay on Jake's level. But for him? Everything just came easy. I would need to put in days of work to pick up something he managed on the first try. He really was a prodigy."

Jet smiled at me, and he looked so sad for a minute that I wished I could tell him Riddick was literally in the shack with us, listening to every word he said.

"Eat," he said, making a lazy gesture toward my untouched plate, indicating that he wanted me to eat while he told me his story.

"Anyway, similar to how you have your little fan club, Jake had a crew that used to watch him surf, too," Jet explained as I took a syrup-soaked bite of pancakes.

"Whenever he did some cool new stunt, his fans would lose their minds. *Did you see that?! That was ridiculous!*"

He chuckled as if he could literally still hear the crowd cheering for his friend.

"It kind of became a coined term. *Ridiculous.* Over time, it was shortened to *'That's ridic!'* Which morphed at some point to *'That's so Riddick,'* in reference to Jake. So, that's how his nickname came to be. That's why he's Riddick."

I swallowed my bite of pancake and frowned.

"I'm sorry... for your loss," I whispered, and he met my gaze, his dark eyes soft and full of a wistful kind of sadness.

"Thank you," he said quietly. "I miss him all the time. We were... We were really close."

The way he said it made me feel strange. Like they were closer than friends.

I glanced over at Riddick, but I couldn't read his expression at all. His jaw was tight, and he had stood up from his seat on the couch as if he wanted to say something or join in somehow.

"I wasn't kidding when I told you that you remind me of him when you surf. Watching you yesterday..." He cleared his throat roughly, and I noticed his eyes were glassier than they'd been when I first came in. "It was like he was still alive."

I didn't really know what to say to that, so I just reached out and laid my hand on top of his, giving it a squeeze.

He glanced at my hand, then met my eyes, a slow smile spreading across his face.

"Sorry," He chuckled, though he didn't pull away. "I said I was gonna coach you, and here I am bumming you out."

"You're not bumming me out," I assured him. "Losing someone you love is hard. I get it."

Jet was staring at me with a soft smile tilting on his perfectly shaped mouth. He leaned closer, and I blinked as I felt his breath skate across my lips.

He smelled like cinnamon and spice, whereas Riddick was more sea salt and coconut. The hair on the back of my neck stood on end when I realized how close we were and how intimate this moment was suddenly feeling.

"Thanks, surf star," he said softly, and his eyes dropped to my mouth. He chuckled. "You've got some syrup right—"

CRASH!

We both jumped, and I threw myself away from Jet, whipping toward the sound. Riddick was standing next to my now-shattered floor lamp, which he'd clearly knocked over intentionally.

He was *pissed.* His fists were clenched at his side, and the muscles in his jaw flexed uncontrollably.

"That was weird..." Jet mused, frowning at the broken lamp. He got up and wandered over to inspect the base, no doubt trying to figure out how it had tipped over like that when neither of us was anywhere near it.

"Uh, yeah. Super *weird,*" I agreed, glaring at Riddick over Jet's shoulder.

Riddick looked like he wanted to snap at me, but I just raised my eyebrows at him in challenge, and he shut his mouth.

"You got a broom? I'll help clean this up," Jet mumbled absently, and I gestured to the tiny broom closet next to the bathroom.

"We need to talk, Finn," Riddick said firmly. It was freaking me out that Jet couldn't hear him at all, and he was speaking at a regular volume.

"Not now," I hissed.

"*Obviously* not now, but when he's gone, we need to discuss this."

My blood was boiling. I was so hurt and fucking angry with him. I wasn't ready to have a productive conversation.

"I said not now."

Jet was already on his way back with the broom and a dustpan. I gave him what I hoped was a normal smile, and Riddick darkened further.

"You better not let him touch you," he growled, and my eyebrows flew up in surprise.

He thought I was what... gonna hook up with *Jet?* Five seconds after I found out that the man I thought I was in love with had been lying to me for months?

I'd barely been able to get out of bed this morning, let alone think about fucking someone else.

"Your fan club was right. You really are fucking *ridiculous!*" I hissed, and Jet glanced at me, looking confused.

"You say something, surf star?"

I shook my head and rubbed the back of my neck awkwardly, forcing out a laugh.

"Nah, I was just saying that the draft in here is ridiculous. Stuff's falling off counters all the time."

"Oh... that's super strange. All the windows are closed," he said, though he didn't sound like he was actually suspicious. He was just making an observation as he started to sweep up the mess Riddick had made.

Riddick walked up to me, leaning in close enough that I was flooded with his scent. I could almost taste the salt on his skin and feel the energy radiating off of him. My whole body reacted to his presence, like he was the sun and I was a flower starved for warmth. It took everything in me not to close my eyes and breathe him in.

The memory of his hard body lying on top of mine while he murmured my name over and over again, his fingers exploring every inch of my exposed flesh.

How his scorching lips felt as he worshipped my throat. My chest. My abs. My cock...

The way he always shook and quivered through that first thrust, like being inside me was so fucking good he could barely hold himself back.

The rough sound of his voice when he told me he loved me and that he was proud of me...

How almost every time he touched me, it felt like it was this huge, monumental thing. Like I'd found something safe and permanent. Something that was *mine.*

How the fuck could he not be alive?

Why was this happening to me?

"Have your little lesson with him, but if he lays a finger on you, I'll do a lot more than break a fucking lamp," he growled, and my skin sheeted with goosebumps.

"Be back home for dinner so we can talk."

I couldn't risk Jet hearing a response, so I just glared at him, and he snarled.

"Is that clear, *surf star?* Nod if it is."

I narrowed my eyes but nodded, not wanting him to make even more of a scene. He glared at me for a long moment before turning on his heel. I winced as he slammed the front door open and stormed out onto the beach.

"What the shit was that?!" Jet yelped, spinning to face the door Riddick had left swinging on its hinges.

"Uhh, told you. The draft is crazy. That door blows open all the time."

"Huh..." Jet scratched the back of his head, eyeing the door like he wanted to tighten its hinges.

I shrugged, giving him one of my best dimpled smiles, hoping to distract him.

"Leave that. I'll clean it up later. Wanna hit the beach?" I asked, and Jet's eyes flashed.

"You have *no* idea how down I am. Come on. Show me what you got."

CHAPTER
Thirty-Nine

Finn

The waves were the biggest they'd ever been, and as usual, my emotional response to the terrifying walls of water was *excitement,* not fear.

My board was freshly waxed, thanks to Riddick, so I hit my first twenty-foot wave with sticky feet and perfect form.

It would have been the best day of my life if Riddick had been there to see me do it.

Instead, I was with Jet.

Surfing with Jet was much different than surfing with Riddick.

Riddick was a drill sergeant. He never smiled and he was constantly scanning the beach for threats.

When Riddick trained me, he was always barking orders, frantically reminding me to pay attention, and constantly trying to instill the fear of fucking God into me each time a new wave came in.

Jet was easier. We were similar in temperaments, and he was always smiling. Sure, Jet offered me instruction, but he usually let me do my own thing first, then gave me constructive criticism in areas he thought I could improve. He treated the water with a healthy dose of respect, but he didn't seem to be tense and terrified I might die the entire time like Riddick was.

I wasn't sure if that was because he hadn't suffered the same trauma Riddick had or simply because he didn't care about me as much as Riddick did… which was a sobering thought.

Because I didn't have Riddick there looking out for me, I found that I instinctively took my own safety more seriously. For some reason, I didn't feel quite as safe with Jet. Not because he was doing anything wrong but because he just wasn't as hyper-aware of me as Riddick always was. I hadn't truly understood just how much Riddick was always looking out for me until he was gone.

Feeling off-kilter without him, I found myself actively trying to remember to always scan the horizon, to make sure I was avoiding traps that might drag me out into the death zone and making a conscious effort to strategically plan my path through the pipe so that in the case of an unexpected break, I wouldn't plummet twenty feet.

By the time the day was over, Jet was shaking his head in disbelief, beaming at me.

"You're pretty amazing, surf star," he praised me as we paddled back to shore.

I grinned at him, though it felt strained.

Surfing without Riddick had been unexpectedly stressful. I hadn't realized how much I'd come to rely on him watching my back. I was missing him even more than I had been that morning.

"You're not too bad yourself," I replied as we scooped up our boards and headed back toward the natural stone steps that led up the cliff.

"What are you doing for the rest of the afternoon?" he asked, and I had the feeling that he was asking me to hang out.

Riddick's demand that I be home for dinner was ringing in my head, but I was also pissed enough at him that I didn't want to just blindly obey him as if nothing had changed between us.

"Uh, I don't really have plans," I lied, and Jet beamed at me.

"Cool. I was gonna swing by Jake's grave quickly since it's right around here; then you wanna watch a movie or something?"

"Riddick's grave is close by?" I asked, shocked, and Jet nodded.

"Yeah, we buried him on the property. We figured he would want to be close to home."

Suddenly, I needed to see Riddick's final resting place more than I'd needed anything in my life.

"Can I come with you? To his grave, I mean."

Jet gave one of those soft, gentle looks he sometimes got when he was talking about Riddick, and my stomach warmed.

"I would like that, surf star." He smiled, jerking his head in the opposite direction of the steps.

"Let's go see the legend himself."

Riddick's grave was a simple, old-school tombstone set in a shady corner of the brush. The stone read:

Jake 'Riddick' Whittling.
Friend. Lover. Leviathan tamer.
1986-2024

I frowned, glancing at Jet.

"Lover?"

Jet pursed his lips and nodded. "I told you, we used to be close."

A strange feeling twisted in my gut at this new piece of information.

Had Riddick been so worried about us hooking up because he was jealous of *me?* Or because he was jealous of Jet?

I chewed on my lip, and Jet misread my expression entirely. I jumped as he reached out with his pinky finger, gently curling it around mine.

"And like I said... you remind me of him. *A lot.*"

Heat flushed my cheeks, and I felt my eyes widen.

Okay, that was DEFINITELY a flirt...

Maybe Riddick wasn't being so ridiculous after all.

I cleared my throat and tugged my pinky away, stepping back.

"Jet... I...uhm..." My face was so hot it was embarrassing.

Understanding flooded his expression, and he held up his hands playfully as if showing me he was unarmed.

"Oh, shit... did I totally misread that? I'm usually pretty on point with the gaydar. If you're not into dudes, my bad."

"What? No, it's not that... I've been known to dabble." I chuckled, awkwardly rubbing the back of my neck.

Jet frowned and cocked his head to the side. "You seeing some-one then?"

"Uhm... It's... complicated," I muttered, and he watched me careful-ly, his kind brown eyes searching my face.

"I see..." he said softly. He stepped in closer to me, and I swallowed thickly. His warm, spicy scent filled the space between us, and he curled a finger under my chin, gently tilting my head back. "Well, if someone has *you*, and they're making it *complicated,* then they're probably a dumbass."

A surprised laugh puffed out of me, and I didn't miss the way his eyes dropped to my mouth, that easy, half-cocked grin tilting on his lips.

I stepped away again.

"He can definitely be a dumbass," I mumbled, and Jet let me go, dropping his hand back to his side.

"I have no doubt," he murmured.

We stood there in strangely comfortable silence for a beat before he shrugged, adjusting his shortboard under his arm.

"Maybe we can take a rain check on that movie, then."

"Yeah, I think that's a good idea," I said, digging my toe into the pebbly ground.

"If you ever change your mind and you feel like… *watching a movie,* let me know." He smirked, and I glanced at him, unable to stop myself from smiling.

"Sure… But I probably won't. Change my mind, I mean…"

He clapped a hand on my shoulder and nodded.

"No worries. Still up for shredding again tomorrow?"

My grin widened, and warmth curled in my gut. Jet was a pretty dope dude. "Yeah. Sounds good."

He winked at me and nodded.

"Later, surf star," he said, throwing the *'hang loose'* hand signal over his shoulder as he walked away, leaving me standing at the grave of the dead man I'd turned him down for.

CHAPTER

Forty

Alexa Play: She Keeps Me Warm by Mary Lambert

I watched from the shadows as Jet walked away, leaving Finn standing alone at my grave.

If I wasn't already dead, I would be concerned I might die from the intense, conflicting emotions currently raging in my chest.

Watching Jet touch Finn hurt more than drowning had.

I would take a lungful of saltwater over watching someone else touch Finn's face the way Jet just did.

But... what I was feeling was *wrong*. It wasn't fair to Finn.

Jet would be *perfect* for him.

He was kind, loyal, funny, and, most importantly, *alive.*

I knew I could trust Jet to take care of Finn's heart.

When Jet and I had been hooking up, the only reason things hadn't gotten more serious than they had was because of me.

Jet would have given me anything I asked for.

He *did* give me everything I asked for, including time and space, when I told him I wasn't ready to fully commit to what we had.

He would take care of Finn.

He would never abandon him or make him feel alone in the world...

He was so much better for Finn than I was.

What was that saying?

If you really love someone, let them go?

The thought of letting Finn go made me feel like I was going to die all over again.

He was...

He was like nothing I ever thought I would have in my life, let alone death.

Finn didn't just light up a room... he *was* light itself.

His smiles were pure warmth, and his playful nature made me want to curl myself around him and protect him from anything that might turn his smiles into frowns.

Watching him stand there, staring at my grave with tears in his beautiful eyes, made my chest so tight with emotion that I felt like I might be sick.

His mop of hair was damp and dark from the ocean, and his wetsuit molded to his perfectly sculpted body like a second skin.

Every inch of him was beautiful to me. Every word he'd ever spoken to me was precious. I was *so* irrevocably in love with him that I didn't even know how to properly manage the emotions that welled when I looked at him.

It wasn't a conscious thought, but suddenly, my body was moving. I was drawn to him, like Icarus to the damn sun... because that's what Finn was to me.

Warmth, light, and life.

He was the fire that kept the shadows away.

I'd been existing in darkness until he laid those big, hazel eyes on me, and now I didn't know how to return to my cold and lonely exile without him.

"How long have you been watching?" he asked as I came to stand next to him.

"Since the day we met," I murmured. And it was the truth. The depth of my feelings for Finn held the weight of a planet, and I was an isolated, drifting satellite doomed to orbit him for eternity.

Today was no exception.

I'd seen him catch every wave.

Celebrated every success and stressed over every mistake.

I'd been there, and I always would be, because I didn't know how not to be anymore.

Finn scowled at me, then turned away.

"I turned him down," he said, his voice tight.

We weren't looking at each other. We were both staring at my tombstone.

"Maybe you shouldn't have." My voice came out much lower and quieter than I'd intended.

His head snapped to face me. He dropped his bright pink short-board, fully turning his entire body toward me, and I flinched away from him.

"*What?*" he hissed.

I couldn't look at him. I could barely respond. There was a lump so thick in my throat that it hurt to speak.

"Maybe you shouldn't have turned him down. Makoa is a good man. He would take good care of you."

"You can't be fucking serious." Finn snarled, and I closed my eyes, trying so hard to stay strong and do the right thing.

"Riddick. Look at me."

I couldn't.

He let out a cold, dark laugh. It sounded so foreign on his lips that a chill rolled through me.

"If you're going to fuck me, then throw me away like I'm a piece of garbage, then the least you can do is be a man about it. Look at me and tell me you don't want me, Riddick."

The dam broke.

The lump in my throat cracked, and suddenly, tears flowed down my face. I was angry, heartbroken, and devastated all at once.

I rounded on him with a roar, and I had my hand wrapped around his throat before I could process what I was doing.

Finn didn't flinch. He just met my gaze head-on as I cuffed him the same way I had on that first day, and his eyes filled with a cold fire I had never seen before.

Suddenly, he wasn't sunlight. He was as icy as the waves that had taken my life.

"Say it to my face. Go on," he growled as my fingers tightened around his neck. "Tell me you don't want me."

I knew what those words meant to him.

I knew his father had left him and his mom.

He'd told me that his mom used to always say when he asked her why his father left them alone... Why he didn't want them.

'You're not alone, sweet boy, I'm right here!'

She obviously hadn't known she was going to pass away when she told him that. But still, the damage was done. My baby had been floating through life, feeling completely lost and abandoned by the people who were supposed to support and protect him.

The thought of him believing I would voluntarily toss him away like that *broke* something in me.

Suddenly, I was screaming.

"OF COURSE I WANT YOU!" I roared, and his eyes widened in surprise. "How could you think I don't *want* you? I fucking *love* you, Finn! I'm so fucking in love with you I can't seem to tell the goddamned difference between right and wrong anymore!" I snarled, backing him up until he was pressed against my tombstone.

"Then why the *fuck* would you tell me to sleep with *Jet?*" *he* growled, pressing his throat against my hand hard enough that his beautiful face turned red.

"Because I'm fucking *dead*, Finn!" I yelled. I was inches from his face, and I knew my own face was likely as red as his.

My whole body was so tense I felt like I might shatter into a million pieces. I was so distraught that it was taking everything in me not to squeeze his neck until it snapped.

I wanted to steal his breath away and keep him here with me forever.

The second that thought crossed my mind, my fingers spasmed with horror.

I didn't want that.

I didn't want Finn dead.

I would never want that for him.

Immediately, the tension melted out of my body. Without taking my hand away from his throat, I pressed closer to him.

I brushed my thumb over his pulse, reveling at the feeling of his steady heartbeat. Savoring the warm feeling of hot blood pumping beneath the surface of his skin.

I watched his shoulders rise and fall with each breath he took.

Being alive had never looked so fucking good as it did on my sweet, perfect baby boy.

I rested my forehead against his, and a sob rolled through me.

"He's alive, and I'm fucking *dead*," I repeated, softer this time, my voice cracking as I fought off another sob.

Fucking Christ... I couldn't keep the tears down.

Suddenly, Finn's strong arms wrapped around my waist, and he tugged me into him, pressing our bodies flush against each other. His wetsuit dampened my T-shirt, and I curled into his warm body. He sat back on my tombstone as I buried my face in the crook of his neck, and I shuddered as I fought off another bone-deep sob that threatened to rip through my chest.

Finn's hand slid up my back, and he curled his fingers into my hair, pressing firm kisses into the side of my head as I shook violently against him.

"Shh… It's okay, I'm here. I've got you…" he murmured in between kisses, his hot breath caressing my ear.

"*Baby…* I'm *so sorry…*" I sobbed, and he squeezed me harder. He sniffed softly, and I realized that he was crying now, too.

"I know…" He hummed, stroking my hair gently as he held me. "I know you are."

"I just want what's best for you. You can't be with a ghost, Finn," I whispered, and he squeezed me tighter against him.

"Why not?"

His voice was small, and I shut my eyes and gently kissed the side of his neck.

"Because baby. You're alive, and you deserve to have a long, full life with someone who'd be able to take you on all the adventures you could possibly dream up." I kissed him again, this time on his jaw, shuddering at the rough feel of his stubble brushing against my lips.

"What if all the adventure I need is right here?" he whispered, his voice still that small, fragile version of him. As if one wrong word from me and he could break.

"I can't ask you to stay here with a dead man, Finn. That's… That would make me a fucking monster."

He was kissing down the side of my face now, still stroking his fingers through my hair.

His lips traced down my cheek, his tongue darting out to taste the salt of my tears.

"You're not asking…" he breathed as his hot mouth continued its tender path toward my lips. "I'm offering."

"Finn…" I was shaking my head, but he gripped my jaw and held me steady as he finally slid his puffy lips down the slope of my jaw to catch mine.

I groaned and melted into him; the fireworks that always ripped through my gut at the taste of him immediately sparked to life.

"It's my decision, baby..." He breathed against me before nipping and sucking my bottom lip into his mouth, pulling another moan deep from my chest.

Baby... That was the first time he'd ever called me baby.

"I'm old enough to choose what I want for myself, Riddick," he whispered before plunging his tongue into my mouth and stroking me with a confidence he never had before. His fingers traced down my back, and he found the hem of my T-shirt. He shoved his hands beneath the now damp, cold cotton and slid my shirt up my ribs. His gentleness turned my skin to gooseflesh, and my nipples hardened so quickly it forced a hiss through my teeth.

"And what I want, Riddick... is *you.*"

JAKE
'RIDDICK'
WHITTLING
FRIEND. LOVER.
LEVIATHAN TAMER
1986-2024

CHAPTER
Forty-One

Riddick

Alexa Play: Light Me Up by Ingrid Michaelson

was dizzy, my mind spinning with emotions. Finn's hands on my skin and his tongue in my mouth were making it impossible for me to think straight.

He was sitting on my tombstone with his legs spread wide and his cock tenting the shit out of his wetsuit.

"I *want* you, Riddick. Don't you want me, too?"

"You know I do, baby…" I whispered, biting at his lips and cupping his face while I kissed him.

"Then have me."

I broke the kiss, pulling back to search his face. He was staring at me without a hint of doubt or amusement in his eyes, which had turned a steely grey color due to the cold, cloudy sky.

"Here?" I croaked as the reality of what he was asking rushed through me.

Finn nodded. "Yeah. Here."

"Why?"

He cradled my face in his hands and ran his thumbs over my cheeks, his pink lips a straight line and his flirty dimples nowhere in sight.

"I want to own it. Put it behind us. I want you to fuck me here, and then we'll accept the reality of our situation and move forward. *Together.*"

"You want me to... fuck you? On my grave?"

His lip twitched, and his stormy eyes crinkled at the corners.

"Yeah."

I traced my thumb over his bottom lip, pressing gently to expose his teeth as I thought about what he was asking.

If I agreed to this, it would mean I was agreeing to let him pick me over the life he deserved.

It felt wrong.

It felt fucked up and selfish.

But it also felt...

So.

Fucking.

Right.

I swallowed, knowing in my heart of hearts that I was too weak to say no.

We stared at each other for a long beat, and finally, I gave in.

"Take this off," I growled, tugging at the zipper to his wetsuit, and his eyes flashed with heat as we worked together to strip him down.

I TOOK MY TIME.

Helping Finn out of his wetsuit felt like I was unwrapping a gift. I drank up every inch of flesh, and it felt like I was seeing him for the first time again.

It was always like this when I undressed him.

Being permitted to watch as he exposed all his soft, golden skin felt like such a privilege.

A gift of epic proportions that I just straight up didn't deserve.

And I had *tried* to refuse him. To do the right thing and push him away, but...

He wanted me.

And my baby boy deserved to have anything he wanted. If it was in my power to give it to him, I would.

I honestly couldn't believe he still wanted me.

When he came back home that night and broke down in front of me, mourning my death like it meant he'd lost me... I truly didn't think he would ever let me back in.

I never thought I would ever have the chance to run my fingers over his perfect body again.

Peeling the suit over his shoulders and down his waist, he stood up briefly so I could roll the material down the firm, muscled globes of his ass. He sat back down, resting his bare cheeks against the rough stone of my grave as I gently tugged the rest of the suit off his legs.

I tossed the wet material aside and stood back to look at him.

He looked so effortlessly beautiful, sprawled across my tombstone.

His golden hair was lightening as it dried, and it curled around his ears in soft, golden tufts.

The way his eyes changed to match his environment always fascinated me. Right now, they were gunmetal grey, but somehow, they were still so clear that they felt like pools of Arctic water.

I allowed my gaze to slowly travel down the length of his body, taking in his now *very* broad shoulders that sloped into sculpted biceps. His cobblestone abs were currently scrunched around his belly button from the casual way he lounged on the stone marker. I followed the light dusting of brown hair that led from his navel down to his perfect cock, which was so hard it was pointing directly at his face.

It was getting cold as the afternoon slowly descended in the sky, and a cool breeze cut through the palms surrounding us, causing Finn to shiver.

His nipples darkened and contracted as his skin turned to goose-flesh, and his teeth chattered slightly, causing me to frown.

"Are you cold, baby?" I whispered, stepping between his muscular legs, melting at the way he tilted his head back so that our eyes never broke contact.

"You'll have to warm me up." He smiled, his stormy eyes swirling with mischief. I brushed my thumb over one of his adorable dimples and pressed a soft kiss on his forehead, breathing in his addicting scent.

"I can do that…" I hummed.

Finn smelled like the ocean, but beneath that, he just smelled like *Finn.* It was his own personal brand of human, and sometimes, I just wanted to bury my face under his arms and inhale him because he just smelled *alive.*

Before he'd unknowingly walked into my prison, I hadn't been close enough to touch another living person, let alone smell them, in over a year.

That first day… when I'd had my hand wrapped around his throat, I'd been flooded by his intoxicating *Finn* scent for the first time. I'll never forget the rush that had coursed through me the first time I was suddenly enveloped in a heady cloud of what made him, *him…*

I should have known.

I should have known this impish daredevil was going to take every assumption I'd made about death, life—and everything in between—and turn it right on its fucking head.

Because that's who Finn was.

I should have known nothing would ever stop him from getting what he wanted.

He had dimples that could charm the devil himself, and apparently, even *death* wouldn't stop him from following his heart.

The world didn't deserve Finn Summers.

He was too good for this place, and that scared me more than anything.

But if Finn was brave enough to tame demons disguised as waves and crazy enough to fall in love with a man who couldn't even give him the breath in his lungs... then I could be brave, too.

I wouldn't run from this anymore.

He deserved someone who stayed.

"I love you," I whispered, kissing him softly. He hummed and leaned into me, shoving his cold fingers back under my T-shirt and making my abs contract with the shock of the contact.

"Show me," he murmured against my lips.

"I will," I breathed. "Every fucking day."

CHAPTER
Forty-Two

Riddick

I plunged my tongue into his mouth, relishing in the groan that vibrated out of him as I curled my fingers into his hair.

Controlling his head with my grip, I forced him more firmly against me, slipping my hand around his waist and dancing my fingers over the top of his crease.

My cock throbbed as he arched, his cold fingers hooking into the front of my shorts and sliding them down. Without breaking the kiss, I kicked them off, biting down on his lip so hard my mouth flooded with the tangy taste of his blood.

He hissed, and I groaned, my eyes rolling back in my head at how fucking good it felt to have the privilege of sampling another piece of him.

"Jake..." he whispered. My real name rolled off his lips like it was his favorite word, and my *entire* body reacted to it.

My bare cock surged between us, and I let out a surprised gasp as my balls immediately drew up against me.

"*Fuck-*"

I was ripping my shirt off, needing as much of me to be touching him as possible.

I fisted his cock desperately, wrapping my hand around him and watching carefully as he shuddered and groaned beneath my touch. He rocked his hips back and forth on the headstone in response. I firmly stroked him, hating that my palm was dry and I didn't have any lube with me.

"Spit in my hand, baby."

I held my hand out for him, and he obeyed.

I smeared his saliva over the fat pink head of his dick, tracking every twitch of his abs and marveling at the way his cockhead darkened with a rush of fresh blood as I stimulated it.

I kissed him again as I slid my hand up and down his cock. He thrust himself into me, clutching onto my shoulders and grinding his ass into my grave in his desperation for more friction.

"No lube... I need you to suck me, baby; get it nice and sloppy," I murmured against his puffy lips, and he broke away, his eyes wide.

I'd never let him suck me before. I much preferred pleasuring him as I'd never been much for receiving head. I didn't like the inevitable scrape of teeth... However, I was concerned that just spitting on my fingers wouldn't be enough, and I didn't want to risk hurting him.

"Fuck *yes,*" he breathed, immediately dropping to his knees in the soft grass that grew over my grave.

I looked down at him, and suddenly, I couldn't remember why we'd never tried this before. His perfect face with his big, trusting eyes looked so good peering up at me like this.

My cock bobbed inches from his chin, and he licked his lips... That act alone caused a spasm of pleasure to rocket through my dick, and a thick spurt of pre-cum dripped out of my tip, causing me to groan.

Finn wrapped shaking fingers around my shaft at the base, and he broke eye contact to look directly at my leaking cock.

"You're so fucking big, Jake..." I could feel each word manifest as a puff of hot air. Gently, I thrust myself closer to his puffy, pink lips.

"Let me see how beautiful you look with it in your mouth, sweet boy."

He turned those big eyes back up to me, and my lips parted as his tongue darted out hesitantly.

"You can do this, baby. Get it all wet so I can give you what you asked for without hurting you." It was an order, but my tone was gentle.

I cupped the side of his face with my hand, brushing my thumb over my cheek as I watched him.

Finally, he tentatively wrapped his lips around me, running his warm tongue under the ridge of my head and sucking the pre-cum right out of me.

My muscles locked up, and I quivered as he sucked. Rolling my head back with a deep groan, I threaded my fingers in his soft, golden hair, pressing him closer.

"Open your throat, baby... Let me in..."

He moaned, and it vibrated over the sensitive skin of my shaft, causing a hot lick of desire to zip up through my balls.

I forced his head further down, nearly blacking out with ecstasy as he began to choke on my cock.

His tight throat squeezed and contracted around me as he gagged, and I groaned as a hot rush of saliva began to drip out of the corners of his mouth.

He didn't try to pull back, but when he choked again, I forced him to back off, dragging him away from my cock by his hair.

A thick string of saliva connected his glistening, swollen lips to my dick, and he looked up at me with heavy-lidded eyes and a lust-drunk smile.

"You alright, baby?" I asked roughly, and he nodded.

"More," he whined before diving back down on my dick, swallowing me whole like he'd been sucking cock his whole life.

Heat sparked and pooled in my abdomen, the rush of my orgasm starting up quickly. I struggled with the desire to let him finish me off like this... but he wanted me to fuck him, and that's what I was going to do.

"Finn, stop... You feel too good, baby; you have to stop. I'm gonna fucking come..."

He popped off, looking up at me with swollen lips and a glistening chin.

I was right on the edge. He wasn't touching me anymore, but I was worried I was going to blow anyway.

Hauling him up off his knees, I spun him around and bent him over. He braced his hands on my tombstone and arched his back, exposing his perfect pink hole to me.

Spitting on my fingers, I pulled his ass cheeks apart and rubbed as much saliva over him as I could.

He whined and pressed back into me. I nearly came again as I felt his little hole clench and flutter beneath my fingertips.

"Not gonna last..." I grunted, lining my cock head up with his hole. It flexed again, then softened on his exhale as if he were actively preparing himself for what I was about to do to him.

"Fuck me... I don't care if it hurts, just fuck me, Jake..." he whined, and I plastered myself to his sculpted back, decorating his shoulders with salty kisses.

"I never want to hurt you again, baby...Once was already too much," I rasped, reaching for his crease and easing a finger gently into his saliva-slick hole. I pressed my cock in next to my finger, stretching and rocking softly into him until wet heat enveloped my tip.

He moaned loudly as I slowly sank deep into his ass, pulling back and spreading him open so I could watch my cock disappear into his tight little hole.

We both groaned, and he clenched, squeezing the fuck out of my cock as he spasmed around me.

"Fuck, baby... you feel *incredible...*" I rasped, watching, enthralled as my cock slid in and out of him.

I'd been inside him countless times before, but this felt different.

This time, he knew the truth, and he was giving himself to me anyway, which I never in a million years would have expected, let alone hoped for.

When I had died, I thought I'd lost everything.

I'd hated the universe for taking my life from me, and I'd spent the last year wallowing in misery and self-pity for the life I had lost.

Then Finn found me, and at first, I resented him. His presence on that beach had felt like a cruel joke... a trick. It felt like the universe was handing me one more thing it was inevitably going to take away.

I was sure my worst fears had come true when he walked into the shack that night with a broken heart and cheeks stained with tears.

I thought I'd lost him, and I was truly destined to spend eternity haunting this beach alone.

If you'd given me the choice seven months ago to go back in time and change the past, I would have. I would have listened to my gut and stayed out of the water that day—when the clouds had hung low, and the peaks were shredding the beach with each pass.

I would have chosen to *live.*

But... Now, I wouldn't trade my death for anything. If I hadn't died, I would have never met Finn... And I would die a thousand times more if it meant I got to keep him.

"Jake!" he cried as I fucked into him. He was gripping my headstone so hard his knuckles were white.

I braced one hand on his shoulder and another on his hip as I slammed in and out of his perfect ass.

"Baby, I need you to come for me. Come all over my grave. I want you to paint yourself across my name," I grunted, fighting back the overwhelming explosion of pleasure that was threatening to erupt at any moment.

He reached between his legs and fisted himself, jerking his cock in time with each thrust.

"Jake, tell me you want me..."

"I want you so badly, baby. I've never wanted anyone more than I want you," I promised, though my words slurred and rolled into one another as my orgasm barreled through me.

"*Fuuuuuuck!*" I roared as my dick erupted so powerfully that it almost hurt.

I grunted with each bone-shaking, life-changing pulse. Getting as deep in Finn as I possibly could, I shot pump after pump of cum into his ass.

His orgasm didn't come long after. He sobbed as he jerked himself through it, and he clenched and spasmed around me the entire time.

Hot, thick jets of his release splattered across my tombstone, filling the letters of my name with the evidence of his pleasure.

He was mine.

Even in death, he was mine.

"Promise you won't leave me alone…" He whimpered as he began to come down. "Don't push me away like that again."

I wrapped my arms around him and pulled him back into my chest, my half-hard cock still buried deep in his perfect ass.

I crushed him tight and kissed up his neck and under his jaw.

"I promise, baby. I'm not going to leave you. I won't leave you alone like he did."

He twisted around, sliding my cock out of him with the movement. He buried his face in my chest, and I wrapped him up in my arms, holding him close.

"Baby, you're shaking. Let's get you inside and warmed up. It's cold out here."

He looked up at me, his impossibly large eyes shiny and his cheeks pink and swollen from crying.

"You really mean it? You're gonna let us be together now?" He sniffed.

I nodded. "Yeah, baby. Whether it's right or wrong, you're mine now."

Then... he smiled, and I swear the clouds broke open at that moment, and the sun on his face was the most beautiful thing I'd ever seen.

CHAPTER

Forty-Three

Finn

It was weirdly easy to forget that Riddick was actually dead once I made the conscious decision to just accept it.

Waking up the next morning to find him wrapped around me was just as good as it had been when I'd thought he was alive.

It was honestly even better now because he didn't have a problem coming into town or hanging out with me while I spent time with Jet or Turtle.

Now that I knew, he wasn't worried about me freaking out about them not being able to see or hear him. So, when I surfed with Jet the next day, Riddick came along, too.

It took a little getting used to. Often, he would say something in response to our conversation, and I would have to remember not to laugh or reply.

Sometimes, I slipped up, and people looked at me like I was a little crazy, but I didn't care.

I was just happy to have him around.

It was also interesting to learn about the strange parameters of whatever cosmic rules bound him to our shack. When he passed through the property line, I lost the ability to touch him. I could still see and hear him, but my hand would just pass right through his body when he came to town with me.

He couldn't move or touch things outside of our property line either, but he could in the shack.

He began to fade away altogether if we moved too far out of Stars Cove. He was irrevocably bound to his property and told me he could never really leave.

He informed me that he'd learned there were even boundaries out in the ocean. If he paddled too far out, he lost the ability to control his board.

Unless he was using his teal shortboard.

Apparently, that was the board he'd been using when he died, and it seemed to be just as invisible to Jet and Turtle as he was.

A few days after we promised ourselves to each other on his grave, I'd asked him to tell me about the day he died.

We'd been lying in my bed, and he was gently stroking my hair the way he did every night before I fell asleep.

"Tell me," I whispered and watched his expression carefully, hating the sad look that pinched his brows as he remembered that fateful day.

"I was careless," he explained. "I shouldn't have been in the water to begin with. I didn't trust my gut."

I nodded, understanding now why he was constantly drilling *'when in doubt, don't paddle out'* into my head.

"There was a storm brewing, so the waves were more unpredictable than they usually were, but we figured we would just go out for a few hours and then come back in before the storm fully rolled in."

This reckless version of the overly cautious man I knew felt like a completely different person to me. The Riddick I knew would never let me put a toe in the water if there was a storm brewing. He would have my ass... literally.

As if he could see where my mind had gone, he gave me a small smirk, tracing one of my eyebrows with his thumb and making me shiver.

"I was... a cocky little bastard." He chuckled. "Much like someone else I know."

I grinned at him, curling my toes slightly in response to his gentle touch.

"I guess that's why Jet says I remind him of you. I always thought that was kind of strange, considering you're always so grumpy, and I'm *hilarious.*"

Riddick chuckled softly and shook his head. "Yeah, well. Nothing more humbling than drowning to death." The smile slipped off both our faces and my gut churned uncomfortably.

"So what happened?" I whispered, and he sighed.

"Everything that could possibly go wrong did. I paddled out, trying to catch a solid thirty-footer, but the peak shifted at the last minute, and I was forced to take the second wave that rolled in.

"The next wave came out of nowhere. It was at least seventy feet, and I was close enough to the break line that I was worried it would collapse on top of me if I didn't ride it.

"So, I took a chance... and it was the wrong choice. The wave broke early, and in an effort to not fall to my death, I did my best to stay ahead of it. I was so focused on not wiping out that I didn't realize I was heading straight for the death zone."

I gasped, and he gave me a haunted look.

"I got caught in a double wave hold down, and my board ended up lodged between two rocks. I couldn't even get to the surface because the quick release failed on my tether."

"Fuck..." I breathed. "That feels... cosmically unfair."

He shrugged. "I guess it was my time. The ocean wanted my life, and there was no escaping it. But even now, I panic a little whenever my tether pulls after a wipeout. That's partially why I was so pissed at you that first day when you dropped in on my wave. I was a little triggered after my tether pulled me up."

Guilt rushed through me, and I cupped his face and brushed my lips across his.

"I'm sorry, baby," I whispered, and he let out a soft sigh, wrapping his arms around my waist and pulling me in close.

He buried his face in my neck.

"It's okay. You didn't know," he murmured against me, his breath tickling the sensitive skin under my jaw.

He took a deep inhale as if just the scent of my skin comforted him, and I dropped a kiss on the top of his head.

"I love you, Jake Whittling," I whispered, and he shuddered and kissed me again, just below the ear. I'd noticed that whenever I called him by his real name, he had this deep, visceral reaction to it. I resolved at that moment to do it more often.

"I love you too, Finn Summers." He hummed, and I drifted off, wrapped around the man who'd lost everything but somehow managed to still give me so much.

CHAPTER
Forty-Four

Finn

I saw my first eighty-foot wave on December 28th, 2024.

Flanked by both Makoa and Jake, I watched the Leviathan rise over the horizon like a hulking demon. Its pipe was a great, dark maw, looking to swallow the lives of any surfer foolish enough to try and tame it.

Even Jet's face was grave, his easy half-cocked grin nowhere in sight. I was the only one practically vibrating with excitement.

It was finally time.

I'd worked toward this. I'd been *waiting,* and I was *not* a patient man.

Jet cut me a dark look, his lips pursing as he took in my inability to contain my excitement. My entire body was *humming* with adrenaline as I watched monster after monster continue to roll onto the beach.

"Easy, surf star," he said softly. "Let's not rush into anything."

Jake grunted his agreement just as I whined in protest.

"What do you mean *rush* into anything? This is what I've been training for!"

Jet chuckled, shaking his head, and Jake scowled at me.

"Tomorrow looks like it's gonna be better conditions. Also, I have Kai renting a Jet Ski, so we have a better chance of saving your ass if anything goes wrong."

Jake looked like he might kiss Jet on the mouth, and an unwarranted spike of jealousy coursed through me at the thought.

It was stupid to be jealous. Jet couldn't even see him... but still. I didn't want my man looking at anyone but *me* like he might kiss them, even if the kisses were because Jet was trying to keep me safe... which was pretty much Jake's biggest turn-on.

Safe Finn = Jake boner.

No fake.

"––Turtle here, anyway?"

"What?" I asked, realizing I hadn't heard anything Jet had just said. I'd been too busy thinking about Jake's kisses and safety boners.

Jet chuckled, cuffing my shoulder affectionately.

"What's going on in that head of yours? You're always off on some crazy brain adventure."

I grinned at him, shrugging. "You don't wanna know."

Jet laughed and nodded. "Probably not. Anyway, I was just saying, don't you want Turtle here anyway? I'm sure he's gonna want to be around to watch you ride your first true Leviathan."

My toes curled in my slides at that, and I grinned, nodding.

"Yeah, you're right.

I needed the Turtle Man with me. I could wait one more day.

"Great." Makoa smiled. "Let's hit up the cove for now. You can brush up on your basics. A solid active-rest day is just what you need before your big debut."

"He's right," Jake whispered in my ear, causing me to shiver. "You're getting a little lax on your foot placement."

Makoa had his back to us as we made our way back to the shack, so I was safe to give Riddick the eye-roll he deserved.

"You're such a helicopter mom." I smirked, and he huffed a laugh, his blue eyes shining with mirth.

"You know it, shark bait." He chuckled, slapping my ass hard enough that I jumped and giggled.

Jet glanced back at me, that smile tugging at the corner of his lips.

"What's so funny back there?"

I grinned at him, shrugging. "Nothing. Just more brain adventures."

Jet laughed, shaking his head.

"Crazy fuckin' kid."

CHAPTER
Forty-Five

Finn

"**T**ODAY'S THE DAY!!!!!!" I bleated the second my eyes opened. I launched myself out of bed, and Jake groaned next to me, burying his head in our pillows as I ran through the shack, beaming so big I could have drowned a man in the depths of my dimples. "The sun is shining! The tank is cleaaaaannnnn!"

I sang as I dug through the cupboards for a frying pan, just as Makoa walked in with Kai and Turtle on his heels.

Jet faked a gasp. "GAH! The tank is clean!"

Turtle and I cracked up at Jet finishing my Finding Nemo reference while Kai and Riddick groaned.

Riddick was just coming out of our room in his boxers. He ran a hand down his face as if my antics were giving him a big Finn-shaped headache.

"Are you always this annoying?" Kai grumbled, helping himself to a seat at the table as I enthusiastically cracked some eggs into a mixing bowl.

"Yes," Riddick answered for me as he flopped down on the couch in the living room.

"Finn's an acquired taste," Turtle winked at Kai.

"And if you don't like me, you should acquire some taste!" I chimed.

"HA!" Turtle and Makoa both laughed along with me while Kai and Riddick rolled their eyes at how cheesy I was being.

I couldn't help it.

My entire body was vibrating with excitement. I was short of breath, and my mind was *racing*. All I could do was think about what the world would look like beneath my feet as I surfed an eighty-foot Leviathan.

"I would ask if you're ready, surf star, but that feels like a stupid question," Jet said, sitting down next to Kai while Turtle came to help me with breakfast.

"I feel like I was *born* ready!" I beamed, and Jet smiled back, though there was a bit of concern in his warm brown eyes.

"No doubt," he said softly. I glanced over to find him, Jake, and Kai all staring at me with varying levels of worry on their faces.

I'd gotten to know Kai a little bit over the last few weeks while surfing with Jet. He really was a decent dude; he was just several shades grumpier than even Riddick had been when I'd first met him. I had a feeling it had to do with the fact that he'd been the one to push everyone to surf the day Jake had drowned.

I imagined the guilt Kai felt was enormous. To make up for it, he felt especially responsible for making sure Leviathans didn't take any more lives. So, much like Jake, Kai's grumpiness came from a good place.

He was worried about me.

The fact that he'd rented a Jet Ski so he could save my crazy ass if I wiped out was proof enough of that.

He knew he couldn't stop me from doing it, so he was going to try to keep me safe while I went against everyone's advice and did it anyway.

I was grateful.

But I was also so excited that I felt like I might explode. So, I ignored the giant elephant in the room and whipped out a spatula.

"How does everyone like their eggs?"

MAKOA HAD BEEN RIGHT. CONDITIONS WERE FUCKING *PERFECT.*

The sun was out, so it was even warmer than normal, and after watching the waves for a solid twenty minutes, they seemed to be as reliable and steady as I could hope for on a beach like Leviathans.

"Alright. I'm going in," I finally announced, and Turtle grinned, slapping me on the back enthusiastically.

"Hell ya! You got this, Finn Man!" he cheered, and I smiled at him.

"Thanks, Turtle, catch you on the flip!" I winked and made my way toward the water.

Kai was already dragging the Jet Ski in, and Makoa and Jake followed me into the shallows.

My board was freshly waxed because, of course, Riddick had made sure to take care of that the night before.

When he'd finished waxing my board, he'd crawled into bed and spent the entire night worshipping me. He took his time, bringing me to orgasm over and over, all while telling me how proud he was of me... How he believed in me and how much he knew I was going to crush it today.

I shivered as I remembered how many times he'd made me come.

Did you know if you make a dude come enough times in a row, their balls literally start to *hurt?* I was almost worried I wouldn't get to sleep 'cause Jake had sucked and fucked me so dry I was in literal pain.

Happily, that's what sleep aids are for, and I was feeling well rested, sated, and ready to fuck up some watery hell demons.

I paddled out, Makoa on my left with his sunshine yellow shortboard and Jake on my right with the teal board he'd been riding the day he died. I was the bright pink filling in this surf legend sandwich, and I'd never felt more supported in my life.

Once the three of us were out far enough that we could easily paddle in, I sat up on my board and took in my surroundings. The peaks were always unpredictable here, but right now, they were more stable than I'd seen them in a while.

Kai was bobbing on the Jet Ski a few hundred feet away, watching us like a hawk. Back on the beach, I noticed Turtle had been joined by a few more people. They were far enough away that I couldn't make them all out.

"Did someone tell the Finnatics about today?" I asked Jet, shocked that anyone would let it slip.

Jet shot me a strange look and nodded.

"Yeah, I did. Figured you could use a bit of extra support."

"But… what about not sensationalizing this beach?" I asked, totally surprised.

He shrugged, running his hand through his wet, dark hair.

"What you're doing here… as much as it scares me shitless… Well, I think it's worth something. You worked hard for this day, Finn. You deserve to be recognized for everything you've done to get here. When you conquer this beach, you deserve credit. Just… promise me you're going to show these people that you're the stuff legends are made of and survive this."

I swallowed, my throat suddenly feeling tight.

"I *am* going to survive this," I vowed, my voice coming out raspy.

Makoa met my gaze head-on, and he smiled, nodding.

"Yeah. You fucking *are.* Now, get out there and shred one of these beasts to pieces. Prove to everyone that you're Finn Summers, the Leviathan Tamer."

I glanced over at Riddick and found him watching me with a determined look on his face. He gave me one slow nod.

"He's right, shark bait. If anyone can do this, it's you."

My eyes welled with tears, and for a moment, I wished I was alone with him so I could kiss him before I paddled out.

I cleared my throat and directed my question at Jet, but made sure Jake would know I was talking to him.

"You're gonna be watching?"

I didn't even hear Makoa's response as Jake reached out and brushed his fingers across my chin, his thumb grazing my bottom lip tenderly.

"I'm always watching you, baby," he murmured, and I nodded before setting my sights on the horizon and paddling out to face the monsters that had killed the man I loved.

CHAPTER

Forty-Six

Finn

Alexa Play: Numb by Holly McNarland

The tension and pull of the water beneath my board were reminiscent of a great-scaled beast coiling itself in preparation for battle.

The energy of the building wave was humming through the air and sparking across my skin. I could *feel* the call of the water as it gathered in a great, rushing siphon of devastation.

Allowing myself to be pulled into the frothing mouth of the watery demon, I shuddered with anticipation.

It was *hungry*.

It needed *more*. More salt, more energy, more *lives* to sustain it as it grew and grew at an impossible rate.

A flicker of something other than excitement ignited in my chest as I turned my board, relying on muscle memory to position me in such a way that I knew the water would pick me up and take me for the ride of my life.

As I rose with the swell, I examined the strange feeling, curious as to what emotion this monster had stirred up in me.

Was it fear? Was this what fear felt like?

No.

It was anger.

I was startled, shocked at the strangeness of feeling angry with the ocean.

My muscles bunched instinctively as the surface pulled away from me at an alarming rate.

I was bracing myself against my board, and before I knew it, my feet were planted, and I was upright.

Adrenaline and rage roared through me with as much power as the enormous wall of water that continued to grow at my back.

I was suddenly so high up that Jake and Makoa were mere dots beneath me. It was like time stopped for a long, pregnant moment, and everything froze.

The wave hesitated as I addressed it.

"You killed him," I whispered to the ocean as if it could hear me. Time rippled, and suddenly, the anger I was feeling made sense.

The water—this thing that I *loved*—had also taken something so huge from me that I could barely understand the magnitude of the loss.

Jake and I would never be able to get married or grow old together. We could never go to Australia and check out the surf scene there. We couldn't travel across the states to visit all the different beaches.

We would never ride in surf competitions together. He would never be able to come with me to cheer me on if I ever made it to the Olympics.

Jake would always have to stay here until one day, whatever it was that kept him here, decided it was time for him to go, and he would fade away.

My pink board cut through the water with the force of a blade as I fell back into position, my eyes narrowing with determination.

"I'm gonna fuck you *up*," I spat at the wave, and I could have sworn the ocean laughed at me as I tore horizontally across the now nearly vertical incline of water that was trying to eat me alive.

I was eighty feet in the air. So much adrenaline was pumping through me that I was sure I wasn't breathing.

The second I realized I wasn't, I focused on my breath, remembering what Jake had taught me all those weeks ago.

'The most important thing you can do on this Earth is breathe.'

Inhale.

Carve.

Slice.

The beast roared as it began to close its mighty jaws.

'Breathing properly means you're present.'

Exhale.

Cut.

Slash.

The wave crested, and it began to break behind me. I leaned forward, training my gaze on the end zone, instinctively finding myself a safe place to land.

'Breathing means you're locked in. Focused.'

I was. I was so fucking locked in...

The thunder and crash of the water behind me sent a thrill up my spine. The demon screeched as it cannibalized itself, urging me to press forward even more. I willed my board to go faster, cut deeper.

To make this bitch *bleed.*

I tore out the end of the pipe, catching literal air as I exited the wave. Skipping expertly across the surface of the ocean, I whooped as I landed *exactly* where I had planned.

The momentum of my exit took me halfway to shore and safety. I chanced a glance over my shoulder to relish in the collapse of the Leviathan I had just slain.

I was smiling from ear to ear, my heart racing so fast I was sure that the screaming and cheering crowd on the beach could hear each thump.

But it wasn't them I cared about.

All I cared about were the blue eyes that watched me as I sped toward shore, those full lips that curled into a smile, and the pure look of pride Jake was giving me as I flattened myself on my board so I could paddle toward him.

With each stroke, his voice rang through my mind, and my eyes filled with tears as I made my way home.

'Breathing, Finn, means that you're alive.'

CHAPTER
Forty-Seven

Finn

was swarmed by a crowd of people once I made it to the beach. Turtle launched himself at me with the biggest smile I'd ever seen painted across his face.

"Finn Man! That was gnarly *as fuck, dude!* You didn't just surf that wave; you *slaughtered* it!"

I beamed at him as hands grabbed at me from all sides. The Finnatics were going absolutely bonkers.

Quinn was suddenly with us, jumping up and down with excitement, and Blake appeared too, her blue eyes glistening with tears.

"I can't believe you did it!" Blake cried, pulling me away from Turtle into a big hug. "I'm so sorry I doubted you. That was incredible, Finn!"

Turtle spun around and addressed the crowd, still smiling so big he could have melted someone with how bright his grin was.

"Yo! Three cheers for Finn, the *Leviathan Slayer!*"

Oh my god. My face went beet red as the crowd lost their shit.

Finn! Finn! Finn! Finn!

Makoa and Kai were approaching as I did my best to scoot away from the mob of surf fans, my cheeks so hot they were competing with the glare of the sun.

"Way to go, surf star." Jet clapped me affectionately on the shoulder, and even Kai gave me a small smile.

"Killed it, kid," Kai grunted, his dark eyes shining with approval.

"When you're done celebrating with your fans, come over here. There's someone I want you to meet," Jet hummed close to my ear, and I raised an eyebrow at him.

"Oh yeah?"

He nodded. "Yeah, man. I'm gonna help Kai load up the Jet Ski; come find me after."

I nodded and turned back to the rabid crowd of people still cheering my name.

Kids were literally pushing papers up to me, asking for my autograph, and I felt so flattered and awkward that my face flushed red again.

Jake appeared at my side, and he pressed a soft kiss to my temple and rested a casual hand on my hip.

"You did amazing, baby," he hummed, brushing his thumb over my hip bone as I signed autographs like some sort of celebrity. "I'm *so* proud of you."

I shot him a pleased look, and he smiled at me in a carefree way I'd never seen on his face before. The tightness around his eyes had disappeared, and he looked so much younger. I could see the version of him that Jet had told me about. The laid-back, easygoing version of Jake that had died the day he'd drowned. My heart squeezed in my chest at how much happier he seemed now that I'd successfully conquered Leviathans, and I felt a small twinge of guilt in my chest for how much he must have been worried about me.

"You're gonna make me choke up in front of all these people, babe," I murmured, doing my best not to let the crowd see I was talking to thin air.

He chuckled warmly and leaned in, nipping my earlobe gently, causing me to shiver.

"I'll see you at home. We can celebrate in private when you're done with your fans." He winked before sauntering off toward the cliff face that led back to our shack.

Once the excitement had died down, I made my way over to Jet and Kai, who had been busy winching the Jet Ski onto a trailer Jet had attached to his new truck.

They'd decided to extend their stay to help me train, and Jet had leased the pickup a few days prior after Blake had given him shit for always wanting to borrow her car.

I smiled as I approached, noticing that they weren't alone.

Standing with them was a woman dressed in simple but obviously expensive athleisure.

Jet beamed at me as I approached.

"There he is." He glanced at the woman, who turned to greet me.

She was tanned with blonde hair slicked back in a no-nonsense bun. The clipboard she was clutching had a logo for *Goliath Energy Drinks'* on it.

She gave me a smile and held out her hand.

"Ah, you must be Finn Summers. That was an impressive ride."

I smiled back and shook her hand politely, sending Jet a curious look. He was smiling at me with this strangely excited twinkle in his eye.

"Finn, this is Sylvia Knott. She's a sponsorship recruiter for Goliath."

My brain was whirling as I put the puzzle pieces together.

Goliath was known for sponsoring extreme sports athletes. It was their entire marketing strategy. The fact that a rep from the brand was here, talking to me, meant that... I was being *scouted?*

Sylvia smiled at Jet, nodding.

"Jet informed me that he had some promising new talent and that I wouldn't want to miss your run today. As usual, he was right."

Jet winked at her. "I'm always right, sweetheart."

She chuckled. "That you are."

She turned to face me, "Anyway, Jet's timing was also impeccable. I was in town for Taming Leviathans. We were representing Mike Gurallo for the competition, but he's recently suffered a minor injury, and his sports therapist has advised him to sit this one out."

My eyes widened.

"*The* Mike Gurallo?" I glanced around the beach to make sure he wasn't there. If surf god Mike Gurallo was here, I was going to shit my pants.

She laughed again. "The one and only."

"Oh my *god!* I watch him all the time on Goliath TV! He's a fucking *legend!*"

She nodded. "Yes... Well. Anyway, we were going to cut our losses and pull out, but then Jet messaged me. After watching you surf, I was wondering if you would be willing to discuss signing onto the Goliath team on a trial basis."

It took a minute for my brain to catch up to what she had just said.

"Wait... *what?*"

"Do you currently have representation?" she asked, frowning.

"He doesn't." Jet answered for me since, for the first time in my life, I couldn't seem to get my mouth to make words.

She beamed.

"*Wonderful!* So, what do you think? I know this offer is sudden, but we would rather not pull out on such short notice. I can have a contract sent over to you by the end of the day for review."

"Hold up, hold up... you... as in *Goliath Energy Drinks,* want to sponsor *me* Finn Summers... this weekend?"

"Yes. And maybe for longer, depending on how things work out during the trial period."

Again.

Mouth…words… broken…

Jet jumped in and clapped Sylvia on the shoulder, grinning at me with that sly, wicked smirk on his face.

"Send over the contract, Sylv. I'll look it over with him, and we'll get back to you."

"Great," Sylvia quipped, her eyes no doubt twinkling at the fact that my jaw was literally in the sand.

"Looking forward to hearing back from you, Finn. Jet, Kai… always nice to see you both." Then, she walked away, the wind whipping against her four hundred-dollar windbreaker as she went.

"Well, kid. Guess you really *are* a surf star, after all." Jet beamed at me, and I launched myself at him, whooping like a madman.

"Holy fuck! What the shiz! Did that really happen?"

He was laughing, and even Kai had a smile on his face.

"Yeah, surf star. That really happened. Hope you didn't love bussing tables. Looks like your Sharkies career might be over," he said, rubbing his knuckles into my hair affectionately.

"Congrats, kid," Kai huffed, and I beamed at him.

I couldn't *wait* to tell Jake.

CHAPTER
Forty-Eight

Alexa Play: everything i wanted by Billie Eilish

'd grilled up a steak for Finn while he was celebrating with his friends on the beach.

He did it.

It was over...

He'd survived.

It felt like a rhino had been sitting on my chest since he'd first told me he planned on surfing that beach. When he'd successfully shredded that massive wave and made it to the shore in one piece, I finally felt the enormous, lumbering thing get off and wander into the distance.

Setting the table for my man, I sat down and waited for him to come home. He busted into the shack, predictably full of excitement and energy, and I grinned at him.

"Hey, baby... you hungry?" I asked, and he launched himself at me, straddling me in the chair and showering my face with kisses.

I laughed and wrapped my arms around him, not caring that he was still in his cold, damp wetsuit.

"You'll never believe what happened!" he chirped, and I leaned back, taking in his megawatt smile and adorable dimples.

"What? What happened?" I asked, unable to keep myself from grinning. When he was like this, his energy was infectious. It was almost impossible not to feel excited when he was this pumped about something.

"Jet told this lady from Goliath Energy Drinks that I was riding today, and she wants to *sponsor me* in Tully's surf competition this weekend!"

The smile dropped right off my face.

"What?"

"I'm serious! She's sending the contract over tonight! Wait... why don't you look excited?" He pulled back, frowning at me. I watched his dimples disappear, and I hated myself for being the reason they went away.

I took a moment to sort through the war of emotions that were exploding through my chest.

On the one hand, *Goliath Energy Drinks* was *huge.* Like, *massive.* It was every surfer's dream to be picked up for a sponsorship with them. It was pretty much a career-launching opportunity for Finn.

It was a dream come true for someone like him. I knew because it would have been a dream come true for me when I was his age.

But, on the other hand, the idea of him surfing Leviathans again – so soon after he'd *just* recently survived it – made that asshole rhino come lumbering right back to sit on my chest again.

"I'm excited," I forced myself to choke out. I reached up and cupped his perfect face, running my thumb over his jawline.

He was so amped I could see his pulse jumping in his throat.

Thump. Alive. *Thump.* Breathing. *Thump.* Not. *Fucking.* Dead.

"Really? You seem upset."

"No, baby. I'm not, this is... you deserve this. They're so lucky to have you."

His frown deepened. "I'm not buying it, buddy. Spill. What's grumpifying you?"

I dropped my hands to his hips and tugged him more firmly against me, enjoying the weight of him sitting in my lap.

Resting my forehead on his clavicle, I sighed.

"I'm never going to get a chance to stop worrying about you, am I, baby? Goliath is amazing. I just wish they were sponsoring you for another competition. Literally *any* other competition."

"Oh..." There was a pause, and then he wrapped his arms around my shoulders and kissed the side of my head. "I see."

"I just... I know this is who you are. I know you're not capable of feeling fear. But Finn... *I* can feel fear. All I've felt is fear since I met you."

"Jake..." His voice was strained, and he kissed the side of my head again, nuzzling his nose into my hair just above my ear.

"I don't want you to get hurt," I whispered.

"I won't, baby. Didn't I prove to you today that I could handle it?"

Pulling back, I looked up at his adorably concerned face and rubbed my thumbs across his hip bones.

I wanted to tell him that he did great, but I'd surfed waves just like the one he shredded today dozens of times before it finally killed me.

I wanted to tell him that I believed in him, and I was happy for him, and I loved him so much that when I looked at him, it physically *hurt* me to imagine a world without him in it.

I wanted to tell him that I knew what it felt like to always be chasing the next adrenaline high, but nothing, not even a sponsorship deal with one of the biggest energy drink brands in the world, was worth his *life.*

I wanted to tell him all of this, but it wouldn't change his mind.

Saying these things wouldn't make him reconsider.

They would make *me* feel better, but they would hurt him and make him feel like I wasn't supportive of his dreams or proud of his success.

So, instead, I leaned forward and skated my lips against his, breathing in his intoxicating scent.

"I love you so much," I murmured against him, pressing a soft kiss on his lower lip. He rocked in my lap, and I felt him grow hard as my grip tightened on his hips.

"I love you too," he breathed, and I swallowed that breath, savoring it like the precious thing it was.

I stood up, taking him with me, and pressed kiss after kiss against his lips. He wrapped his legs around my waist and traced his tongue over my mouth as I took him to our bedroom.

I didn't want to ruin this moment for him, so I kept all my worries and my thoughts to myself, burying them deep inside my chest and locking them away.

The only way I was going to be able to make it through this was by losing myself in him.

So, when I laid him down in our bed, and he looked up at me with that trusting, dimpled smile that made my dead heart melt, I let go.

This was his choice, and I was going to support him no matter what he chose to do.

Even if it killed the one person I loved more than anything this godforsaken planet had to offer.

CHAPTER
Forty-Nine

Riddick

Alexa Play: Heal by Tom Odell

"Baby, you made me dinner, and it's going to get cold." Finn hummed against my lips as I crawled on top of him. He was already unzipping his wetsuit and slipping out of it, returning my kisses with enthusiasm.

"We can stop if you're hungry," I murmured, biting his pouty lips as I helped him peel his suit over his ass.

"I'm hungry for something else; I just feel bad you went through all that work to make me a steak…"

"Fuck the steak," I rumbled, pulling back so I could admire his naked body sprawled out beneath me.

He was hard and smooth all over. His beautiful skin stretched tight over the taught muscles that sculpted his perfect form.

I would never get sick of looking at him.

I just wanted to worship him. I wanted to kiss and suck every inch of him and relish the fact that he was here, breathing beneath me.

I sat up and pulled my shirt off before reaching for him again. With flat palms and gentle fingers, I began to slowly map his body with my touch.

He quivered beneath me as I ran my hands over him.

First, I cupped his face, stroking my thumbs over his cheekbones reverently.

"Look at this beautiful face…" I whispered, leaning forward to kiss each of his dimples, enjoying the way he shivered in response.

Next, I slid my fingers down the contours of his neck, brushing his Adam's apple and watching it bob as he swallowed.

I kissed him there too, savoring the small sound he made as my lips grazed the hollow of his throat.

"Jake…"

My heart soared as my name rolled off his lips. They were swollen and wet from all the times I had kissed and nipped them.

"I love it when you say my name."

I sat back again, tracing my hands delicately over his smooth chest, pausing to swirl my fingers around his peaked nipples. The tiny tips of them were firm and taut beneath my fingers, and I spent some time toying with them until his breathing grew choppy.

"Jake, you're *teasing* me…" he groaned, and I smiled, intentionally brushing my fingers over the hardened buds, knowing that my ministrations had likely made them ultra-sensitive.

"Let me take my time with you."

Slowly, I traced my fingertips down his torso, wrapping my hands around his ribs and drinking up the way his abs contracted in response to the graze of my thumbs.

His cock was hard and lying flat against his stomach, and I intentionally avoided it as I continued my path downward.

His skin was hot and flushed now, and he was panting slightly.

"Jake..." he whined as I stroked his abdomen gently on either side of his cock. I watched as his dick surged and flexed as if desperately trying to entice me to touch it.

"I was thinking we could try something new today... but only if you want to," I said, staring directly at his glossy, pink tip. A tiny, glistening bead of moisture had formed on his slit, and I licked my lips.

"What do you want to try?" he asked. His voice was soft and deep, though there was an underlying tone of curiosity there that made my heart flutter with anticipation.

"I thought maybe we could... switch roles."

I met his gaze, gauging his reaction. I don't know why I expected him to laugh or make light of it, but he didn't. He was looking at me with something close to reverence on his face.

"I didn't think that would be something you would want," he whispered, reaching out to brush his fingers against my cheek. I nodded, biting my lip.

"Normally, I don't," I admitted, rubbing my thumbs over his hip bones and watching his dick surge against his abdomen again. That tiny bead of pre-cum grew and dribbled against his tight stomach.

"But I want... I want to experience everything with you, baby," I said, my voice cracking slightly.

If anything were to ever happen to you, I don't want to have any regrets.

The words I couldn't say out loud hung heavy between us, and he swallowed.

We stared at each other for a long moment, and I felt like I was drowning on dry land. My eyes pricked, and his filled with a sense of understanding.

"Nothing's going to happen to me, Jake."

How he knew where my head was at, I'll never know, but he did. He always did.

I swallowed, clearing my throat and forcing myself to smile at him.

I leaned forward and kissed him gently.

"I know that, baby," I lied. "I just want to know what it's like to feel you inside me. Even if we just do it once."

Finn cupped my cheeks and kissed me back, his warm tongue soft and pliant against mine as I sipped from his mouth, greedily accepting the comfort he was offering me.

"We don't have to if you don't want to," I rumbled between kisses.

"Of course I want to." His words were little promises, dusting over my mouth like a gentle sprinkle of confetti.

I sighed in relief, pressing my forehead against his.

"Thank you," I breathed, and he traced my cheekbone with his fingertip.

"Don't thank me. I'm so... I don't know. It means a lot to me that you want to do this with me. Have you ever bottomed before?"

I chuckled and shook my head. "No. There's never been anyone I've wanted to do it with."

Finn looked absolutely shocked, and then his features softened into something so tender and precious that I could have wept from the intense feeling of adoration that welled in my chest.

"So... in a way, we'll be each other's firsts?"

I nodded, kissing his warm cheek right above one of his adorable little dimples.

"Yeah, sweet boy. You'll be my first."

CHAPTER

Fifty

Finn

Alexa Play: Anchor by Novo Amor

My feelings for Jake were already so strong that sometimes they overwhelmed me. The fact that he was trusting me with something like this felt like such a huge honor. I was so full of emotion that I was shaking.

He noticed immediately and buried his face in my neck. Gently, he nipped and sucked, his breath puffing just below my ear, making my toes curl.

"You're shaking," he murmured, and I nodded, swallowing hard in an attempt to push back the strange buzzing sensation that was curling in my gut.

"This feels... huge," I whispered, and he nodded, leaving one more kiss on my jaw.

"Like I said, we don't have to..."

"I want to," I said firmly, and he smiled at me as I pressed a hand gently against his sternum. His chest hair was somehow both coarse and soft at the same time, and I rubbed my lips over his collarbone as I gently pressed him off me and onto the bed.

He allowed me to guide him, leaning back on his elbows as I switched our positions. My fingers were shaking as I hooked them into the waistband of his shorts, sliding them down his hips to expose his perfect, hard cock.

My mouth flooded with saliva at the sight of it, and my breath caught in my throat. I didn't think I would ever get used to seeing him fully naked.

He was perfect.

The blueprint.

He was the type of man that I was sure an artist would die to paint.

I wasn't an artist.

Not even close.

But even I could see he was beautiful.

Everything about him was masculine, rough, and rugged, but when I met his gaze, there was a softness there. He was looking at me in a way no one else ever had, and I felt my eyes prick with tears as the room seemed to shrink around us.

It was just me and him in the world, and the very air itself was buzzing with anticipation.

I grabbed the lube off the end table and placed it on the bed beside us before positioning myself between his strong legs.

"Finn..." His voice was like gravel, and it sounded like he was speaking around something hard in his throat. "You okay, baby?"

I looked up at him from between his legs, knowing that my eyes were probably full of tears, and I nodded.

"Yeah... just... feeling a lot," I grunted, leaning forward to kiss down his stomach. The hair here was even softer than the hair on his chest. His cock surged between us as I gently licked and sucked a path down his happy trail.

I paused to leave gentle kisses down his shaft, reveling in the soft groan of pleasure he let out as I ran my tongue over every ridge and vein.

"*Fuck*, baby... that mouth of yours..."

I nibbled around the base of his cock before gently sucking his sac into my mouth. He jerked beneath me, fisting his hands at his sides and rolling his hips as I pulsed him gently.

The deep tremor in my bones hadn't subsided, and when I nestled between his legs, guiding his muscular thighs up, I could barely get my breathing under control.

I'd never seen him spread out like this before, and I hooked my thumbs in his crease, gently spreading him open to expose his hole to me.

"Finn..." he groaned as I brought my mouth closer. The sight of his hole flexing and tightening was so erotic I felt a deep pulse in my balls just from looking at him.

"Has anyone ever kissed you here before?" I asked, marveling at how I could literally see his body react to my breath as I spoke.

He shook his head and swallowed loudly. "No, baby. Just you."

That was all I needed to close the distance. I gently licked him, and my eyes rolled back into my head as the muscle contracted against my tongue.

"*Fuck, Finn...*" *he* groaned, and I licked him again, slowly tracing a lazy circle around the perimeter of his rim.

Now, *he* was shaking. His muscular legs quivered on either side of my head as I flattened my tongue to massage him more thoroughly.

"Yes, baby...just like that— Fuck..."

Even while bottoming, he knew just how to praise me, and his words drove me to gently wiggle and work my tongue inside him.

He gasped, and the tight ring of muscle clenched around my tongue as I penetrated him, his hands suddenly fisting my hair and holding me tighter to his hips.

I kissed and sucked and licked, sliding my tongue in and out of him as he slowly softened to let me in deeper.

Soon, my entire world narrowed down to Jake and the sounds he made as I pleasured him with my mouth. Nothing else existed but the taste of him and the breathy moans he made as I kissed him.

Pulling back, I looked up to find him staring down at me, completely blissed out.

"Baby... you're fucking amazing..." he breathed, and I placed a gentle kiss on his cock before reaching for the lube.

"*You're* amazing..." I whispered as I coated my fingers before reaching back between his legs.

Starting with one, I teased his rim again gently before slowly easing into him. His heat swallowed my finger, and he groaned loudly, his cock thickening even more and rising up off his abdomen as I stroked him.

I stared in awe at where my finger had disappeared into the man I loved, and my eyes welled again.

I couldn't believe he was letting me do this to him. I hadn't even thought to ask. This felt so *intimate.* He was giving me a part of him that he'd never given anyone before, and that alone was enough to make my chest feel tight.

Giving my finger an experimental wiggle, my heart skipped a beat as he rolled his hips into me, urging me to press deeper. I grazed what felt like a firm bundle of nerves, and he barked out a shout of pleasure, his hand reaching for my hair again.

"Oh fuck..." he rasped, his eyes rolling back into his head. "There... *fuuuck....* that's..."

My heart was slamming against my ribs as he writhed beneath me. I was hot and cold all at the same time. His reactions were so open and *visceral.*

I was making him do that.

I was the reason he was so out of control and lost in ecstasy.

Me...

Licking my lips, I allowed him to grip my head as I methodically worked my finger in and out of him, curling gently to touch that firm bundle each time I penetrated him.

Carefully, I added another finger, slowly opening him for me and internally working myself up to what came next.

He was such a *man*, and seeing him speared onto my fingers was such a powerful sight that I could barely breathe. My cheeks were flushed, and I cleared my throat, glancing up at his face again hesitantly.

"Do you think you're ready for more?" I whispered softly, and he nodded, rocking his hips urgently into my hand.

"Fuck, yes, Finn. I need you, baby. Put your cock inside me." Listening to someone so dominant and authoritative basically *begging* for me to take him was what caused me to lose the ongoing battle I'd been having with my emotions.

A hot tear slid down my cheek, and I smiled, nodding.

"Alright, just give me a minute."

I reached for the lube with trembling fingers and coated my cock. He watched me with heavy-lidded eyes, his feelings for me painted on each line of his face.

With shaking legs, I positioned myself over him the way he'd done to me countless times before.

I pressed my cockhead against his soft, prepped hole and met his gaze.

We stared at each other as I slid my tip firmly against him, absorbing the way the tension released from his body as he relaxed himself for me.

He said my name, and my muscles quivered as I pressed forward, both of us letting out choked moans as his wet heat finally enveloped my tip.

The scorching pressure of his ass squeezed my cock as he bared down, and I swallowed hard, sinking into him as slowly as I could.

"Jesus Christ, Finn... baby... that's..."

"It's *so good...*" I whined as inch after inch of my cock disappeared inside him.

"Kiss me," he begged as I bottomed out. I didn't hesitate to lean over his chest to do as he asked.

His hot tongue lapped at mine, and we moaned into each other's mouths as I ground my hips into him.

I bumped something inside him that made him writhe and curse beneath me, his hands finding my ass cheeks and driving me deeper into him.

"Move, I need you to move," he hissed, each word spoken directly into my mouth.

I nodded, unable to respond as he was now aggressively sucking on my tongue.

I flicked my hips, and the sensation of his scorching channel sliding against my cock made my eyes roll back.

"Need...to...fuck you..." I gasped, and he squeezed my ass harder, his fingers likely leaving deep bruises with the strength of his grip.

"Yes... do it. Fuck me. Go hard." His words were broken and disjointed, each one carried out through a desperate gasp. One of his hands slid into my crack, and he worked himself into my ass as I fucked into him, causing me to cry out in surprise.

"Need to...touch you," he groaned as he pressed his fingers inside me. They slid in and out with each thrust of my hips, and my already fractured mind grew even more dizzy.

My body was moving without my permission. I gripped his shoulders and slammed into him *hard*, the bed hitting the wall with the force of the thrust.

"Fuck yes, Finn... so good. That feels so *fucking good.*"

In and out, in and out.

I was shattering, my mind melting with the twisting whirlwind of sensation blending with emotion.

"Gonna... come..." I hissed as I continued to drive into him. He rose up to meet me, urging me into him harder with the vice grip he had on my ass.

"Do it. I want to feel you come inside me," he growled in my ear, and the raw, broken need in his voice sent me over the edge.

"Jake! *Fuck!*" I screamed his name as I erupted, and he stroked my prostate with the hand that was still buried inside me, milking my orgasm out as I came.

"That's it, Finn… fill me up." He bit my earlobe and sucked on it as I finished.

I whimpered and sobbed, my body going limp and weak as my strength left me with my orgasm.

"Good, Finn… You did so good, baby," he murmured before rolling me off him onto my stomach.

"Jake… what…"

I felt lube dribble across my bare ass cheeks, and he roughly stuffed it into my already well-prepped hole.

"Need to fuck you," he grunted, and I whined, arching to give him better access as he lined himself up with my ass.

He shoved himself inside me, and I screamed as he pegged my already sensitive prostate.

He let out a deep, rumbly moan as he sank all the way into the hilt, stretching me so much I felt like I might split in two.

"So good, Finn, baby, you take my cock so well…" He was gritting each word out through clenched teeth as he rammed in and out of me. Faster and faster he went until I felt him swell and start to spasm. He snarled as he came inside me, his voice splintering through the thick air of the room. I clenched intentionally, squeezing the cum out of him as his cock throbbed so violently I could feel each pulse.

"Good boy… Good boy, Finn…" he repeated, over and over, as his thrusts began to slow.

Finally, he collapsed on top of me. Our sweat-slicked bodies slid against each other as I buried my face in my pillow, and he bit down on the side of my neck.

"I love you so much, baby… It doesn't even feel like enough to say it," he murmured in my ear from behind.

I whimpered beneath him, shivering in ecstasy and wishing I could find the energy to speak and tell him I felt the same.

We lay there like that, with him inside me for what felt like forever, and I realized in that moment that I had probably just experienced what would likely be the happiest day of my life.

I was happy.
I was loved.
I was home.

I was happy.
I was loved.
I was home.

CHAPTER
Fifty-One

Finn

The day of the surf competition came quickly.

It felt like I blinked, and then I was suddenly standing on Leviathans Beach, staring at the biggest crowd of people I'd seen since moving here.

The beach was packed. There was even a news van and reporters there to televise it. Goliath had outfitted me in a new wetsuit, and it was the most expensive thing I'd ever owned.

They'd wanted me to use a new gunboard, but I'd refused. I had my pink shortboard with me, and the thought of switching it out felt like I was betraying it or something.

"It's an inanimate object, surf star." Jet had laughed.

He didn't get it, clearly. This was my favorite board, and it hadn't failed me before. If I was going to do this, it would be on a board I felt comfortable on.

The crowd was buzzing with anticipation, and I was right there with them. However, my inner circle was not as excited.

The weather had turned. This day was a far cry from the blue skies and even tide I had ripped previously.

Today, the sky was a dark, angry grey, and the peaks were cold and sharp. Within the first hour, I'd seen two massive double-up waves crash onto the beach, which seemed to alarm Jet and Kai.

Don't even get me started on Jake.

His entire body was tense. He'd been stiff as a surfboard next to me when I woke up, and the muscle in his jaw kept pulsing.

I could tell he was holding back a slew of warnings and protests about me surfing on a day that wasn't perfect conditions, but he kept them to himself, and I was thankful.

"If it wasn't safe, they would postpone the competition," I assured him over breakfast, and he'd just given me a dark look and nodded.

His silence spoke volumes.

It would have been easier to brush off his grumpiness as him just being his usual paranoid self if I hadn't been getting the same tense vibes from Kai and Jet.

Even Turtle was on edge.

"Finn Man, some of these waves are looking rough, bro," he said, eyeing the third sixty-foot double-up that was currently demolishing the death zone. The majesty and power of it sent thrills of excitement through my entire body.

I shrugged. "It'll be fine. I'll be careful. No one else looks like they're planning on pulling out," I said, trying to stay positive.

The other surfers were all doing their pre-surf rituals. I'd seen several surfers who were personal idols of mine, and I was having a hard time not acting like a star-struck uber-fan.

Even Mike Gurallo had come to watch, and he shook my hand!

I, of course, forgot how to speak again, and I'm pretty sure he thought I had brain damage or something, but I was too busy eyeing up the swells to worry about that right now.

"Yeah, well. Most people are fucking morons," Kai grumbled. He, unlike Jake, hadn't kept his thoughts to himself.

He'd told me straight up and in no uncertain terms that I was an idiot for riding today.

When I'd looked to Jet to call off his dog, he'd just pursed his lips and admitted that he agreed.

Thanks for the support, assholes.

Sylvia walked up to us, her shiny clipboard in her hand and her expensive running shoes crunching in the black rocks that made up the beach.

"You ready, Summers?" she asked, giving me a smile.

Finally, someone who was just as amped as I was.

"I was *born* ready," I grinned at her, and she beamed at me.

"Hell yeah. That's what I want to hear. Follow me; the lineup is being announced."

I nodded, saying goodbye to my unofficial team. They all watched me go with worry painted on their faces.

"Good luck, Finn Man," Turtle said, his voice softer than normal and his brown eyes full of concern. I frowned at him.

"Hey man, I'm gonna do great. No stress." I winked at him. "Let's have a bonfire with Shelly tonight to celebrate."

He gave me a tentative smile and fist-bumped me.

"Hell yeah, man. Let's do it."

I nodded and saluted the guys before following Sylvia to where the other athletes were gathered around an official-looking dude with a headset.

She wrapped her hand around my shoulders and gave me a squeeze.

"How you doing? You okay? Nervous at all?"

"I know this is gonna sound like I'm trying to flex, but I'm not," I chuckled. "But I don't get nervous. I don't feel fear. It's a whole thing."

She looked at me, surprised. "Wow, really?"

I shrugged. "Yeah. I process fear as excitement. When I was a kid, I couldn't understand what held people back from doing epic shit, and my mom had to literally explain what fear was to me." I laughed, and Sylvie looked impressed.

"Well, we clearly hit the jackpot with you, Summers. You're gonna go places in this industry."

I beamed at her, giving her a dimple-popping smile.

"I hope so! This is like a dream come true."

"What the fuck is *this* joker doing here?" a nasty voice interrupted our conversation, and I turned around to see Kyle Tully glaring at me.

Oh yeah. Forgot about this guy.

"Bro, close your mouth; you're gonna burn someone's retinas off with those teeth," I grumbled, trying not to smirk at how red his face got.

Sylvie snorted next to me, and we exchanged an amused look.

"How the fuck did you get into this competition? You didn't even try out! I would *know.* My dad organized this!" He puffed out his chest like nepotism was something to brag about.

"Relax, Tully. Don't hurt yourself. Save that aggression for the waves, yeah?" I brushed him off, already bored with whatever this altercation was.

"Kyle, focus!" a man who I assumed was his coach barked.

"No! I want to talk to someone about this. That man *assaulted me!* He shouldn't be allowed to compete."

Sylvie raised an eyebrow at Kyle but then spoke directly to his coach.

"Get him under control. This is unprofessional."

Tully's coach nodded, grabbing him by the arm and tugging him away.

"Let's go, Kyle. You're gonna get yourself disqualified."

I had to resist the urge to flip him off as his coach manhandled him to the other side of the lineup.

Somehow, I didn't think *that* would be professional.

"What a little prick," Sylvie muttered, scribbling something down on her clipboard.

"Tell me about it," I mumbled when the official headset man finally started talking.

We were all assigned to our respective heats. If you don't know what a heat is, it's basically a timed set where multiple surfers compete at the same time.

As I was officially a Goliath athlete and they were the competition's biggest sponsor, I was given a big fat shiny number one.

I cheered silently to myself about the fact that I was going to be up first. However, my excitement was squashed when Tully was assigned to the first heat. Likely because of *nepotism*. *Yay.*

But I didn't let it get to me.

He could eat my ocean spray. I was gonna set the bar so fucking high they would be naming the next competition after me.

Sylvie walked me to the shoreline, running me through how the process was going to work.

She pointed to the west side of the beach. "Line up starts there; they want the first heat out in five. They're running with a flag system," she explained. "Green flag means heat is in progress, and y'all can catch waves. Yellow flag indicates the last 5 minutes of the heat, signaling you need to wrap up your strategy. Red flag means the heat has ended; no waves you catch after this are going to be scored. Got it?" she asked, and I nodded, basically bouncing on the balls of my feet in anticipation.

"Got it. I'm so fucking ready!"

She smiled at me, chuckling.

"Alright. Good luck, Summers. Make us proud."

I winked at her.

"You bet!"

Another Goliath rep called her name, and she left me to strap on my tether and get in the water.

"Hey, baby." I glanced up from fucking around with my ankle strap to see Jake standing next to me.

He had his teal board with him and was in his swim trunks. He never wore a wetsuit, and I assumed it was because the dead didn't get cold.

Suddenly, the world fell away, and it was just me and Jake.

"Hey," I breathed, smiling at him so big I felt like my face was going to split in half. "You coming out there with me?" I asked.

He gave me a soft smile that was a little too sad for my liking.

"Of course I am."

"Really?" My eyes pricked, and for a second, I felt weirdly lucky that no one but me could see my boyfriend. It was fucking sick that he could come out to the lineup with me and see me off before I started my heat.

"Yeah, baby. Wouldn't miss it for the world."

"Fuck, I love you."

He grabbed my chin and pressed a soft kiss to my mouth. I closed my eyes and inhaled his coconut scent.

"Mmm. That's all the luck I need, babe," I hummed against his lips, and he chuckled.

"You're going to need more than luck." He pulled away and turned his gaze out to the ocean.

The violent peaks crashed and roared in the distance, white eruptions of seafoam rupturing in deadly bursts.

It was easy to imagine the barrels of each wave as hungry mouths, looking to devour those of us foolish enough to venture out.

Fucking sick.

"The double-ups are savage today," Jake commented, his tone level but dark.

"Yeah, no kidding."

He shot me a loaded glance.

"Remember your training. When in doubt, don't paddle out. Even if you only catch one wave during the heat, it's better to catch one perfect swell and execute it well than risk a wipeout trying for multiples that are high risk."

I nodded. "Yeah, got it."

"Alright. Let's go, shark bait," he grunted, adjusting his board under his arm.

"Let's go slay some Leviathans." I grinned, and together, we paddled out into the chop.

CHAPTER
Fifty-Two

Finn

Alexa Play: Golden by Harry Styles

The clouds rolled overhead in tandem with the nearly black walls of water that surged before us.

There were four of us in the lineup, waiting for the green flag to drop.

I could feel Tully's eyes burning holes into the side of my head as we bobbed in the waiting zone.

"Ignore him. Focus on you. Lock in," Riddick growled next to me. I say Riddick because he was not Jake right now. This was the man I had first met that day months ago when I'd first come to Stars Cove.

Intense. Serious. Not one ounce of amusement or softness in his face.

He was almost angry.

Angry with the ocean, and maybe a little angry at me for doing this, though I suspected a lot of his anger was just for Tully.

"Focus on your breath. The last two waves were clean. If the next one that comes in starts to peak before the break zone, take it."

Riddick's instructions were humming through my body, and my mind was whirling a mile a minute. I felt that snapping sensation in my chest that I always got right before something life-changing was about to happen to me.

It was like I could see the waves form before they even began to swell. My mind cataloged my path, and I invented my ride strategy at the speed of light, connecting dots that only I could see.

"Flag's dropped," Riddick whispered in my ear. "Go!" he barked just as the next wave started to form. It was a good one. The water began to curl right before the break zone in a way that told me it would be a safe one to ride.

My body went into autopilot, and I was moving before anyone else had even registered that the flag was up.

Mine.

My entire body coursed with adrenaline as I caught the swell and reversed into it, mounting it like a fucking dragon tamer, riding his monster into war.

Up, up, up, I went as the wind and the water roared around me.

It peaked.

I dropped.

The rest was history.

I fucking shredded through the thing like a sword cutting through flesh.

My feet stuck to my signature pink board as if it were a part of me. It was magical. Every move came easily—a rehearsed dance.

I laughed as I carved through the belly of the beast, whipping out every trick in the book.

Before the wave curled, I tilted up and caught air off the lip, sticking my landing and barrel riding through the rest of the run.

I knew the aerial would be huge points, and I couldn't wipe the grin off my face as I executed a perfect cutback, extending my run for another glorious ten seconds.

I exited the wave directly back where I started, saving me paddle time and setting me up to catch another one before the heat was over.

"Damn, Summers! You're a tough act to follow!" Devon McAlphie congratulated me as I resumed my place in the lineup. Devon was a big wave surfer who'd made his name surfing Jaws in Hawaii. Doing my best not to fangirl, I grinned at him, giving him an up nod.

"Thanks, man!"

Tully was sputtering with fury, his beady eyes bouncing back and forth between Devon and me, clearly bristling at the easy camaraderie.

"I'm up," Devon winked at me, and I gave him a hang loose sign.

"Good luck out there."

Devon laughed. "Fuck luck, never needed it." Then he paddled out to catch the next monster swell. I watched in awe as he held back on his entry, executing a late drop that looked so smooth you could spread that shit on toast.

"Damn, that was sick," I breathed as Riddick paddled up next to me.

"Devon's good people. I surfed with him a bit in Hawaii."

I nodded just as Tully started running his mouth.

"You're a piece of shit, Summers. You think you're so fucking badass, but you're just a wannabe. Leave the surfing to the real professionals and go back to the East Coast. No one wants you here."

I shot him a cool grin and shrugged.

"That's not what Quinn said last night." I smirked, and Riddick snarled at me.

"Don't engage with him! Fucking focus!"

I chuckled, turning away from Tully, whose face was now a satisfying shade of purple.

As fun as it was to get Kyle all worked up, Riddick was right. I had a surf competition to win, and the next wave rolling in was a beauty.

"Later, toothtastic; my ride's here." I winked and paddled away, catching the Leviathan with just as much ease as I had the last one.

Riddick caught the wave with me, and I immediately knew this ride was going to be more challenging than the previous run.

The wave unexpectedly formed a second ripple, and I realized a few moments too late it was going to turn into a double-up.

"The barrel's splitting! Hit the crest and catch the inner tube!" Riddick bellowed to my right, but I was already ten steps ahead of him.

My mind mapped out my route effortlessly, and I caught a floater over the first break so I could drop into the second barrel safely.

"Fuck yeah, baby!" Riddick praised me as I entered the greenroom of the inner tube. He was right behind me, cheering me on, and I had never felt so alive.

"They're going to go nuts for that floater!" I yelled back to him as I prepared to execute another cutback so I could land back at the lineup.

I was setting up my pivot when suddenly, Tully dropped in front of me, fishtailing a carve that pulled the water away from my board.

Without the water to keep my board latched in, there was nothing I could do to recover.

"FINN!"

Riddick's booming voice was the last thing I heard before I fell.

Eighty.

Feet.

Down.

CHAPTER
Fifty-Three

Finn

Alexa Play: Only by RY X

I f you've never wiped out before, there are no words I can use to describe how disorienting it can be.

There is no up or down.

There's no air.

No shape or form.

It's all sensation and sound, but even the sound has no discerning features.

It's a relentless rush in your head that prevents you from getting your bearings.

The only thing you can see is the color of the ocean and flashes of foam that seem to rip right through you, tossing your body around like a rag doll.

It's disorienting when it happens with a normal wave.

This wasn't a normal wave.

This was a Leviathan.

The first thing I felt was the impact.

I hit the water with so much force I felt bones break, and the breath was forced from my lungs. The quick release snapped on my tether, and my board tore away from me, removing my lifeline back to the surface... Not that I was sure I would have been able to follow it up anyway.

I went into shock pretty quickly when I realized I couldn't move either of my arms.

Shock is a weird thing.

Your brain feels calm and slow, and everything around you moves like it's suspended in gelatin. You can't really process that you're in pain.

It's the calm before the storm. Usually, after the shock wears off, people descend into a delayed bout of hysterics.

I had this thought briefly as the ocean swallowed me up and pulled me deeper.

Cold liquid claws curled around my broken body and dragged me into the washing machine, like a predator hauling its prey into a den.

I tumbled and rolled underwater for what felt like forever before my brain started to catch up with the reality of what was happening to me.

"FINN!"

I could hear Riddick... which I vaguely understood shouldn't be possible.

I was under water.

I couldn't breathe or hear anything other than the endless rush of the ocean.

My body wasn't working properly.

I was drowning.

For some reason, that thought came as a shock to me.

I was drowning... I was really *drowning.*

The ocean pulled me deeper and deeper, and I was helpless to stop it.

My vision flickered in and out as the undercurrent had its way with me, and I blinked, ignoring the sting of salt water in my eyes.

Jake was swimming toward me, his caramel hair floating like a halo around his head.

He looked terrified.

I tried to reach for him, but my arms still weren't working.

Were they broken? Both of them?

"FINN! Baby boy, fuck, you need to swim up. The surface is this way!"

How was he speaking underwater?

He reached for me in an attempt to guide me to the surface, but his hands passed right through me.

How far out had the water dragged me?

"No... no, no, no, FUCK! Finn, you have to swim, baby, *please!*"

I shook my head, jerking my head toward my torso, trying to tell him I couldn't move my arms.

His gaze traced my body, and his already pale face went even whiter as he realized I couldn't move.

A strange feeling sparked in my chest.

It was a horrible feeling. A freezing shot of something that felt close to excitement but wasn't.

A slow, cold realization unfolded in the deepest recesses of my mind.

Fear.

I was feeling *fear.*

I was afraid.

I was afraid because I was going to die.

Jake...

I opened my mouth to say his name, but only bubbles came out, taking my last breath to the surface with them.

"Baby, no, don't try to speak. You need to preserve your breath..."

His hands cupped my face.

I could almost feel him now.

The panic in his blue eyes was so bright his irises looked like little underwater flames.

"*Jake...* I'm... I'm *scared...*" I whispered.

My words were audible. They shuddered around us, and I knew it was over at that moment.

"Shh, I know. I know you're scared, baby. It's okay. Just focus on me. Look at me." He was clearly doing his best to stay calm, but the look of pure horror on his face betrayed his smooth, even tone.

"I think... I think I'm dying," I whimpered. My voice sounded shocked, even to me.

Jake pulled me into him. Was it weird that I could kind of feel him now? A great shudder wracked through his body as he kissed my face. He held me while we floated in the endless dark abyss that I now understood to be my tomb.

"It's okay, baby," he lied, and I choked on a sob.

A bright light started to form in the water behind him. It seemed to be calling to me, but I was afraid of it.

That word felt strange in my head.

Afraid.

"There's a light," I whispered, and Jake looked startled.

"You can see a light?" He glanced over his shoulder, looking hopeful, but his face fell as he scanned the abyss.

He couldn't see it.

He turned back to me, frowning. "Is it calling you? Go to it, baby. I can help you get to it if you need me to."

I shook my head.

"No...no... what about Turtle? What about you? I can't go, I'm not ready."

"Baby, you can't stay here just for me. You need to pass on."

I shook my head again, the decision solidifying like a hard weight in my heart.

"No. I can't. I can't leave you here all alone." The words were broken, but as soon as they left my mouth, the light flickered, then faded, leaving us alone in the dark, cold depths of the ocean.

"Sweet boy..." Jake breathed, brushing his thumb tenderly over my cheek. I looked up at him, taking comfort in his familiar face.

"Jake... I don't want to die."

"I know, baby." His voice cracked, and he looked like he was in so much pain. I knew his heart was breaking.

"Please don't leave me," I whispered. "I don't want to die alone."

He wrapped his arms around me and buried his face in my neck, his entire body shaking with grief.

"You're not alone, sweet boy. *I'm right here.*"

Those were the last words I heard before my soul peeled away from my broken body.

CHAPTER
Fifty-Four

Riddick

Alexa play: Already Gone by Sleeping At Last

After Finn died, I could touch him again, and I gently guided his spirit to the surface with me.

"Don't look down, baby. Eyes on me," I'd urged him. His body was still floating beneath us, rolling and tumbling uselessly in the undercurrent.

I'd seen my body after I died, and I didn't want him to have to go through that experience. The sight of my own body floating in the water, tied down to my board, still haunted me in my dreams.

He clung to me, his beautiful eyes wide and glassy. No matter what I said, he couldn't respond. He simply nodded or obeyed when I gently told him what to do, guiding him through each step until we were back on the beach.

It was *chaos*.

Sylvie was screaming at the rescue team to get more people out there. I knew they weren't aware he was dead yet, as they kept using the word *rescue* instead of *recovery.*

Finn was despondent, standing next to me in a clear state of shock as the people around us rushed in every direction.

I turned just in time to see Kyle exit the water, clutching his board and looking a little shaken.

Rage like I had never felt before rolled through my chest, and I had never wished I was corporeal more... which was saying something.

If I had been able, I would have killed him with my bare hands.

However, Jet—being the fucking beauty that he was—attacked Kyle for me.

The kid didn't know what hit him.

Within seconds of him exiting the water, Jet shot at him, moving like a dark streak across the pebbled sand.

"You fucking BITCH!" Jet roared, slamming his fist directly into Tully's face.

Kyle didn't see it coming and immediately buckled, falling to the ground.

Jet was on top of him, rage carving every line of his usually kind face.

He slammed blow after blow into Tully's head. Jet was screaming.

"Do you know what you've done! He could be *dead! What the fuck is wrong with you!"*

Two large guys with 'SECURITY' written across the backs of their uniforms pulled Jet off of Kyle. Jet fought against them, still clearly blind with rage and devastation.

Kyle groaned and tried to get up off the ground, but he didn't get far.

Kai took his turn.

He descended on the kid while Jet tried to fight off security, getting in a few punches of his own before more men in black T-shirts swarmed him, too.

Turtle was running forward, trying to get to Kyle next, but more security flanked him, protecting the little asshole from further assault.

"You fucking dropped in on him! That's my best bro! You fucking bitch!" Turtle was screaming, tears streaking down his cheeks.

"Turtle..." Finn croaked next to me, reaching for his best friend in what I think was an effort to comfort him.

The team of security carted the bruised and bloody Kyle Tully away, and Turtle collapsed to his knees, burying his face in his hands, a frustrated roar reverberating out of him.

"That's my best friend!" he cried into his hands as Blake appeared, gathering him into her arms.

"That's my best friend..." he repeated over and over.

And there wasn't anything we could do but watch.

CHAPTER
Fifty-Five

Riddick

Alexa Play: Autumn by Paolo Nutini

It took hours for them to find Finn's body.

The ocean had pulled him much farther out than anyone had expected, which explained why I hadn't been able to touch him to bring him up to the surface.

They'd needed to execute a recovery dive to find him, and I overheard some of the rescue team saying that the chop had been so bad they almost lost another person when one of the Sea-Doos was rolled by a rogue Leviathan.

The sun was setting by the time his body was found.

"Baby, you don't need to see this," I whispered to Finn, who I'd wrapped up in my arms hours ago.

He clung to me. Wordless and shaking. I heard him swallow as a Sea-Doo appeared, dragging a sled attachment with it.

What could only be Finn's body was wrapped and strapped to the sled, and he shuddered violently at the sight of it.

There was an inhuman wail, and Turtle rushed to the sled. He threw himself on top of it, sobbing and screaming Finn's name over and over again.

"I have to… I have to go be with him," Finn croaked, tugging away from my embrace.

"Okay, baby. We'll go together," I whispered, and he looked at me with so much trust and sadness in his eyes that my throat closed up.

"Thank you…" he whispered.

I nodded, my voice cracking as I spoke. "Of course."

We approached the sled and an inconsolable Turtle. A few people tried to pull him away, but he threw them off and curled around Finn's body as if his touch alone could bring him back to life.

"Finn… please… no… we gotta have that bonfire. You *said!* You said we were gonna chill later. We were gonna celebrate. Shelly and I need you, man. Please! You can't be dead. You *can't be.*"

"Turtle Man…" Finn whispered, dropping to his knees next to the sled. Finn's body was wrapped in a black, waterproof tarp, and I sent a silent thanks to the recovery team for that small blessing.

Finn reached out to touch Turtle's hair. His fingers passed through him, but he stroked him just the same.

"It's gonna be alright, brother," he whispered as Turtle shook and sobbed over his body. "You gotta take care of Shells for me, okay? Take her to Hawaii… I'm sure you can get her on a ferry or something."

Pride swelled through me at Finn's brave attempt to comfort his friend.

I wasn't sure if Turtle could sense him there on some level, but he slowly calmed down as Finn continued to stroke his fingers through his hair.

Jet appeared, his expression dark. He had tear streaks on his own cheeks as he reached out with a bloody hand to touch his grieving friend.

"Hey, man. Come on. Let's let the paramedics get him out of here. You can come crash with Kai and me tonight."

Turtle looked up at Jet with swollen, red eyes. He looked lost.

"I can't leave him, man. He wouldn't want to be alone."

"Hey..." Jet said softly, crouching down next to Turtle. "He's not alone. My buddy Jake's looking out for him."

Turtle sniffed and dragged his wrist across his puffy, tear-stained cheeks.

"Yeah? You really think so?"

"I know so, man. Jake'll make sure he's alright."

"He's right," I said softly, even though they couldn't hear me. "I'm here. I'll make sure he's never alone."

Finn looked up at me, his own eyes finally welling with tears. I hated to see him cry, but tears were a good thing. It meant he was processing what had happened to him.

"You promise?" Finn sounded so small and broken.

I nodded, giving him a sad smile.

"If you'll have me, baby, I'll take care of you forever."

He came to me, succumbing softly to his tears as Jet led Turtle away to where Kai was waiting by their truck.

Finn wrapped his arms around me, and I tucked him into my chest, kissing the top of his head softly.

"You're alright. I've got you," I murmured against him as he cried quietly in my arms.

I love you.

I love you.

I love you.

You're not alone, baby. I'm right here.

EPILOGUE

Jet

Alexa Play: Coastline - Vancouver Sleep Clinic Remix by Hollow Coves, Vancouver Sleep Clinic

5 years later

Leviathans was officially closed to the public after Finn's death. What should have filled me with a sense of relief only made me feel bitter.

It felt cosmically unfair that it had taken the deaths of two of the most talented surfers the world had ever seen to finally drive the point home.

Kyle was convicted of voluntary manslaughter and was sentenced to 5-10 years in prison. His defense attorney had attempted to reduce the charges to involuntary manslaughter, but both Devon and Sylvia testified against him, claiming that he had shown clear signs of aggression toward Finn and had dropped in on his wave intentionally.

As far as I knew, that little fucker was still in jail, though he was likely to get out soon due to the strings his father had pulled in an effort to get him out early on good behavior.

He also had a lifetime ban from all professional surfing events, so I could at least rest easy knowing he couldn't hurt anyone else the way he'd hurt Finn.

The Tully family needed to pay significant restitution to Finn's family for damages. Since Finn didn't have any living relatives that anyone knew of, it went to Turtle, who Finn had named as his primary beneficiary on his Sharkies benefit plan.

This was the closest thing Finn had for a will, so Turtle was now a very financially comfortable surf rat.

Turtle used that money to buy Finn's shack.

He refused to live in it and instead turned it into a memorial for his friend.

"I want people to remember him. I want them to know what happened here," he'd told me after he'd signed the papers.

"We won't let them forget," I promised, and Turtle nodded.

"No the fuck we won't," he vowed.

Several months after the wake, Turtle confided in me that he and Finn had always planned to take Shelly across America, surfing all the beaches they could find.

We'd spent several years after Finn's death doing just that. I even managed to get that stupid van to Hawaii, where Turtle shredded up the local beaches with Kai and me, living out his and Finn's dream. Blake came with us, and after we'd torn up most of the beaches in every state that would have us, Turtle asked her to marry him.

He asked Kai and me to be the best men in their wedding, and it was one of the most beautiful nights of my life.

We went back to Stars Cove to have the wedding and to *tell Finn the good news' as* Turtle put it.

Visiting Finn felt like coming home, in a way. We'd buried him next to Riddick, just outside of Leviathans, and I went with Turtle the first night we made it back to the cove.

Turtle had insisted that Finn's stone be simple when we'd chosen it. I remembered going through the same process for Jake, and I understood.

Neither Jake nor Finn ever had a ton of money or even seemed to care about money.

They didn't want flashy things. They'd only wanted to surf and live their lives conquering waves that most people wouldn't even dream of trying to tame.

Which is why the inscription on Finn's stone read:

Finn Summers

Leviathan Slayer

2003-2025

On our first day back in the cove, Turtle had laid a hand on Finn's headstone. His eyes were full of tears as he told him all about our adventures with Shelly and, finally, about his engagement to Blake.

"I told you Mrs. Turtle had a nice ring to it," he'd said so softly it made my eyes well with tears.

Turtle and Blake got married on Finn and Jake's private beach.

It was a small ceremony with only close friends and, of course, all of Finn's Finnatics who never stopped loving him.

Kai and I stood next to the happy couple as the sun set behind their modest marriage arch, and we watched with pride in our eyes as they said their vows.

There had been magic in the air that night. I had such a warm, comforting feeling for the entire ceremony that Finn was somehow there, watching his best friend get married to the woman of his dreams.

I felt Riddick there that night, too.

I liked to believe that what I told Turtle that day was true.

In my mind, Finn and Riddick were together. It was a tragedy that they hadn't met when they were both alive. They were different in many ways, but I knew if they'd known each other, they would have developed the same strong bond I had with each of them, and now Turtle, as well.

After the wedding, we collectively decided to permanently move back to Stars Cove. Turtle finally moved out of Shelly and bought a place in town with Blake, claiming that Shelly was too old to keep up with all the 'little turtles' he planned to make with his blushing new wife.

However, every Saturday, Turtle, Kai, Blake, and I religiously gathered and surfed Jake and Finn's private beach.

It made us feel close to them.

After a long day playing in the ocean, we usually used Jake's old charcoal grill to make dinner and had a bonfire to honor them.

Every week, without fail, Turtle always talked to Finn as he lit the fire.

"See, Finn Man? Told you we would have that bonfire to celebrate."

I could almost hear Finn's laugh every time he said it. I usually imagined Jake's soft chuckle next to me, too.

The crazy thing was, on warm summer nights, when the light from the moon hit just right, sometimes I swore I could see the two of them surfing together.

Every time I caught the distinct silhouettes of Jake and Finn bobbing on their boards in the ocean, my heart stopped. It was like I could really hear their deep, content voices trickling in with the tide as they teased each other.

Though I could never make out their faces, I always liked to think that they were happy and that they were laughing and smiling along with us.

The End

WANT MORE FINN AND RIDDICK?

END NOTES

I'm not crying – YOU'RE CRYING!

Jk, I'm totally crying. Oh god… honestly, while writing this I made it through Finn's fall with dry eyes, but when Turtle broke down I lost it.

Once again, my morbid obsession with themes of death seem to have taken the wheel, and we've all been totally raked over the coals as a result hahah – I'm not even sorry. :'D

I think what hurts so bad about Turtle's reaction is – we as the reader know that this was the only way Finn could be with Jake forever. As much as we want that for them, the price of that happy ending is Turtle's happiness… and if any of my characters deserve happiness, it's Turtle.

He's absolutely the best. Everyone deserves a friend like him.

Turtle wasn't the only character that was touched by death in this story.

Jet and Kai were still mourning the loss of Jake when Finn met them. I designed them to represent different stages of grief. Kai represents the earlier stages of grief (denial/anger) and Jet represents acceptance.

Jet's willingness to try to move on from the pain of losing Jake by pursuing a relationship with Finn shows us that as horrible and consuming as grief can be, it is possible to move on and heal in time.

It obviously didn't work out between them, due to the fact that Finn was very much taken by none other than the object of Jet's grief, however, I like to believe that in a different universe where Finn wasn't able to see Jake, he and Jet would have actually been happy together.

Jake was right. Jet *would* have taken good care of Finn and he genuinely is an awesome person. I'm glad Turtle had him as a friend to help him heal and find acceptance.

Finn himself is still struggling with the grief of losing his mom while the story is unfolding. What's interesting about the stages of grief is they're not linear and an individual may revisit each stage multiple times. We see this with Finn's cyclical bouts of depression that pop up annually on the anniversary of his mother's death.

Jake is grieving too, however, he's grieving the loss of his own life. We see him heal from that grief over the course of the book as he moves slowly through the stages. He starts off angry and closed off, and slowly he opens up to Finn and finds acceptance through his love for our happy-go-lucky little sea puppy.

Along with themes of death and its devastating impact it had on the living people we leave behind, this book was also heavy on themes of loneliness and abandonment.

The intentional abandonment from Finn's father coupled with the loss of his mother has resulted in some serious trauma on his end. Finn's abandonment issues make him the perfect counterpart for Riddick, who is desperate for connection.

It's almost like the universe knew they were going to need each other and the stars aligned just so to make that happen. (It's me. I'm the universe. I made the stars align... every time Jake curses the universe he's cursing me LOL.)

But seriously, I wanted to play with this concept of fate with this book. Obviously I knew how it was going to end, and I liked the idea of Finn being fated to meet his demise on this beach.

However, I didn't want his death to be just another way the universe let him down. On the contrary, I wanted his death to open an eternity of happiness and comfort from someone who loves him unconditionally.

That's why, as sad as this story is, I still consider it a happy ending.

Riddick and Finn are together now – forever – doing exactly what they loved to do everyday while they were alive.

I can't think of a happier ending than that. <3

ACKNOWLEDGMENTS

As always I need to thank my best friend Lauren for the absolutely *killer* playlist. I think this is my favorite one you've ever done for me! I've been listening to it on a loop! Also, Diem, for always being a lil eggish cheer leader!

Special shout out to Brandon and Julia – the psyche ward group chat brings me so much joy and I love you both so much. Also, thanks Brandon for always giving my MM's a solid advance screening/sensitivity read. You're feedback and thorough reviews after every each book of mine you read are so special (I save screen shots of them lol)

Alina May – sorry I made you sob with this one lmfao, but thanks for always reading my shit even at the risk of being traumatized hahaha.

Jules - my gorgeous lil book dragon, thanks so much for having me over for the launch party and always being so supportive of my writing and my dreams <3

Rhiann, my illustrator! The cover! The artwork!!! Ugh, you truly bring my characters to life so perfectly every time. The details you add always blow me away and I love you so much! Please follow Rhiann on instagram if you're not already! (rhearons_art)

Of course, my lovely PA and Editor, Taylor. I have no idea how I did this before you! Please never leave me *Sob.*

And finally, as always, Michael and Tartar Sauce, for being the best support system an egg could ask for.

STAY CONNECTED!

Follow Alex on socials

Tiktok/Instagram: @alexandrastpierrebooks
Patreon: patreon.com/Alexandrastpierre
Facebook: Alex's Lil Psycho's facebook group
YouTube: @AlexStPierreBooks (Lil Psycho Book Den)

ALSO BY ALEXANDRA ST PIERRE

Dark Romantic Fantasy
The Origin's Daughter Series
(Primarily M/F)
Book 1: The Origin's Daughter
Book 2: The Dominion of Sin
Book 3: The Queen's Shadow

Dark Paranormal Romance
The Murder and Mayhem Duet
(MF, MM, MFM)
Book 1: Deathtrap
Holiday Novelette featuring Shem + Gabe (Available on alexandrast-pierre.com)
Book 2: Hellcat (Coming Oct 2025)

Dark Romance
The Silent Hollow Series (Shared world with Alina May)
(MM, MF, FF)
The Mercenary and the Mortician

Standalones
(MM)
Chasing Riddick